LARA ADRIAN

"Action-packed, sexy and enticing...Lara Adrian's wild imagination and creativity is amazing."
—Reading Divas

"With an Adrian novel, readers are assured of plenty of dangerous thrills and passionate chills."
—RT Book Reviews

"Ms. Adrian has a gift for drawing her readers deeper and deeper into the amazing world she creates."
—Fresh Fiction

DONNA GRANT

"Donna Grant has given the paranormal genre a burst of fresh air..."
—San Francisco Book Review

"Time travel, ancient legends, and seductive romance are seamlessly interwoven into one captivating package."
— Publisher's Weekly

"Dark, sexy, magical. When I want to indulge in a sizzling fantasy adventure, I read Donna Grant."
—Allison Brennan, New York Times bestselling author

LAURA WRIGHT

"Wright launches a powerful series with a rich mythology, page-turning tension, and blistering sensuality."
–Publishers Weekly (starred review)

"Wright knows how to lure you in and hold you captive until the last page."
–Larissa Ione, New York Times bestselling author

"Complexity of emotion is what makes Laura Wright's books so engrossing."
–Sizzling Hot Book Reviews

ALEXANDRA IVY

"Ivy creates such vivid and complex characters, their emotional struggles feel real even though their exploits are supernatural. A true gift to the genre."
–RT Book Reviews (Top Pick)

"Delivers plenty of atmosphere and hot-blooded seduction."
–Publishers Weekly

"Oh, so hot and wonderfully dangerous."
–Gena Showalter, New York Times bestselling author

MASTERS
OF
SEDUCTION
Volume 2

LARA ADRIAN
DONNA GRANT
LAURA WRIGHT
ALEXANDRA IVY

ISBN: 099164753X
ISBN-13: 978-0-9916475-3-8

MASTERS OF SEDUCTION VOLUME 2
© 2015 by Obsidian House Books, LLC
Cover design © 2014 by CrocoDesigns

PRICELESS: HOUSE OF EBARRON
© 2015 by Lara Adrian, LLC

BOUNDLESS: HOUSE OF DROHAS
© 2015 by Donna Grant

DAUNTLESS: HOUSE OF TREVANION
© 2015 by Laura Wright

RECKLESS: HOUSE OF FURIA
© 2015 by Debbie Raleigh

www.MastersOfSeductionAuthors.com

Available in ebook and print. Unabridged
audiobook edition forthcoming.

CONTENTS

PRICELESS
House of Ebarron

Lara Adrian

CHAPTER ONE

Sorin, Master of the Incubus House of Ebarron, leaned back on the velvet divan in his private office as warm, eager hands worked his silk tie loose, then began to unfasten the buttons of his crisp white shirt.

Another pair of hands slid over his thighs and groin, zeroing in with fevered enthusiasm on the erection that strained against the fabric of his expensive black suit. Behind him stood a third female, whose fingers played in his wavy golden hair as she leaned over him, her naked breasts bobbing above his upturned face like fruit, ripe for the plucking.

He let out a deep sigh, settling into the effortless pleasure that the captain of Ebarron's Watchmen had procured for him for the evening. Sorin had to admit, Milo had fine taste in women.

The trio of human females his personal bodyguard had sent up to the penthouse from Ebarron's elite casino downstairs were beautiful, seductive, and clearly intent on fulfilling Sorin's every wicked desire.

His body responded instantly as they began to undress him. Already his cock was rock hard, rampant behind his zipper. Lust swamped his acute demon senses, from both his own carnal need and that of the three lovely women vying for his favor.

Sex was a powerful drug for any red-blooded male, but especially for one born of the Incubi race. They lived for sex—would die without it, in fact.

Sorin and every Incubus demon like him fed on the energy of their partner's sexual release for sustenance. For life itself. But they fucked for the pure, debauched pleasure of it.

Yet the Master of Ebarron could not have been more bored.

As enticing and arousing as his companions were, they were just three more nameless faces in a sea of women eager to land in the billionaire casino owner's bed. Like the rest of the mortal world, the females had no idea Sorin's wealth was the least remarkable thing about him.

As for his interest in them, Sorin would forget these three the moment they finished with him and left the room. Hell, they were all but forgotten by him now, even with their hands and mouths doing their best to please him.

A hundred distractions tugged at his attention. Matters concerning the family business and his role as the head of venerable Ebarron House. A role that had also come with an unending awareness of his responsibility for the family's treasury, an obscene fortune in artifacts, arcana, and priceless trinkets, which had been wagered and won, bought or collected by the males of his line over thousands of years.

Like the griffin that was the Ebarron sigil, Sorin's family was fiercely proud of their hoard—and famously protective of it as well.

Sorin's thoughts snagged on other issues that weighed on him now too, not the least of which being the persistent unrest and rumors pertaining to the highest seat of power in all of the Incubi realm. The Obsidian Throne was the only thing standing between the gates of Heaven and Hell. The truce struck between the Incubi and the angels, overseen by a council of Nephilim priestesses known as the Three, had forever been a fragile thing.

Whispers of ineffectiveness concerning the current Sovereign on the Throne were hardly new, but reports coming out of the Incubi Houses of Gravori, Romerac, Vipera and Xanthe in recent weeks indicated corruption and collusion of the worst kind.

Bloody damned hell. If boredom with his lovely but forgettable companions wasn't enough to kill his urge to fuck and feed before he'd even gotten started, visions of war between the Incubi and the angels certainly was.

He couldn't have been more relieved when a knock sounded on the office door. "Enter," he commanded to his Watchman posted on the other side.

Milo opened the heavy panel, the dark-haired Incubus's expression sober. "Pardon the interruption, sir. We, ah…we have a situation in the casino."

It was all the reason Sorin needed to extract himself from the three women draped over him. Immodest as any demon, he stood up, began tucking himself back in, zipping and buttoning his disheveled clothing.

"What kind of situation?" Sorin crossed the room to meet his captain at the door. *Christ, could the seasoned Watchman's face look any more uncomfortable?* "What the fuck is going on down there?"

Milo cleared his throat, kept his voice low enough for Sorin's ears only. "Korda Marakel just walked into the casino."

Sorin's answering curse was dark and vivid. The male was from another Incubus House, and not a Master like Sorin, but one of several lower-ranking cousins of Marakel's Master, the very Incubus who now sat on the Obsidian Throne.

Sorin had once considered Korda Marakel a friend, but now his hackles rose at the mere mention of his name. "Where is the son of a bitch?"

"The roulette room, sir."

"Alone?"

The Watchman shook his head. "No, he's with a female companion. A Nephilim."

Sorin's anger flared, spiking toward outrage. "You don't mean he's come back here with—"

"No. Not her." Milo's quick reply spared Sorin from uttering the faithless bitch's name.

Although it had been five years, the betrayal by his former friend, with the woman Sorin might have taken as his mate one day, still sat on his tongue like acid.

Not that he'd ever take Greta back. After learning she'd allowed Korda to seduce her, Sorin had raged more at his own stupidity for letting the Nephilim into his life, than he had out of any kind of emotional pain that she was gone. She'd made a fool of him, squandered his trust.

And he gave no one the chance to do it twice.

As for Korda Marakel, friendship across House lines was a sometimes tenuous thing in the Incubi realm, but especially when one of those Houses was that of the current Sovereign. Not to say there weren't a few honorable males among the Marakels, but treachery seemed to run deep in that bunch of demons.

The same could be said of their arrogance.

If Korda thought he could walk back onto Sorin's turf with impunity, he could think again. "Who's the female with him?"

"Never seen her before, sir."

"You're certain?"

"Positive." A smirk tugged at the corners of Milo's mouth. "She's not the kind of woman a man is likely to forget."

"Show me." Irritated now, and not a little curious, Sorin gestured to the sulking playthings left behind in his office. "Have one of your men escort the ladies out after they've dressed and collected their things."

Milo gave him a nod. "Consider it done."

The captain of the Watchmen made the call while Sorin and he strode the length of the lavish corridor toward the penthouse elevator. They stepped into the glass lift and descended through the heart of the elegant Ebarron building, toward the casino twelve floors down at ground level.

Built into the side of a mountain nestled deep in the Carpathians of Romania, Ebarron's casino and family fortress was exclusive in the extreme.

Incubus magic protected the place better than any amount of security, rendering it impossible to find on any map or GPS coordinates. Even if outsiders did learn the precise location of the stronghold, unless they could teleport, the terrain itself would keep them away.

As such, the casino catered mostly to Incubi and other, lesser-ranking demonkind, and it was rare that patrons arrived—or stayed—without the Master of Ebarron's knowledge and approval.

Milo stopped the elevator on the broad, balconied second floor, whose galleries overlooked the grand playing halls and gaming salons below. Sorin didn't wait for his Watchman to show him to the balcony poised over the roulette room. He prowled there in irritation, across the hand-loomed Persian rugs and sleek, veined-marble floors, to the edge of the balcony.

Down below, standing among a small, glittering crowd gathered around the green table of the high-stakes wheel, was Korda Marakel.

The tuxedoed, dark-haired Incubus had just lost a bet on the wheel and was scowling as a pile of his chips were swept away by the croupier. By rough estimation, Marakel had just surrendered more than ten thousand euros to Ebarron's bank.

Sorin could hardly contain his smile. He didn't need the money, but the satisfaction of taking something from his old rival was its own reward.

He stared as Korda snapped impatient fingers at one of the cocktail servers carrying a tray of filled champagne flutes. The demon grabbed one in each hand, and when he turned to offer one to the woman beside him, Sorin's gaze followed too.

Damn. Milo was right when he said the Nephilim was something to see.

Tall, long-limbed, with ample curves in all the right places, the platinum blond stood beside Korda Marakel in form-hugging black pants and a matching long-sleeved top sliced far between her breasts in a generous vee. Stiletto-heeled black leather boots rode up her calves and just over her knees. Her long, pale white hair was gathered off her face in a sleek ponytail that gleamed like gossamer silk under the casino's soft lights.

Milo strode up to the balustrade next to Sorin and slanted him a knowing grin. "I don't suppose you've ever seen this Nephilim before either?"

"No," Sorin replied. And what a damned shame that was.

Even from the floor above, he could see that she was beautiful—arrestingly so. Creamy skin, full pink lips, and a dark-lashed gaze that moved over her surroundings with an unmistakable confidence and intellect.

Where the other Nephilim and human females in the casino wore bright colors, sparkling gowns, and expensive jewels just screaming for notice, this woman in body-skimming black needed no embellishments to draw the eye of every man in the place.

Sorin found himself studying her. Fixating on her with an interest he could hardly deny.

Desire flickered through his veins as he watched her bring the slender glass to her mouth. Lush lips parted over perfect white teeth as she took a brief drink. Watching her pretty mouth and throat work suddenly made everything male in Sorin—everything dangerously, carnally Incubus—crackle with rapt, unswerving attention.

Korda Marakel seemed equally entranced with his companion. Leering openly, he leaned in close and whispered something against her ear. She smiled, but the curve of those mesmerizing lips seemed too tight to be genuinely amused.

Marakel didn't seem to notice. Or maybe he didn't care. Crowding her body even more where they stood at the roulette table, he petted her silky platinum hair with a lover's caress. His fingers slid around to her cheek, and the grin he gave her was profane, purely sexual.

Before Sorin could bite it back, a low, disapproving growl rumbled over his tongue.

Marakel must have shocked the poor thing with whatever he suggested next because she recoiled from him, teetering unsteadily on those sky-high heels. With her sudden, awkward wobble, the drink in her hand slipped through her fingers and crashed to the floor.

Champagne exploded in all directions, splashing her and Marakel both. The Incubus sputtered a string of curses as he tried to brush the spilled alcohol from his tux and white shirt.

Sorin grinned. "Couldn't have happened to a better man."

Champagne dripping off his chin, Marakel was furious. He bellowed for help from one of the nearby servers while his lovely companion cautiously backed away from the ruckus.

She didn't seem clumsy at all as she withdrew from the table. And the look on her pretty face was nothing close to contrition.

No, the slight tilt of her lips told a different story altogether.

"Shall I have them both removed from the premises, sir?" Milo asked, chuckling from beside Sorin now.

"No. That won't be necessary." His gaze locked on to the intriguing beauty, he watched as she slipped out of the roulette room to the main parlor of the casino. "I'll handle this personally."

CHAPTER TWO

Ashayla hurried out of the crowded gaming room, her sleeve and fingers soaked with spilled champagne. She wasn't embarrassed for what she'd done. She sure as hell wasn't sorry. Especially considering she'd doused the demon on purpose.

He had been dropping innuendos and suggestive comments all evening, despite the fact that she wasn't remotely tempted to take his bait. The lewd remarks and none-too-subtly roaming hands were annoying, but Ashayla deflected the Incubus's advances without too much concern.

She was a Nephilim, and she could handle herself well enough. She had no interest in playing games— his own or the ones taking place in the casino. Ashayla was focused on a bigger prize, and she wasn't going to let her unwanted but necessary "date" faze her.

That is, until the sex demon suggested he might console himself over his losses at the roulette wheel by making her his Thrall for the night. The thought sent a fresh spike of outrage through her. The bastard was lucky all she'd had in her hand at the time was a glass of champagne.

The prospect of losing control of her body and

mind under the influence an Incubus's sexual power was no laughing matter. Their kind was dangerously alluring *without* the benefit of the ability to bend any female's will to their own. Add in the hypnotic force of the thrall, and there wasn't a woman alive—full human or half angel like her—who could resist them.

Even the dark-haired demon who'd brought her to Ebarron's casino had a certain coarse sensuality that some females might find attractive. Ashayla wasn't one of them.

She didn't know anything about him beyond his first name, Korda. Nor did she need to know anything more. They'd met only last night, after she'd arrived in Bucharest from the States. Ashayla had gone into the city and its after-hours nightclubs with the sole purpose of hiring an Incubus to bring her to the exclusive casino.

She'd learned the House of Ebarron's family business and residential stronghold was located somewhere in the Carpathian Mountains, but it wasn't exactly the kind of place you'd find in any tour guide. And to get there, she'd needed to find a demon to teleport her onto Incubus soil along with him.

Korda had seemed willing enough to take her there. He'd seemed almost too willing, as if the five hundred euros he'd demanded in exchange for the favor—an amount twice as high as she'd budgeted— had been merely an afterthought.

If she hadn't worked so hard and saved so long for this trip—this *quest*, to be more precise—it wouldn't have stung so much to watch her hired companion throw away her money at the tables along with a huge sum of his own.

Then again, she didn't try to fool herself that her purpose for being in Ebarron's domain wasn't going to come at a steep price. Nor without a great deal of risk.

Stealing from an Incubus House, particularly the formidable one she planned to cross tonight, was no easy feat.

Not that the obstinate, arrogant Master of Ebarron had given her any other choice.

Ashayla pushed open the gold-trimmed mahogany door of the ladies' room on a huff of indignation. Ebarron's enormous wealth was evident on every silk-covered wall and framed original work of art. It shone in every inch of polished, snow-white marble under her booted feet and in every gleaming fob and fixture, right down to the restrooms of their lavish casino.

The fortune the House had amassed over the centuries was obscene, so what would it hurt them to part with one insignificant item in their treasury?

"Greedy bastard," Ashayla muttered as she entered the restroom.

Several elegantly dressed women stood at the mirrors primping, while others chatted quietly on tufted velvet chairs and divans in the restroom's lavish parlor. Most of them were human, with a few Nephilim here and there.

All heads turned as Ashayla stormed in, reeking of spilled champagne and pulsing with combined disgust for her Incubus companion and the one at the helm of Ebarron House.

She didn't belong here. Nephilim or not, she was

an outsider in this opulent place and these women knew it. Could they see that in reality she was a twenty-nine-year-old struggling accountant from Chicago who'd just spent her last five hundred euros merely for the chance to get in the door of this rarefied world?

Could they detect her determination, or the sheer desperation in her plan for being there?

Ashayla stared right back, defiant.

These women and their disapproving, superior gazes didn't matter. Only one woman's opinion of her mattered, and that was Ashayla's grandmother. The aging Nephilim had been Ashayla's only family since her own mother had died when Ashayla was a child.

Back home in Chicago, now it was Gran who was dying, after more than a hundred years of living in the mortal realm. She probably had no more than mere weeks left, growing more frail and faded with each passing day. The thought put an ache in Ashayla's chest. It also renewed her resolve to see tonight's plan through, no matter what.

In all their years together, Gran had never asked anything of her granddaughter. But a few months ago, as the old Nephilim recognized that her time was drawing thinner, she'd become fixated on an heirloom pendant that had fallen out of the family's hands nearly two decades ago.

That Ashayla's mother had been the one to lose the pendant—sold it to a local pawn shop without Gran's knowledge, in fact—only made it harder to bear Gran's increasing worry over the piece.

Gran wanted the pendant back. She talked of

little else lately. She wanted to see it again, to hold it in her hands before she died and know that it was returned to where it belonged.

Against all odds, Ashayla had managed to track the semiprecious gemstone necklace from the pawn shop to a jewelry dealer across the country who later sold it to an antique shop in Canada, who then sold it in a lot of other baubles and trinkets to a private collector. That private collector, she'd eventually discovered, was the House of Ebarron.

Ashayla had thought her search was over. She sent a message through Nephilim channels to the Master of Ebarron, explaining the situation, but her request to buy the pendant back was denied. She sent another, better offer. Another refusal.

She tried again and again over the past five months, but each time, her request was denied. According to the responses from Sorin Ebarron, he was in the business of collecting items of value and interest, not trading them. As he'd so succinctly stated in his final written reply, treasure won by the House of Ebarron was never surrendered.

Ashayla probably shouldn't have sent her final message, but the arrogance and disregard of Ebarron's Master had pissed her off like nothing ever had in her life.

How dare he refuse a dying woman's request? What kind of cold-hearted bastard was the Master of Ebarron?

Really, he'd left her no alternative.

Gran would have that pendant in her hands before she took her last breath, no matter what Ashayla had to risk to get it back. Nothing—and no one—was going to stop her.

Determination steeling her, Ashayla strode to one of the polished marble and gold-fitted sinks to wash the alcohol off her hands and clothing. Her reflection gazed back at her, mouth grim with resolve, cobalt blue eyes unflinching. Not that she wasn't nervous too.

She was undertaking an enormous risk, plotting to steal from Ebarron's famed treasury.

But she hadn't come empty-handed.

Hidden in one of her tall boots was a small vial of Nephilim magic. The black market potion had cost her nearly a full year's wages—all of her savings, gone. She could always make more money. Gran's time, however, was limited. And Ashayla's mission to bring her some peace before she passed had run up against a very stubborn, uncompromising roadblock named Sorin of Ebarron.

So, she had traded her savings for a single dose of magic that promised to render her invisible—completely incorporeal—for eight full minutes on demon soil. Not even the strongest Incubus security spell could prevent her from entering Ebarron's treasure room.

Now all she had to do was slip away by herself to find it, swallow the elixir and step inside the vault like a ghost.

Then hope to hell she could find Gran's pendant and hightail it out of the casino without getting spotted by Ebarron's Watchmen or anyone else.

All in under eight minutes.

The plan had seemed reasonable enough all the times she'd played it through in her mind. Risky as fuck, but doable. Now, she felt a niggle of fear slide up her neck.

If she failed to find the pendant? If she got caught...

She didn't want to consider either of those scenarios.

And the further she delayed in getting started, the worse the chances that her companion or someone else at the table was going to notice she'd been gone for too long.

Steeling herself for what she had to do, Ashayla dried off and stepped out to the hall. Instead of heading back to the roulette room, she went the opposite direction, deeper into the sprawling corridors and sumptuous antechambers of the place.

Research and rumors both speculated that the House of Ebarron kept their treasure secreted somewhere beneath the grand casino. Ashayla strolled nonchalantly, but with purpose, pausing to admire some of the priceless masterworks framed on the walls while surreptitiously taking note of the dozens of dark-suited Watchmen posted all over the casino.

She drifted farther along a promenade of elegant arches and vaulted ceilings, bypassing a trio of pretty little Monet paintings with barely a blink of notice as she concentrated on the positions of Ebarron's guards. They were everywhere. Big, muscular Incubi whose shrewd eyes scanned the crowds like vigilant hawks.

As she strolled deeper into the corridor, toward the casino's private salons, the challenge of what she was up against really began to sink in. Every ornate door and passageway seemed to have its own dedicated security detail.

Dammit.

There would be no slipping past any of Ebarron's Watchmen without their notice.

Which meant she'd have to use the dose of magic even before she located the treasure room, leaving less time to retrieve the pendant and make her esc—

"Are you lost?"

The deep, unrushed voice halted her in her tracks. Shit. Speaking of Watchmen keeping an eye over every corner...

Ashayla forced a smile and slowly pivoted her head to look at the guard. "I was just, ah..."

Good lord, he was gorgeous. Standing well over six feet tall, he was golden-haired, tawny-skinned, and had a breathtakingly handsome face that would have seemed more suited to an angel than a demon-spawned Incubus.

Ashayla's throat went suddenly dry. The rest of her started a slow, heated melt as she stared at him, her female body responding of its own volition to the sex demon's presence. Her pulse sped toward a gallop. Heat climbed up her throat, simultaneously spreading lower, over her breasts and down to the core of her body.

She tried to ignore the carnal awareness that ran up her limbs and into her blood, but his allure was startlingly powerful.

And she could tell that he wasn't even trying to affect her. If this was his sexual pull at rest, what would he be capable of with the added strength of his thrall?

She damned well didn't want to find out.

Like all Incubi, his age was impossible to pinpoint. Outwardly the Watchman in his black suit and crisp white shirt appeared to be in his thirties. In truth, she knew he could be much, much older.

When she seemed incapable of speaking, he folded his arms over his muscled chest, piercing her with a suspicious, topaz-colored stare. "I asked you a question. What are you doing out here?"

He spoke with an air of total authority. And that low rumble of a voice was made even more arresting by the hint of a Romanian accent, which rolled off his tongue like dark, red wine.

Ashayla summoned her composure enough to make up a feasible excuse. As anxious as she was to get away from him, she also didn't want to give him reason to think she had anything to hide. Nervously, she licked her lips.

"I was just admiring some of the art." She gestured to a moody Post-Impressionist painting in front of her, an obvious, but rare Van Gogh. "I've never seen such an impressive collection up close like this before."

This painting, like all the others on the silk-covered walls in the palatial casino, was clearly an original, one that any museum would have kept protected from the public by a thick glass case and yards of velvet ropes.

Not Ebarron. They displayed their spoils out in the open, close enough to touch.

As if they were certain no one would ever dare.

The arrogance was staggering.

Ashayla forced a placid smile. "I would've

expected priceless pieces like this to be under lock and key somewhere. In the House's treasure room with the rest of Ebarron's legendary hoard, maybe."

It was a desperate fish for information—even a small hint—about the vault she needed to locate. But the Watchman didn't seem inclined to take her bait.

He approached now, his gait smooth, his body moving with a big cat's coiled strength. "Isn't it better that they aren't hidden away? Out here, everyone can enjoy them."

Ashayla scoffed softly under her breath. "Or maybe the House of Ebarron just wants everyone else to see what can never be theirs."

The Incubus's dark-lashed eyes narrowed. He moved in close to her, standing beside her in front of the painting. His scent invaded her senses—spicy, warm, and utterly male. She felt his scrutiny of her deepen, and she cursed herself for letting the remark slip.

"I've never seen you here before, Nephilim." The weight of his gaze was a physical thing. Probing. Heated. Far too compelling. "You're American?"

She really didn't want to have this conversation with him. The last thing she needed was to create a lasting impression on one of Ebarron's guards, let alone raise questions about herself she had no intention of answering.

"I should get back to the roulette room. My date is waiting for me—"

The Watchman's shrewd gaze held her. "How long have you known Korda Marakel?"

Ashayla froze. How could he possibly—? Oh, of course, she reasoned in the same instant. Security cameras. The casino was probably equipped with countless eyes in the sky.

One more hurdle she'd have to clear.

"I only met him recently. In Bucharest," she replied, figuring it was safest to stick to the truth. Or something close to it. She licked her dry lips. "I'm here on vacation and the famous Ebarron casino is something I've always wanted to see. Korda offered to show it to me."

"Is that so?" The Incubus tilted his head, seeming even more intrigued. His penetrating topaz gaze assessed her in a way that made the sensual buzz in her veins vibrate into the very center of her being. "Can I presume that you've come here to play, Miss…?"

The way he asked the question, the way he coaxed her to give him her name, put an uninvited, heatedly erotic image in her mind. Tangled sheets and soft moans, his dark gold head buried between her spread thighs.

Holy shit.

Was he doing that to her deliberately, or was it her own imagination running hot and wild?

Ashayla blinked hard. She stepped back, needing the distance.

This man was more than dangerous. She had to get away from him at once and hope he found another woman to distract him while she tried to figure out how to do what she needed to do.

She anxiously licked her lips again, then cleared her throat. "Like I said, I have to go find my…um, Korda. Which way is the roulette room?"

"I'll take you there."

"No." She shook her head, started to take a step away from the Watchman. "You don't need to do that. I'm sure I can find it on my own."

His mouth curved into an unfriendly smile. "I insist."

Given little choice, Ashayla fell in beside him and walked in silence to the gaming room where Korda waited. It didn't escape her notice that the Watchman snagged the attention of every pair of eyes in the place—female and male alike. The people in the casino stared at him in open curiosity.

In deferential awe.

And suddenly a terrible dread settled over Ashayla.

She'd made a mistake talking to this Incubus, letting him see her in the casino.

"Korda," he muttered from beside her as she accompanied him to the roulette table. It was more of an accusation than a greeting.

Ashayla's hired date grinned around her with a smugness she didn't understand. "Have you come to kick me out on my arse, old friend?"

"No. I have a more interesting idea." The Watchman who was no Watchman motioned to the croupier. "I've decided to play a few rounds."

"Yes, Master Sorin. Of course."

Ashayla stood there in stunned silence, not even certain she was breathing.

She felt wooden, torn between contempt and utter defeat, as the Master of Ebarron—her despised nemesis of the past five months—moved into place on the other side of her at the table.

CHAPTER THREE

As Sorin took his place on the other side of the woman, sandwiching her between himself and Korda where they stood at the roulette table, he swore he felt the air temperature drop a few degrees.

Back in the gallery corridor, there had been heat in her captivating dark blue eyes when she looked at him. Her creamy cheeks had flushed pink as they spoke, and he'd felt her desire for him like a physical caress.

Being an Incubus, Sorin's senses were highly attuned to sexual interest and arousal. A few moments ago, the Nephilim had been throwing off both like hot sparks.

Now? It was as if she blocked him with a wall of ice. With barely restrained contempt, if he had to guess.

Interesting.

Most women would trample each other to get near one of the Incubi Masters. Not her. He was positive he'd never met the female before, yet it was clear enough that she detested him.

Why? He was eager to find out.

He was even more eager to feel her desire again. To taste it.

To taste *her*.

The approving growl that worked its way up his throat made her inch slightly farther from him. Sorin didn't allow her the distance. He edged her way as the croupier spun the wheel and took the first bets at the table. Korda made a cautious wager on a split. Sorin called a single number and slid half his chips onto black.

Beside him, the Nephilim arched a slender brow. He could see her mentally calculating the tens of thousands of euros he'd just staked on the wheel, but she didn't so much as glance at him. Not even when Sorin allowed the outside of his thigh to brush against hers.

But he caught her sudden intake of breath at the contact. He detected the sharp spike of her heart rate at the same time, and it was all he could do to refrain from touching a lot more of her as the ball rattled in the slowing roulette wheel.

Oh, she wanted him, even now.

But she was determined as hell to deny it—to herself and to him.

Because of the Incubus on the other side of her? Sorin doubted that. She didn't seem interested in Korda Marakel either.

So, what kind of game was she playing?

She stared straight ahead, ramrod still, as the roulette ball found its pocket and the croupier called the winner. "Twenty, black. Congratulations, Master Sorin."

He won the next spin too, and all of the players but Korda Marakel retreated from the table with their pockets emptied into Ebarron's bank.

Korda was down to his last few thousand in chips. The Incubus gave a low chuckle as he toyed with his dwindling stack. "What is this, old friend? Some kind of revenge for what happened with Greta?"

Sorin smirked at the attempted jab. "If I'd been after revenge, you would've paid it a long time ago, *old friend.*" Now the Nephilim glanced at him, confusion in her night-dark eyes. Sorin held her curious gaze but spoke to the demon beside her. "You're in my House now. If you sit down to play, you'd better be prepared to lose."

To his surprise, she scoffed quietly. "No doubt especially in your House."

Her accusation was so unexpected, it took him aback. Sorin cocked his head at her. "Are you implying that Ebarron would stoop to cheating?"

"You tell me." Her expression was placid, unreadable.

Maddeningly so.

As the croupier put the wheel in motion and called for bets, Sorin reached over and took the Nephilim's hand in his.

She sucked in a sharp breath as his fingers closed around hers. "What are you—"

He drew her hand toward him without explanation, feeling her pulse jackhammer under his fingertips. Their contact felt electric, hardening him in seconds.

Her eyes were wide now, uncertain. But underneath her confusion, curiosity flared. The chilly front she tried to erect between them couldn't hide the heat that still burned inside her.

Sorin smiled a dangerous smile. He was a man accustomed to getting what he wanted, and right now, he couldn't think of anything he wanted more than to make this icy blond female combust in a screaming, soul-shattering orgasm. He could do it right now, with the power of the thrall, but where was the challenge in that?

"You seem to think I don't play fairly," Sorin murmured as he brought her fingers down onto his pile of chips, his own hand still covering hers. "So, I want you to place my next bet."

"No, I—" She shook her head. Even though his grasp was loose on her, she didn't try to pull away.

"You and I both know this is what you want." His grin deepened with meaning, and he could see she was smart enough to catch his innuendo. "Go on," he demanded. "My fortune is in your hands."

Her soft features froze over a bit at his remark. The instant Sorin relaxed his hold on her, she shoved an entire stack of chips across the table onto the red number five.

On the other side of her, Korda chuckled, then bet the same amount on a black number.

The black won.

Sorin didn't miss the female's pleased reaction as his chips were swept away. "I assume that answers your question about the integrity of my House."

She turned a frosty look on him. "Not especially. After all, what have you actually lost here? You've only transferred Ebarron's treasure from one pocket to the other."

He grunted. "True enough, but losing at anything isn't something I enjoy. I'm not in the habit of giving up what's mine."

"So I've heard."

"Have you. From whom?" Damn, the woman was practically hostile toward him now. "Do you know me? I asked your name earlier, but you didn't tell me."

When she stood in stony silence, Korda answered for her. "Told me her name's Asha."

"Asha," Sorin said, testing it on his tongue. "Asha, what? And where are you from?"

She swallowed, but her dark blue eyes were locked on him in defiance. "Asha...Messenger," she said, her reply too measured to be truthful. She licked her lips. "I came here from New York."

Sorin studied her. They most certainly had never met, and untrue or not, there was something vaguely familiar about her name.

Although she was withholding something more than that from him and he knew it. As a gambling man, he watched for tells and he easily recognized when someone was keeping their cards close to their chest.

And Asha Messenger from New York had a chest he very much wanted to explore.

He wanted to discover all of her tells, explore every last creamy inch of her. In scorchingly intimate detail.

Which meant it was time to get rid of Korda Marakel.

Sorin glanced at the croupier and gave a subtle nod of his head, an unspoken command that sent the roulette wheel spinning. As the ball was let loose, Sorin leaned around Asha to look at the other male.

He gestured to his enormous pile of chips, which dwarfed his opponent's. "All or nothing. Are you in?"

Korda stared at him, hesitant. Skeptical. But as anticipated, the Incubus's greed got the better of him. He called his number and slid his entire holdings onto the table.

Sorin did likewise, putting all of his chips on the same red square that Asha had picked a moment ago.

She slid him a questioning look. "That number already lost once."

He cocked his head. "Worried for me?"

She snorted. "Not in the least."

Instead of watching the ball as it clattered and bounced from pocket to pocket on the slowing wheel, Sorin watched Asha, utterly transfixed. She held her breath, her lower lip caught between her teeth. Her dark blue eyes followed the ball, a frown creasing her delicate brow.

"Come on, black," she whispered. "Keep going...keep going."

She slanted an arch glance at Sorin, and he chuckled.

When was the last time he'd met any woman with courage enough to not only bet against him at something, but to openly taunt him as well? And this defiance was coming from a Nephilim who knew damned well he was not some lowly Incubus cousin from the Ebarron line, but Master of the House.

He should have been annoyed at her lack of deference for his rank. Instead he was fascinated.

"Number five, red," the croupier announced.

Asha exhaled a disappointed sigh. Korda

Marakel was far more vocal. He cursed harshly and pushed away from the table, raking a hand through his dark hair. "That spin was rigged. It had to be."

"There's only one cheat in this room, and it's not me. You took your shot. You lost." Sorin gave an idle shrug and met his rival's glare. "And this table is now closed for the night."

Fury exploded from Korda. "You son of a bitch! I demand another chance to win back my money."

His outburst drew plenty of attention from the other tables in the roulette room. Several of Ebarron's grim-faced Watchmen moved in from their posts before the situation could escalate any further. Milo led the pack of lethal Incubus guards.

At Sorin's nod, the captain of the Watchmen dropped a firm hand on Korda's shoulder. "It's time for you to leave now."

"Gladly," he grumbled. "Asha. Let's go."

She didn't move.

Sorin looked at her, waiting for her to fall in with her so-called date. He arched a brow in question. Her hesitation seemed conflicted, as if part of her couldn't get away from him fast enough, yet another part of her could not compel her feet to move.

Sorin was more than happy to handle the indecision for her. "Show Marakel out. The lady will be staying for as long as she likes. As my personal guest."

Milo and the other Watchmen obeyed at once, escorting the sputtering, bewildered Incubus from the roulette room and out of the casino.

When it was just the two of them standing at the table, Sorin turned his full attention on Asha.

Leaning an elbow on the tall table, he held her midnight blue gaze. He couldn't help but smile that he had the intriguing female all to himself. "So it seems you *are* interested in playing after all."

Her chin notched up a degree. "I don't like games."

"Yet here you are." He lowered his voice to a private level, a grin tugging at his lips. "Even if you don't want to admit it to me, I think you enjoy taking risks."

Something sharp, shrewd, glinted in her eyes. "I'm certainly not afraid of it."

"No," he said, chuckling. "I can see that you're not."

Fuck, she was an enticing female. He'd noticed that plainly enough on first glance from the balcony earlier tonight, and again in the gallery promenade.

Now that he was alone with her, close enough to touch, close enough to breathe in the sweet, warm scent of her skin, Sorin couldn't tear his eyes from her. He'd already considered a hundred different ways he wanted to have her.

All he had to do was convince her that she wanted him too.

"How about a private round, Asha of New York?" He indicated the roulette wheel and the croupier, waiting for instructions. "Care to take me on at the table, just the two of us?"

She considered, then gave a small shake of her head. "I don't have any money. I spent everything I had just to get here."

Sorin was undeterred. "I'll extend House credit to you. No strings attached."

LARA ADRIAN

At his silent signal, the croupier gathered several tall stacks of chips and slid them in front of Asha. Her brows lifted, but when she looked at Sorin, her eyes were full of wariness. "Why would you do this?"

"Because you intrigue me, and I'm not ready to let you go just yet."

"I intrigue you," she said, cautious now. Suspicious. "What exactly is that supposed to mean?"

"You arouse me." Sorin leaned toward her, leaving bare inches between his mouth and hers. "I want you, lovely Asha, and I'm trying to decide how best to seduce you. Is that exact enough for you?"

Some of her defiance fled at his bold candor. She was no timid mouse, but she didn't seem able to hold his gaze now. She glanced away from him, down at the small fortune in front of her. "And if I say I want to leave?"

"Then go now. Take the chips with you and cash them in. No one will stop you."

She gaped at him. "You'd actually let me walk out of here right now with more than twenty thousand euros?"

"I would, yes."

She shook her head and exhaled a short laugh. "Then apparently you're the one who likes taking risks."

"No, Asha." He reached out and stroked his fingers down her silky cheek, unable to resist touching her. "I like to win."

He gave the croupier a nod and the wheel started to spin. Asha didn't move. Hell, as far as he could tell, she barely breathed beside him as Sorin waited

30

for her to either accept his challenge or reject him outright.

An unspoken but palpable tension crackled between them, ratcheted up even tighter with each rotation of the wheel. Without taking his eyes off her, Sorin placed his bet.

"Your turn," he prompted her softly. "Last chance to run away."

She swallowed, her gaze locked on his. A torrent of emotions roiled in her dark blue eyes. Uncertainty. Mistrust. Outrage. Contempt.

And yes, desire.

Sorin had made his share of wagers during his life, had learned to read people on a glance. And yet this woman mystified him. He wanted her to stay right now the way he needed air to breathe. Yet he prepared himself to watch her gather up her chips and glide out of his life as mysteriously as she'd appeared.

But she didn't leave.

Asha reached for a large handful of chips, then hesitated, her slender fingers hovering over the stacks. The look she swung on him was pensive, as though she were calculating odds of her own. Then she gave a small shake of her pale blond head. "I've come too far to run away now. I'm in."

Sorin grinned, more than pleased. "Good."

The Nephilim blew out a quiet curse and called her number. Then, to his surprise, she took her hands away from her chips. "I'm in, but I'm not interested in your money."

CHAPTER FOUR

If the sexual heat pouring off Sorin Ebarron had been powerful before, the moment those words left her mouth the air turned instantly electric. Erotic energy surged off the Incubus, vibrating somewhere deep inside Asha's core.

As Sorin stared at her, a low, predatory sound curled up from his throat. His topaz eyes flared with avid interest.

"Do tell," he said, that unnerving gaze sharpening, penetrating her. "What do I have that might interest you more than my money, delectable Asha Messenger from New York?"

Hearing him speak her name like that—a name that was mostly a lie, given to Korda Marakel as a small bit of self-protection—helped jostle her out of the spell of Sorin's innate allure.

Only Gran called her Asha. Her last name wasn't Messenger either, and although she'd flown to Bucharest from New York City, Ashayla had lived in Chicago all her life. If Sorin Ebarron knew any of those things, he'd know for certain who she really was. And he would probably just as easily guess why she was really there tonight.

His full lips curved with wicked curiosity. "Don't keep me in suspense. If you want to alter our wager, you have to do it before the ball stops on the wheel."

Oh, God. She must be out of her mind to think she could play games with this demon, let alone win at them.

But she had to. She meant it when she told him she'd come too far to run away now. Whether she'd realized it at the time or not, she'd been all-in the moment she stepped foot in the Ebarron casino tonight.

She couldn't back down now, no matter how dangerous the stakes.

"Okay." She swallowed, summoning her courage. "If I win, I want you to let me take one item from Ebarron's treasure room."

"What?" The request obviously took the Incubus aback. He blinked—or was it a flinch? Then his tawny brows crashed down in a scowl. "Out of the question. There are too many priceless things in there. And besides, treasure won by Ebarron—"

"Is never surrendered. Yes, I know." Ashayla forced herself to hold his thunderous stare. "Afraid to take the risk, Incubus?"

"Not at all." He leaned in close now, breathing her in. Dissecting her with his shrewd gaze. "The question is, will you be willing to pay my price if I win?"

As if to punctuate his challenge, the roulette wheel began to slow. The quiet rattle of the ball made the moment feel endless, time stretching to a crawl along with her indecision.

She thought about Gran back home, about the

prospect of letting the most cherished person in Ashayla's life pass to the next with a burden weighing so heavily on her frail shoulders. Gran was desperate to have the pendant back in her hands. And Ashayla was determined to be the one to bring it to her.

She lifted her chin, refusing to let the demon intimidate her. "Fine. What do you want from me?"

Ashayla didn't expect him to move as quickly as he did. She didn't anticipate the sudden heat and strength of his hand as it wrapped around her nape and hauled her toward him.

And she sure as hell was not prepared for the moment his mouth crashed down on hers in a fevered, dizzying kiss.

When she parted her lips on a small gasp, Sorin took full advantage. His tongue pushed past her teeth in a sweeping, erotic claiming that practically melted her where she stood.

He held her firmly as his kiss deepened, igniting a desire in her that she was helpless to deny. Her nerves tingled everywhere their bodies brushed together. Her breasts felt heavy and tight, aching for his touch. Her sex ached even more. With just one kiss, she was wet and melting, longing for more.

Sorin's spicy male scent invaded her senses like a drug, saturating her self-control until all she knew was this man and his devastating effect on her.

This Incubus she despised, yet desired in a startlingly powerful way.

When he finally released her, Ashayla was panting, every inch of her on fire.

"My price is you," he announced thickly. "You, for the rest of the night. I trust I've left no doubt as to what's at stake."

She rubbed her swollen lips with the back of her hand, furious that her mouth—and other parts of her traitorous body—still throbbed with pleasure from his unwelcome kiss.

Ashayla glanced to the slowing roulette wheel and the ball that would determine her fate tonight. Everything rational screamed for her to get as far away from Sorin Ebarron as fast as she possibly could. Even while everything female in her arched toward him against her will.

Sorin leaned close to murmur near her ear. "One final chance for you to end this ruse now and run back home where you belong, little Nephilim."

His smile was as profane as it was playful. The arrogant bastard.

Ashayla bared her teeth as she skewered him with a glare. "Fuck you, Incubus."

"Excellent. Then we're agreed." He chuckled, looking gorgeous and wicked—and far too confident. "I accept your wager...with pleasure."

~ ~ ~

Lust spiraled through him after that hot, uninvited kiss.

It staggered him, in fact. Sorin could not recall the last time a woman had enticed him so thoroughly. Never, if he was pressed to name one.

Now all he could think about was how quickly he could get Asha Messenger naked beneath him in his bed.

Or rather, Ashayla Palatine.

That was her real name. And she wasn't from New York, but Chicago.

He knew it now with a certainty that infuriated him almost as much as it intrigued him. As soon as she mentioned the treasure room, all the pieces clicked into place.

Damn. He should have realized even sooner, but he'd been too caught up in his carnal pursuit of the Nephilim to stop and think with anything other than his very enthusiastic cock.

He had received more than a dozen letters and emails from one Miss A. Palatine over a five-month period, all concerning a certain bauble that had been in the Ebarron vaults for nearly twenty years. After Sorin's refusal to sell it back to her, the Nephilim had gone from imploring to indignant to downright insulting.

And now here she was, in the flesh, on Ebarron soil.

Very delectable flesh, from what Sorin could ascertain.

In all the times he had imagined her—and there had been many—he'd envisioned a dour little church mouse with a voice to shrivel even the lustiest Incubus's allure. Instead, Ashayla Palatine was a tall and luscious, defiant temptress.

One who'd arrived tonight under false pretense, besides.

As wildly attracted to her as he was, Ashayla's true purpose for coming to his domain was the thing that now captivated Sorin the most. Before he let her out of his sight tonight, he would unravel every one of her secrets.

If he could undress her and have her screaming his name at the same time, so much the better.

Idly tapping his index finger on the tallest stack of his chips, Sorin watched the slowing wheel. He heard Ashayla's inhaled breath as the ball bounced from pocket to pocket. Felt her go utterly still beside him on the final clatter that sealed her fate.

The croupier called the winner.

Sorin.

Ashayla stood wooden, staring at the table as Sorin dismissed the croupier with a casual lift of his hand. "That will be all for tonight, Carl. Thank you." As the tuxedoed casino worker stepped away to leave them their privacy, Sorin swiveled his head to look at Ashayla. "I have to admit, this has been a most memorable night already...Miss Palatine."

She swung a stricken glance at him.

"Yes, I know who you are. And it doesn't change a thing. You made a deal, Ashayla."

She scoffed beneath her breath. "A deal with the devil, if you ask me."

Sorin smiled, gave a mild shrug. "Nevertheless...I mean to hold you to it."

He held out his arm to her. She didn't take it. She hardly moved. Sorin half-expected her to cry foul or bolt like a frightened doe. If she had, maybe he would have shown her mercy and let her go.

Maybe.

But she did neither of those things.

Shoulders squared, chin held high, she looked at him with ice in her midnight blue eyes. "The rest of the night and not a minute more," she said. "That was the price. Nothing more."

"You know the price, Ashayla."

She regarded him the way she might look at something that had crawled out from one of Hell's sulfurous abysses. "What do you mean to do? Rape me, or use the thrall to do the work for you?"

He deflected her barb with a cool shake of his head. "There won't be any need for such heavy-handed tactics. Before the night is over, you'll be begging me to take you. After that kiss a moment ago, I'm guessing you're more than halfway there already."

"I'm sure you'd like to think so." She pinned him in a seething stare, even though her cheeks flamed with color. "Since you know who I am, it shouldn't come as any surprise to know that I despise you and everything your House stands for. If you think that's going to change because I was foolish enough to gamble against you tonight, you're sorely mistaken."

He met her outrage with a calm, level glance. He reached out, unable to resist stroking his fingertips over the deep pink flush on her face. "I said you're going to want me between your legs, sweet Asha. I didn't say you had to like me."

CHAPTER FIVE

Crude. Overbearing. Despicable.

Seated alone in an elegant dining room inside Ebarron House's living quarters, Ashayla mentally recited a litany of condemnations for the demon Master who'd brought her there about an hour ago. Sorin had personally escorted her from the casino to the private elevator that carried them up to the Incubi stronghold a dozen floors above, then he'd left her by herself without a word of excuse or explanation.

As she waited, dreading what might come next, she couldn't help reliving the time she'd already spent in Sorin's company.

She couldn't help recalling the way he teased her, taunted her, even charmed her—all against her will. The memory of his kiss still blazed on her lips, on her tongue. Just the thought of his hot, demanding mouth on hers made liquid heat pool in her core.

But he was wrong if he thought he could seduce her. No matter what she'd wagered tonight, she had no intention of giving herself to him willingly.

She would rather chew off her own arm than give the demon that satisfaction.

Arrogant. Infuriating. Bastard.

He may have won their bet, but she hadn't forgotten why she was there in the first place.

Reaching down to her boot, she slipped her fingers inside the black leather to where the small metal vial of Nephilim magic was concealed. Still there. Maybe this awful detour could be used to her advantage. Maybe there would be an opportunity to slip away from Sorin later tonight and search for the treasure room.

Or maybe she should use the potion for her own self-preservation and escape before the Incubus returned to collect on her debt.

As her fingers curled around the vial, the massive double doors opened across the room and Sorin strode inside.

"I apologize for leaving you here by yourself for so long. Family matters required my attention." He said it as if she was a guest invited for tea and he the polite host.

Ashayla casually brought her hands into her lap and shrugged. "I hope you didn't rush back on my account. You could've stayed away all night as far as I'm concerned."

He grunted, the corner of his mouth quirking. As he approached the table and took the seat at the head of it to her right, several Incubi servants in formal attire followed from outside the room.

The men wheeled in two large dining carts draped in white linen and loaded with dome-covered dinner plates and fine china table service for two. On another cart came a chilling bottle of champagne and sparkling crystal glasses. The servants began efficiently arranging the silver and glassware on the table in front of Ashayla and him. They placed one covered plate in front of her, another in front of Sorin.

It was lovely, all of it. And oh…it smelled delicious, even from under the polished silver lids.

She swiveled a suspicious glance on Sorin. "What's the meaning of this?"

"Dinner. I thought you'd be hungry."

Was he kidding? "No." She shook her head. "You can't actually expect that I'm going to sit here and eat with you like I'm your guest and this is…what, some twisted kind of date?"

One tawny brow lifted. "Would you prefer we skip the formalities and head right to my bed?" Sorin's handsome face was placid as he looked at her, but dark power stormed in his penetrating gaze. "Or shall we have the meal cleared away and make use of the table instead?"

Ashayla snapped her mouth closed before she could wade any further into his snare. She sat in mute outrage as the servants hastily finished setting the table.

When they left and closed the doors behind them, she glared at him. "I suppose you enjoy humiliating women in front of your household staff?"

"Not at all," he said, his tone solemn. "Not ever."

She scoffed. "I see. Only me, then."

"Not even you, Asha. I have the utmost respect for any female in my care or safekeeping. As for my staff, this is an Incubi House. Talk of sex and pleasure doesn't shock them, I assure you. I could've spread you beneath me right in front of them and they wouldn't have batted an eye."

The image leapt into her mind with instant, vivid clarity and she swallowed. Hard.

"Heathens," she muttered, even as the thought of being pinned to the table under Sorin's strong body wreaked havoc on her thoughts and sent arrows of heat streaking through her veins. "If that kind of behavior passes for respect in your world, it's no wonder so many Nephilim prefer to live among humans instead of being a mate to one of the Incubi. Is that what happened with Greta?"

He drew back at that remark, frowning in question. "You don't know anything about that."

"Back in the casino, Korda Marakel made it sound as if she was important to you. Was she?" Asha studied him. "Is she still?"

His sharp, short exhalation was dismissive. Derisive, even. "Greta was a brief, pleasant diversion from my duties, and a family-approved candidate as my mate. At least she was, until she started fucking any Incubus who would have her. Including, finally, my former friend, Korda. I cut them both out of my life five years ago. I haven't looked back since."

He chuckled darkly after he said it, those unnerving eyes holding her in an oddly amused stare. Asha stared right back, utterly confused.

Lord help her, but she did not know what to make of this man at all. "You can laugh over losing a lover and a friend? Are you crazy, or just that callous?"

"Neither." He leaned forward, his elbows braced on the edge of the table. "I find it funny to realize I was more disappointed when your letters and emails stopped coming than I was when Greta moved on with Korda."

Now it was her turn to laugh. "I don't believe that for a minute. I'm pretty sure I called you a selfish, pompous jerk in the last message I sent you."

"Actually, you called me a selfish, pompous jackass. One who, and I quote, obviously doesn't have an ounce of compassion in his Hell-spawned body."

Asha bit her lip, recalling that heated final reply with fair accuracy herself. "I don't hear you denying it."

He shrugged mildly. "No, you don't. What about you?"

"What about me?"

"You're a beautiful woman," he pointed out. "Headstrong and reckless, obviously. Opinionated and judgmental too—"

"Gee, thanks."

"—but lovely," he said. "So why hasn't another man—another Incubus—convinced you to become his mate? Don't bother to deny it. I checked into your family background after your first letter arrived."

"You what?"

He shrugged again, utterly unapologetic. "I was…curious. I am curious, Asha. Do all of the Nephilim women in your line despise my kind?"

"Of course not."

"Do you?"

She frowned. "No. I don't despise all of your kind."

He grunted. "I see. Only me, then."

A twinge of guilt pricked her to hear her own words tossed back at her, but she shut it down just as swiftly.

No, no, no. She was *not* going to let him make her feel that her dislike toward him was misplaced. After five months and a dozen denied requests for him to show one tiny ounce of sympathy for the wishes of a dying old woman, Sorin Ebarron had earned every bit of her resentment.

After his profane wager that had landed her in his hands for the duration of the night—God help her, in his *bed*—Ashayla had even more cause to despise him.

She shook her head. "Why wouldn't you just give the pendant back?"

"The piece belongs to Ebarron now. That's why. We acquired it honestly and fairly, the same way we've acquired every other piece of jewelry, art and arcana in the Ebarron treasury."

Indignation flickered inside her as she watched him calmly reach for the champagne and pour some into her glass as if the discussion was over. "That pendant is my grandmother's. It never should have been sold at all. Haven't you amassed a large enough hoard without this one item? How deep is Ebarron's greed that you won't part with a single trivial piece?"

"Value is a relative thing. And if we forfeited every bit of treasure each time someone expressed regret over losing it to us, the House vaults would be empty." He offered her the filled crystal flute, but instead of letting go when she reached for it, Sorin's fingers closed over hers. His grasp was light, but firm. Startlingly possessive. "Why would I let go of something I won fair and square?"

Rattled by the contact as much as her body's reaction to it, Ashayla pulled out of his hold and exhaled a short, frustrated sigh. "We're not talking about priceless treasure. We're talking about a simple, polished stone on a silver chain. It's hardly worth anything beyond sentimental value and you know it."

"I know no such thing. I know only what you've told me. That it's a family heirloom supposedly sold by mistake a long time ago, and now a dying old Nephilim is suddenly desperate to have it back before she pushes out her last breath. Maybe the person I should be asking about all of this is her."

"Don't," Ashayla murmured, wounded by his cold tone. "Don't speak of my grandmother so dismissively. You don't know anything about her. She raised me. She's all the family I have in this world. You have no right to talk about her as if her life and the things that matter to her are not important."

He'd gone silent as she berated him, solemn. When he finally spoke, his deep voice was quiet with sincerity. "Forgive me. I didn't realize—"

"No, you wouldn't have. But now you do, so leave her out of this." Her tone was still bitter, her heart still stung and defensive.

She took a drink of her champagne, missing Gran like crazy now. Hoping she was okay back home without Ashayla to look after her.

Sorin moved his chair out and stood without speaking. As Ashayla took a larger sip from her glass, she felt, rather than saw, him come around to the other side of her.

As formally as the most meticulously trained server, he unfolded the crisp white linen napkin and gently placed it on her lap. Then he lifted the dome from her dinner plate, revealing a gourmet meal of roasted chicken, perfectly steamed vegetables and aromatic sauce.

"Please," he said softly. "Relax and enjoy your meal, Asha."

He returned to the head of the table, resuming his place without another word. They ate in a strangely companionable silence, and she found it difficult to keep from stealing glances at him as he carved his meat and drank his champagne.

She couldn't deny her attraction to him on a physical level. With his glorious golden hair, arresting topaz eyes and that wickedly sensual mouth, to say the Incubus was handsome was an understatement. And his body...even in his conservative dark suit and white shirt, it was more than obvious that Sorin Ebarron was six-plus feet of lean, muscled perfection.

Worst of all, he knew it.

Looking at him at the table beside her, dining with him as though they weren't engaged in an impossible standoff, Ashayla would have preferred his infuriating arrogance and demonic swagger.

This thoughtful, civilized man in the room with her now was more dangerous by far.

Finally given some peace, Ashayla realized she was hungry after all, and her dinner, as she suspected, was amazing. She finished most of it a few moments after Sorin had cleaned his plate completely.

They drank the rest of the champagne, then he rose and walked over to help pull out her chair. "Shall we?"

"Shall we, what?"

"Come with me, Asha."

Oh, God.

Left with little choice, she stood up and faced him, uncertain. Nervous to find out what was to come next.

CHAPTER SIX

With his broad palm hovering possessively at the small of her back, Sorin guided her out of the dining room and down a long hallway. Like the casino a dozen stories below, Ebarron's mansion fortress was opulent and awe-inspiring. Rare art decorated every wall space and corner. Intricate parquet flooring gleamed beneath her feet.

Sorin led her deeper into the sumptuous Incubus stronghold, his warm hand at her spine generating heat she felt like a brand. They passed a large banquet room filled with other Incubi and several beautiful women, all dressed in sophisticated clothing and conversing in hushed, serious murmurs over a generous spread of food and wine.

Most of the females were Nephilim, Ashayla noted, as more than a few heads turned to look at her in question or surprise as Sorin shuttled her past the open doors without a word of excuse or introduction.

As for the males in the room, they all bore the golden good looks of the Ebarron line, though none seemed quite as commanding a presence as Sorin. A fact that only made sense, considering he was the Master of his House. She wasn't familiar with the intricacies of Incubi politics, but she'd learned enough here and there to know that each of the nine surviving Houses was ruled by the strongest, most capable male of their line.

Not to mention the most ruthless.

Sorin smoothly guided her along the length of another labyrinthine corridor. No one was in this part of the fortress, and each step seemed to carry them deeper into a world she was unprepared to face. Was he taking her to his bed now? Or did he have some other game in mind?

Ashayla awkwardly cleared her throat. "Where are you taking me?"

His voice was dark velvet beside her. "You'll see."

She braced herself as they finally paused in front of a set of ornately carved double doors. The dark wood was emblazoned with the Ebarron griffin and a fluid script written in a language she assumed would date back to the first generations of Incubi, eons past.

Sorin opened the doors without preamble and swung them wide. "After you."

She glanced into the darkness, confused. Then she heard a soft click behind her as he turned on the switch and light flooded the massive treasure room.

Ashayla whirled on him. "All the rumors say this room is located beneath the casino."

"Of course they do. Who do you imagine started those rumors?"

His smile was unreadable, somewhere between pride and cautious scrutiny as he gestured for her to enter ahead of him. Ashayla walked inside, not even sure she was breathing as she took in the sight of thousands of rare works of art and sculpture, busts and figures made of precious metals and cases of glittering, priceless jewels. Scores of vibrant tapestries and rolls of parchment scrolls filled another part of the expansive room.

"It's incredible," she gasped.

Sorin's reply was matter-of-fact. "Yes, it is."

She gaped at him. "It's an obscene fortune."

"Yes."

He started walking ahead of her, heading toward an opened clear case at the far end of the massive collection. When he stopped in front of it, Ashayla glanced down at what it contained and her breath caught in her throat for a different reason.

"Gran's pendant."

She'd only seen it a few times when she was child, before her mother pawned it. But she would recognize the tear-shaped, light blue cabochon stone and the modest silver chain anywhere.

It was right there in front of her now. Close enough to touch.

Close enough to take.

Did he mean to give it back to her now?

She looked up at Sorin in question.

If she thought she might find softness in his eyes, that hope vanished the instant her gaze met his. His voice was equally unyielding. "Tell me what this pendant really means to you, Asha."

"I did tell you, numerous times. It belongs to my gran—"

He made a sound of impatience in the back of his throat. "I don't think it does. It's an unusual piece. An unusual stone, if not particularly remarkable. And a chain made of silver? Everyone knows that material is one of the most toxic to the Incubi."

She had no idea what he was talking about. "It's been in my family for generations. It would still be with us, if my mother hadn't pawned it. If she hadn't been…"

"What?"

Ashayla shook her head. When she tried to avoid his gaze, Sorin reached out, his fingertips light under her chin as he guided her eyes back to him. "If she hadn't been what, Asha?"

"Desperate for money." The words crept up, bitter as bile. "Desperate for her next fix."

Sorin frowned. "She was an addict?"

What was the point in trying to deny it now? Her mother was gone, dead long ago. Ashayla nodded. "From before I was born, according to Gran. My mother might have been Nephilim, but she had her own kind of demons inside her. Gran said my mother was a little mad, even before her addictions took hold of her."

"You never mentioned any of this when you wrote to me."

"Air my family's shame to a stranger?" she asked softly. "Plead for pity?" God, she would never do either of those things.

Sorin studied her. "You never mentioned it."

"Would it have made a difference?"

He didn't answer. For a long moment, he didn't say anything at all. Then he heaved out a sigh. "It doesn't matter what either of us might have done before. This is now, after you've come to my House under false pretenses. Compassion isn't part of this equation."

His level tone stung her worse than had he bellowed at her. She shook her head, trying to think of a way to explain herself, or to justify her reasons. "Sorin, you have to understand—"

"Understand that you didn't accept my decision, so you thought you would defy it instead? You've lied to me about your name and your intentions. I can only guess what you thought you were going to do once you got here." His sharp-edged features seemed to harden even more as he spoke. He brought his hand toward her face, but despite his cold words and glacial gaze, his fingers were tender when they lit on her cheek. "I'm not a fool, Asha. If you make the mistake of thinking I am, you'll also find I'm not a forgiving man."

She licked her lips, swallowing the tangled knot of guilt and fear that had lodged itself in her throat.

Sorin exhaled a slow sigh as he stroked her jawline, his thumb caressing the sensitive skin below her chin. "But I'm not a monster either. Before you think about testing me any more than you already have, I'm prepared to alter the terms of our deal."

"What do you mean?" Her voice trembled somewhat as he continued to trace his fingers along her tingling skin. Her heart rate galloped, everything female in her captivated by the potency of his stare and the gentle coaxing of his touch. "Alter the terms...how?"

A smile slowly lifted the corner of his sensual mouth. "You owe me the night in my bed, and that's a debt I fully intend to collect. But since you claim you don't desire me, I propose a new wager."

She didn't trust that glimmer of a smile. It was too diabolical. Too classically Incubus. "Dare I hope, one that doesn't require me to sleep with you?"

"Oh, this has nothing to do with sleeping." Now he smirked. "You insist you don't desire me—"

"I don't." The blurt lacked fire, even to her own ears. She tried again, giving her voice more steam. "I don't care what we wagered tonight. I won't ever want you."

He inclined his head in acknowledgment. "And I am certain you do, and you will."

He stepped closer to her, his large body and sinfully intoxicating scent sapping all of the air from the room. Ashayla had nowhere to go, no hope of escaping his demonic allure.

He didn't touch her, but his hooded, knowing gaze was enough to ignite the embers of awareness that had been smoldering since she'd first laid eyes on him in the casino.

And he knew his effect on her. Knew it all along, and now he planned to put her to the test.

"Deny it all you want," he murmured. "I'm willing to bet that before the sun rises, you'll not only want me, you'll be begging me to take you."

"Ha." She scoffed, hoping she sounded sufficiently appalled. "In your dreams."

"So prove it. Resist me." At her skeptical look, he gave a small shrug. "If you can, then in the morning you're free to leave with the treasure you came here to steal from me."

He knew? God, of course he knew. She wouldn't

insult him or herself by trying to deny it.

Still, she didn't trust him. He was an Incubus, after all, and he already warned her that he was not a forgiving one.

"I don't believe you. It sounds too easy." She shook her head. "It sounds like a trick. You're going to manipulate me somehow. Enthrall me?"

"No tricks," he said. "No use of the thrall or any other means of coercion or force. Just you and me, Asha. In my bed. For the rest of the night."

"You're serious." Was he really going to make it so simple for her? Sure, he was attractive. Seductive, even. But she was determined to walk out of this situation with her pride intact. And she would do anything—resist anything—to bring Gran's pendant home to her.

"All right, then. Deal." She thrust out her hand to him. "I accept."

"Good." He took her fingers into a firm, warm grasp that didn't let up for a long moment. Those fiery topaz eyes bored into her, full of confidence and wicked determination. "Make no mistake, though. Before dawn, I promise I *will* make love to you, Asha." He drew her closer, until her breasts mashed against the hard, muscled planes of his chest.

Lowering his head to hers, he spoke in a velvety growl, his lips nearly brushing hers with each illicit word. "I mean to have my cock inside you, my name rolling off your tongue on a pleasured scream. But I will accept your submission through free will and nothing less."

He kissed her then, just the lightest, teasing nip at her mouth, and she nearly combusted where she stood. Desire flooded her body and limbs. Her pulse galloped, and everything female in her arced toward him for more. More contact. More heat. More inflaming promises of what he wanted to do with her.

Oh, God. She was doomed.

She closed her eyes, wishing for a deeper kiss even as her survival instincts howled in alarm.

Sorin's breath gusted against her on a low curse. His hand went around to her nape, guiding her deeper into his embrace, deeper into his consuming heat. Then his mouth came down on hers, gently this time. Reverently.

Ashayla couldn't think.

She couldn't summon even a shred of resistance...

Until she realized they weren't alone in the room anymore. Someone cleared his throat behind them near the open double doors.

Sorin tore his mouth away from hers on a snarl. "What is it?"

A handsome, elegantly suited Incubus with short golden hair and breathtaking features not unlike Sorin's stood in the doorway. Ashayla recognized him as one of the people gathered in the salon when she and Sorin walked past a short while ago. He took his time looking at her now, his expression curious, questioning. Friendlier than Sorin's could ever be.

"Radu," Sorin acknowledged. All the passion of a moment ago was instantly replaced with a different kind of tension now. "Has there been any change in him, brother?"

The other male gave a grim nod. "He's awake.

He's pissed as hell." Dread and weariness edged his voice. "He's calling for you, Sorin."

CHAPTER SEVEN

Sorin raked a hand through his hair and blew out a sharp sigh.

He couldn't ignore the unpleasantness that awaited him elsewhere in the family stronghold, but he didn't have time to stow his pretty guest somewhere while he took care of the problem.

He sure as hell wasn't about to leave Ashayla with his charming, better looking younger brother. Radu was already having a hard enough time taking his eyes off the stunning blond Nephilim. While Sorin was arguably not the most suitable protector of her virtue, he'd be damned before he let his shameless sibling get within arm's length of her.

"I'll handle it." He took Asha's hand in his, and on a muttered curse swept past Radu with her in tow. "Tell Milo to meet me outside the chamber."

Asha's long-legged stride kept up with Sorin easily, but he could feel her confusion in every step they took together. "What's going on?"

He doubted she'd really wish to know. He could only imagine what was going on in the chamber where they were heading. They had barely turned the corner of the long corridor that led to the private cell when a tremendous, animalistic howl shook the floor beneath their feet.

Ashayla startled, throwing him a wild glance. "What was that?"

"My father."

She didn't ask anything more, not even when another furious roar erupted from within the closed chamber. Sorin brought her to a halt outside the barred door and turned to face her stricken expression. Milo arrived at that same moment, the captain of the Watchmen giving Sorin a knowing nod as another crazed shout went up, followed by the crash of something shattering against the floor.

"Take her to my quarters. Wait with her there," he instructed the guard. To Asha he said, "You'll be safe with Milo. He'll look after you until I'm through here."

"Um, okay." She seemed to consider for a moment. Then she stunned him by reaching out to place her hand on his forearm. Her light touch was tender, halting. "What about you, Sorin?"

"What about me?" He scowled as a litany of foul curses sounded on the other side of the heavy door.

"Will you be safe in there?"

Her question took him aback completely. He stroked the side of her face.

No one ever worried for him. He was a formidable male. A powerful Incubus, the Master of his House. The eldest son, he'd been the one expected to shoulder every responsibility and problem without hesitation or failure.

So he had, all his life. Never questioning his role. Never requiring accolades or soft reassurances.

And yet here was this woman who'd been little

more than a name on paper to him until tonight—a beautiful, courageous woman whom he'd given little cause to care what might happen to him—looking at him now with genuine concern.

He wanted nothing more than to pull her into his arms and kiss her just then. Hell, he wanted to do a lot more than that. And he would, as promised, before the night was over.

But right now his duty called him to deal with the bitter old demon imprisoned in the room behind him.

Pivoting around, he released the heavy lock bar and opened the door. The room inside was dark, but not dark enough to conceal the shriveled form standing in the center of the large chamber in loose-fitting linen pants and a long tunic.

And not dark enough to conceal the gaunt face and wild eyes of the madman who'd been Ebarron's Master for centuries, until Sorin forcibly took his seat a year ago.

Behind him, Asha let out a small gasp. Sorin turned back to her, caressing her cheek on a throttled growl. "Go with Milo. You don't need to worry about me."

~ ~ ~

He was gone for more than an hour.

Ashayla sat on an oxblood leather sofa in a large salon inside what she assumed was Sorin's private apartments in the massive Ebarron stronghold. His Watchman waited with her in measured silence, standing across the room like a statue until the door opened and Sorin strode inside.

He was scowling fiercely, but to Ashayla he seemed more weary than anything else. His broad mouth was drawn at the corners, his sharp topaz eyes dulled with fatigue and stress. He dismissed Milo in hushed tones, then closed the door behind him as the Watchman departed.

"I need a shower," he murmured, scrubbing a hand over his head and jaw. He arched a brow at her in invitation. "You're welcome to join me, if you like."

He was trying to be light and casual, trying to return to their banter from before he'd been summoned to his father's heavily locked room. She couldn't play along after what she'd heard and seen outside that chamber, but she followed him into the adjacent bedroom. "Is he all right, Sorin?"

"He's insane, as you might've guessed. And he's furious with me for petitioning the rest of the family to see him ousted from power as Master of Ebarron, so I could take control."

"Why did you do it?"

"It was best for the House." His tone held little inflection. When he pivoted to face her, as guarded as his expression was, she also saw weariness. There was a sadness in his grim features that she suspected he let few others see in him. "My mother was the one who asked me to challenge my father's seat as Master. She came to me two years ago—not long before she died—and pleaded for me to step in."

"Because he wasn't well?" Ashayla guessed.

Sorin nodded. "That had long been a concern of hers, yes. Mine as well. But also because now more than ever, the Incubi Houses need to be strong, united. If the angels in their Conclave and the Three in their temple are plotting an insurrection, or manipulating our Sovereign to light the first spark, then we all need to be ready for what comes next."

"You're talking about war between the Incubi and the angels?"

"If the Houses don't stop it first, Asha, I could be talking about war between Heaven and Hell."

She swallowed the dread that crept up her throat. Although her life in Chicago was far removed from the one Sorin referred to, she knew enough from talking with Gran over the years to understand the danger of corruption on the Obsidian Throne, the highest seat of power in the Incubi and Nephilim realms. The Incubus who ruled from it as the Sovereign held authority over the portals of both Heaven and Hell. If the Throne were to fall, there would be no holding back the chaos that would follow.

Sorin gave a grim shake of his head. "My mother loved my father as only a mate can, but she also loved Ebarron and wanted the House to thrive for future generations. I had no interest in serving as its Master, least of all while my father was still alive. But she was right. Duty comes first. The House and all who live under its protection come before anyone else. So, I presented my case before my brothers and cousins and they agreed that I should step in."

"How did your father take the news when your mother told him what she'd done?"

Sorin gave a vague shrug. "He doesn't know. She didn't want him to know it was her idea, so neither of us told him and no one else knew. My mother was killed a few months later, when her car swerved off one of the mountain passes. After she was gone, I didn't see the point in tarnishing his feelings toward her."

"But he thinks it was you, Sorin. He thinks it was your idea to push him out of the way." Ashayla shook her head. "Why let him think the worst of you?"

"It would've destroyed him more to know that she felt him unfit to lead. He was bad off already. I saw no need to add fuel to the fire."

Sorin spoke like a man used to shouldering heavy burdens without complaint. His actions seemed equally unfazed. She watched as he began to undress, his suit coat slung over the back of a chair across from the bed before he started unbuttoning his white shirt.

"Your father looks very weak. Is he dying too?"

He nodded gravely. "His madness worsened after my mother died. He probably doesn't have much time left now. The family's looked after his comfort as best we can, but it's…difficult."

"I'm sorry." Ashayla had heard about the mating bond between Incubi and Nephilim, of course. It was eternal, and since Incubi relied on their Nephilim mates exclusively for sustenance, separations were almost always a fatal sentence for the one left behind. "Sorin, I'm sorry for him and for everything you're dealing with."

She felt awful now, as selfish and unreasonable as she had believed Sorin to be. She'd been so obsessed with making Gran happy by getting her heirloom back, Ashayla never stopped to consider the burdens Sorin might be faced with as Master of Ebarron House.

He had his own personal struggles to contend with, his duties as head of his family and their business interests, all of it compounded by the demands and increasingly dangerous politics surrounding the fate of the Obsidian Throne.

Sorin shrugged, then stripped off his shirt. Although she hadn't intended to let her gaze stray so long on his body at that moment, it was impossible not to notice the magnificence of him. She'd suspected he'd be big and athletic and gorgeous underneath his refined clothing, and he was. Beyond gorgeous. Smooth, golden skin wrapped bulky shoulders and beefy pectorals. His chest was broad and strong, his abdomen rippled with lean muscle.

She couldn't keep her mouth from watering at the sight of him. Her cheeks flamed, and a liquid yearning pooled in the center of her being. No doubt about it, this male had been made for sin.

When he reached for his belt and zipper, she had to remind herself that she wasn't interested. More to the point, she was determined to hold him to their new bargain, so the less she warmed up to him—the less she saw of his magnificent body—the better.

At his knowing glance, she forced herself to look away. "I'll, ah...I'll be in the other room."

Damn him for chuckling as she pivoted on her heel and practically fled out of his presence.

She resumed her seat in the salon as the water hissed on in the en suite bathroom. She absolutely did not want to picture Sorin Ebarron lathering up naked under the spray, but no sooner had she told herself to avoid thinking about it than her mind eagerly went to work flooding her head with a vivid play-by-play.

Ashayla stood up and started to pace the hand-woven rugs in her tall, high-heeled boots. Would he come out of the shower and begin his seduction of her? He promised not to force her in any way, but how could she be absolutely certain of that? Could she trust him at his word alone?

What would he do if he discovered the vial of Nephilim magic secreted in her boot? Dread went tight in her chest. He would be furious, for sure.

What if he took the vial from her?

It was a risk she couldn't chance, even if she fully intended to win Gran's pendant back according to the terms of Sorin's new deal.

With the shower running in the other room, Ashayla crept into the bedroom and carefully tucked the pinky-sized metal vial between the mattresses on the enormous, four-poster bed. She took the opportunity to peruse the Incubus's living quarters, from the gleaming dark-wood furniture and leather seating, to the art-covered, millwork walls.

A collection of trinkets and masculine jewelry lay in a small tray on the bureau, much of it bearing the Ebarron griffin sigil. His closet was a room of its own, filled with suits and other fine clothing befitting a rich, spoiled playboy.

Yet he wasn't at all how he appeared on the surface.

She was seeing that now. He was a complicated man living a complicated life. A solitary life, despite the family members who occupied the Ebarron stronghold with him and the business that kept him surrounded by beautiful people every night.

Not to mention all of the adoring female companions a man like him was certain to attract wherever he went.

Why that thought should put a twinge of disapproval in her breast, she had no idea.

"Already making yourself at home, I see."

Sorin's deep voice made her spin around to face him.

And, oh, God...that was a terrible mistake.

He stood there with a white towel in hand, but the rest of him was absolutely, gloriously naked. His golden hair was slicked back off his face, still wet, curling at the ends that kissed his strong neck. His smooth skin glistened with tiny droplets of water that just begged to be licked off him.

Every inch of him was perfectly carved, from his broad shoulders to his powerful chest, trim waist, and long, muscular legs. Good lord, even his feet were beautiful. His physical perfection bordered on angelic, he was so delectably formed.

But if there was any doubt this demon male had been spawned for a carnal existence, his cock left no question at all.

It jutted out fully erect, as large and magnificent as the rest of him.

Desire kindled low in her belly, turning her insides to melted heat. Her sex clenched with need, pulse throbbing with a sudden, heavy beat, as if all of her female senses recognized what they wanted even as she struggled to deny it.

Ashayla swallowed thickly. She lifted her eyes after a long moment and found him watching her intently. Heaven help her, she could barely breathe from the power the sight of him stirred in her.

Panicked, she tore her gaze away. Her voice was little more than a croak as she swiftly gave him her back. "Do you always parade around naked like that?"

"When I'm fresh out of the shower, yes. Do you always blush like a virgin when you see a naked man?"

There was humor in his voice. And, curse the Incubus, enough masculine pride for ten men—none of it misplaced.

"I'm not a virgin," she replied, feeling oddly indignant that he would suggest she behaved like one. "It's just that I've never seen...never been with..."

"Never been with an Incubus?" He grunted, sounding surprised. Sounding pleased. "Don't worry, I'll do my best to make it memorable for you. Especially now that I know the reputation of my entire species is at stake."

Even though the thought of Sorin doing his carnal best with her sent anticipation spiraling through her, Ashayla barked out a caustic laugh. She swung back around to face him. "Are you this confident in everything you do?"

"Yes." His topaz eyes gleamed under his arched brows. He dropped the towel and stalked toward her.

Oh, God.

Ashayla held her breath as he came up close, his

nudity impossible to ignore when she could feel the heat of his bare skin radiating through the barrier of her clothing. Without warning, he reached around and freed her hair from its ponytail at her nape. Then he gently took her face in his hands and kissed her. His mouth brushed over hers, soft but firm, commanding.

She wanted to resist. She wanted to be strong, but his tenderness undid her. She gave in on a moan, telling herself she could have this moment of pleasure without forfeiting the bigger prize.

She would be strong later. Right now, she was melting…and utterly lost to the taste of his kiss.

She wrapped her arms around his neck and parted her lips for his questing tongue. His erection was massive against her abdomen, as hard and unyielding as granite, but hot and enticing. Calling to everything female inside her.

She could hear his heartbeat galloping, feel it throbbing against her breasts as her own heart banged against her ribs in a similar tempo. He swore something ancient and profane, his voice rough with desire, his warm breath skating across her chin and cheeks with every searing exhalation.

Fire licked through her veins as he continued his erotic assault on her senses, need pooling deep within her core. He was right; she wanted him. She desired him with a wild yearning she could scarcely reconcile.

Wager to lose or not, in that moment, if he'd taken things any further, she would have been powerless to refuse him.

The depth of her arousal swamped her, so much

that she hardly noticed he'd paused until she heard his low, rumbling growl. His voice vibrated against her parted lips, sending a shiver of electricity into her veins. "It's time, Asha."

When she drew back, feeling a sudden spike of uncertainty—of dread for what she might surrender to him—Sorin's blazing topaz eyes darkened with merciless intent.

"We made a deal," he murmured thickly. "And I want you in my bed now."

CHAPTER EIGHT

He was so racked with desire for her, it was all Sorin could do not to tear off Ashayla's clothes right where she stood.

She might not have resisted. The way she kissed him just now left little doubt that all of her protests and denials were nothing more than words. Flimsy words she hadn't so much as attempted to voice when she'd wrapped her arms around him on that erotic little mewl of rising need.

Sorin was Incubus, but even had he been born a mortal man, the sweet scent of her arousal would not have escaped his notice. She wanted him. She was wet for him, after just one fevered kiss. He knew it, and the awareness of that fact turned his stiff cock to granite. His blood was surging through his veins, drumming with the demands of his demon nature.

Take her. Give her the pleasure she craves.

Claim the price she agreed to pay.

But the terms they'd struck earlier tonight left no room for interpretation. Sorin said he would only have her if she willed it. No tricks, no games. No coercion of any kind.

He'd promised to have her begging for him to be inside her, and as much as he wanted to break that pledge right now, he wouldn't. He wasn't accustomed to refusing his demonic nature, but this female had pushed him to do many things outside his norm tonight.

On a low, rolling growl, he reined in his hunger for her.

Barely.

Sorin took her hand and led her out to his bed. Only now did he feel a slight resistance in her. Where her fingers rested against his large palm, they tensed. The sudden lurch of her pulse made him pause beside the king-sized four-poster and turn to face her. "We had a deal, Asha. You, in my bed. For the night."

She drew in a shallow breath and her eyes traveled down the length of his nude body, lingering the most on his jutting cock. "You said you wouldn't—"

"And I won't," he finished for her. "Not unless—and until—you tell me that's what you want. Me, inside you. I won't lie and tell you it's not what I want." He chuckled ruefully, indicating his aroused state. "I guess that's more than a little obvious."

"No, there's nothing little about it," she murmured, and to his astonishment a glint of wry humor sparked in her indigo eyes.

He smiled, much too pleased by her appraisal. "Get undressed, Asha."

"Undressed?" She said the word as if he'd just asked her to shave off her eyebrows. "That was never mentioned as part of this arrangement."

Sorin shrugged. "I don't go to bed with clothing on. Tonight, neither will you." He tilted his head at her. "I can help you, if you wish."

"No." She gave a shake of her head, her loose platinum hair sifting around her shoulders. "No, I'll do it myself, thanks. I think I'll be better off keeping you at arm's length."

"It'll be difficult to do that when you're lying up against me all night. " He smirked and took a seat on the mattress. "Or beneath me."

Her cheeks flushed a delectable shade of pink. "We'll see about that."

"Yes, we will." He nodded toward her with his chin. "Now, take them off, Asha."

"Are you going to sit there and watch me?"

He grinned. "Yes, I am."

For a moment, she didn't move. Just stared at him in quiet contemplation. He wondered if she would refuse his command. In truth, she could have. This wasn't part of their deal, disrobing in front of his greedy gaze.

But instead of crying foul or hiding in the other room to protect her modesty, Asha bent over to unzip one of her tall, black leather boots, holding his level stare with one of her own. Courageous. Defiant.

Sexy as hell.

With a soft rasp of the zipper's tiny metal teeth, she took off one spiked boot, then the other.

Sorin admired the way her breasts swayed and swelled with her movements, the deep vee of creamy skin and cleavage making him yearn to put his mouth on her. His hands too.

Would her nipples be cherry red like her lips, or pale peach like the blush that still rode on the apples of her cheeks? He couldn't wait to find out.

His cock leapt in agreement as she straightened and began to unfasten her long-sleeved black top. One by one, the tiny buttons holding it together in the front fell away. Beneath it, she wore a black satin-and-lace bra that made his teeth ache with the urge to lunge off the bed and chew through its delicate clasp so he could taste her without delay.

No force, he reminded himself sternly. No taking what she hadn't given him, so he clamped down on his desire and searched for patience.

It wasn't easy.

No, in fact, it was the hardest damned thing in the world to refrain from pouncing on her like the libidinous Incubus he was.

Ashayla glanced at him as the last button popped free, baring her chest and torso to his fevered gaze. Her waist was an hourglass, trim but curvy, flawlessly pale and smooth.

Sorin's mouth watered. His cock throbbed, standing at full attention as he waited for her to continue. She unzipped her form-hugging black pants, pushing them over the generous flare of her hips. More black satin and lace tempted him here as well, in the form of skimpy bikini panties that that barely covered her sex.

Lust slammed into him as he watched her step out of her pants and stand before him with just those two scraps of fabric concealing her from his hungered eyes. He met her gaze, unable to hide his appreciation for her form.

"You're stunning, Asha." His voice scraped out of him like gravel. "But don't stop there. Please, keep going."

She exhaled a shaky breath, but kept her attention locked on him as she reached between her breasts and popped the clasp on her bra. The satin parted, then fell away completely as she slowly shrugged the straps off her shoulders and down her arms. She let the bra drop to the floor with the rest of her clothing, then lowered her hands to her sides.

"Peach," he mused thickly, admiring the perfection of her breasts. His cock was on the verge of exploding and he hadn't even touched her yet. He hadn't tasted her body yet, or her release. "The panties too, Asha."

As she peeled the lacy black fabric off, Sorin had to fist his hands in the sheets on either side of him to keep from reaching down to stroke away some of the painful tension from his cock.

Holy hell. What kind of idiot had he been to vow he wouldn't push her into making love with him? That he would hold himself back until she was begging for him?

All of his boasts incinerated to ash as he drank in the sight of her nudity.

This female owned a piece of him whether she knew it or not. Her letters over those many months had made him curious about her, but it was the woman who strode into his casino tonight who'd captivated him the way no other had before.

She'd challenged him, confounded him. Defied him and denied him.

And now, if she didn't let him touch her, taste her—fuck her—in the next few moments, he would be the one reduced to begging.

On a groan, he swung his legs up onto the mattress, sweeping aside the sheet and coverlet to make room for her beside him. He held out his other hand to her. "Come to bed, Asha."

He didn't know whether to feel relief or regret when she stepped forward and placed her fingers in his open palm.

~ ~ ~

It should feel strange, standing naked in front of Sorin with nowhere to hide. Nowhere to escape his searing, seductive stare.

It should feel dangerous, seeing this powerful Incubus Master waiting for her on the bed. Immense. Fully aroused. Every hard inch of his tempting body sculpted of inhuman strength and dark, carnal intent.

It should feel wrong, taking his outstretched hand, walking toward him willingly, eagerly. So swamped with desire, her heart was running at a gallop, threatening to burst.

It did feel strange.

God help her, it did feel dangerous too.

But when she looked at Sorin, when she held his hooded, hungry eyes and let him guide her onto the bed with him, nothing about it felt wrong.

And that was the thing that terrified her most.

He'd been right—she did want him. Right now, she couldn't think of anything she wanted more.

No. Not true. Ashayla mentally shook herself out of the daze of her desire.

There was something she wanted more.

Something she needed even more than the pleasure that waited for her in Sorin's arms.

The pendant.

The peace and happiness it would bring Gran to know that it was finally returned to the family before she passed.

Which meant giving in to the desire Sorin ignited in her was not going to happen.

"So beautiful," he murmured, cradling the side of her face in one broad palm while his other hand skimmed down the front of her, coaxing her to lie down beside him. His gaze was tender on her, but his grin was pure Incubus. "I've held a lot of priceless things, but never anything as lovely as you, Asha."

His remark hit her like a splash of cold water. A much-needed one.

"No." The word wrenched out of her on a moan as she bolted upright. It would be so easy to surrender to him, but she couldn't. She would not fail tonight, no matter how difficult he made it to deny her own feelings. "No, this isn't happening."

She scrambled out of his arms and into the center of the big mattress, pulling the edge of the sheet along with her and holding it up to her breast like a shield.

Sorin came up on one elbow, frowning. "What's the matter? Where are you going?"

"*This* is the matter," she said, gesturing to the space between them. "I agreed to spend the night in your bed, Sorin. I even agreed to do it without my clothes on, which, for the record, was a totally Incubus way to bend the rules even further in your favor."

His grin held no remorse. "You could've refused at any point. Don't pretend you didn't know what you were getting into when you took me on tonight."

Oh, she knew. What she hadn't been prepared for was the way he managed to touch more than just her body or her desire.

She wanted him with a need she could hardly resist, but even worse than that, she realized she genuinely liked him. She wanted to know more about him, more about his family and his life. She wanted to know everything about him.

After just a few hours in his company, she was beginning to care for him deeply.

She couldn't wait for morning so she could walk out of Ebarron's treasure room with her prize, yet there was a part of her that knew she was going to remember this night for the rest of her life.

There was a part of her that already regretted everything that could never be between them.

"Come." He reached out to her. His deep voice was coaxing, but there was unspoken command in his heated gaze. "You can't sit there all night, Asha."

"Maybe I will." She forced a shrug. "Technically, I am still in bed."

One tawny brow winged up. "Now who's bending the rules?"

"It's called compromise, Sorin. Ever hear of it?"

He grunted. "I lead. Others follow. That's how I prefer it."

"Arrogant man," she chided with a roll of her eyes. "It's good this arrangement is only for one night. Any longer and all you and I would do is lock horns."

"Oh, I promise that's not all we'd do." He leaned back against the headboard, thighs loosely parted, all of his muscles and masculinity on full display.

Ashayla had to wrench her gaze away from him. All she wanted to do was lie down next to him again and feel his strong arms wrapped around her.

She wanted to feel that large, powerful body pressed against the length of her as he thrust inside her, filling the hot ache that hadn't abated since their kiss.

No, it had only intensified the longer she was with him. Near enough to touch. Near enough to inhale his unearthly scent of spice and power and sin. All of which made her hungry to taste him.

As if he followed the line of her thinking, he made a deep, raw sound in the back of his throat. Ashayla licked her lips, and he was in motion even faster than she could register his movements.

He pulled her back down onto the bed beside him, at the same time smoothly rolling himself up onto his arms so he was covering her. Face to face. His warm, solid chest against her soft, sensitive breasts. His heavy hips pressing into the tops of her thighs. She felt his rigid cock too, the searing, powerful length of it nestled against her mound.

Ashayla panted beneath his weight, beneath the blazing intensity of his heavy-lidded gaze. Her pulse banged against her ribcage, not out of fear or resistance, but out of complete and consuming need.

Without warning, he bent down and took her mouth in a fierce, hot kiss. His tongue pushed past her lips on a moan, sweeping inside to tangle with hers. Lust ignited inside her like a wildfire, singeing all of her nerve endings. While lower, all she knew was a wet, demanding ache to be filled by this man. This Incubus. This incredible male.

He released her mouth on a snarled curse, looming above her like the demon he was.

God, he was so handsome. So heartbreakingly, hellishly beautiful. And he was hers.

In that moment, with nothing but heated, naked skin between them, Sorin, the forbidding Master of Ebarron, belonged to her.

As she belonged to him.

"Say it," he rasped. "I need to hear the words, Asha."

She closed her eyes, tried to look away so he wouldn't see how raw her need was, but he brought her gaze back to him with his fingers resting gently below her chin.

"You know our deal, Asha. Tell me you want this—that you want me inside you—or push me away now."

"Sorin…" She could do neither. What little resistance she'd had was long since evaporated. But her determination to make it through the night without giving in to him, without losing their damnable wager, kept the truth from falling off her tongue.

She wanted this, yes.

She wanted him inside her so keenly it hurt.

But the price was too high. His price, the one he placed on their time together. She knew she was as much to blame for where they had ended up now. After all, she'd been the one to seek him out with the intent to take what he hadn't been willing to give her.

Part of her wished he would use his Incubus allure to put her under his thrall. At least then she'd have someplace to hang her guilt when she returned to Gran empty-handed.

But Sorin was more honorable than that. If she'd doubted it at any time tonight, she saw him demonstrate that honor now, in the way he held her so tenderly, patiently, even while his entire body was hard and straining with lust.

"Say it," he whispered fiercely, his lips brushing against hers as he spoke. His mouth trailed down her chin, then along the sensitive line of her jaw, sending electricity arcing into her veins. His breath skated against the shell of her ear. "Give me the words, Asha. Leave neither of us any room for doubt."

Oh, God, she couldn't take the yearning.

She couldn't walk away from this moment, or from how he made her feel.

Nor would she lie to him by pretending she could deny what was happening between them now.

"Yes," she gasped. Then took a breath and pushed the words out again. "Sorin, yes...I want this. I want you. I need you...inside me."

Triumph flashed across his face like lightning—quicksilver, white-hot. Jagged and powerful.

Then, on a savage curse, his mouth crushed down on hers.

CHAPTER NINE

He didn't realize how thorough Ashayla's conquest of him was until he'd been holding her in shaking arms, demanding her submission. Christ, pleading for it.

When she said the words out loud—that sweet, breathless admission that she wanted him, needed him inside her—Sorin nearly roared his pleasure.

Claiming her mouth with his, he let his passion for her take the reins.

He shifted his weight off her so he could let his hands roam freely over her warm, creamy skin. From her delicate throat to the hard-peaked nipples of her sumptuous breasts. Then down the soft plane of her abdomen to the tantalizing rise of her mound and its trim little nest of gossamer curls.

Sorin groaned as her silky wetness met his questing fingertips. "So ready for me," he murmured roughly against her mouth. Her juices slicked his fingers as he teased her cleft and clit. Her breath deepened, and the warm peaches-and-cream scent of her arousal filled his head, more potent than any drug. "I have to taste you, Asha."

He moved down the delectable length of her body, pausing to lavish her breasts with hungry kisses, drawing on her nipple with his tongue and teeth until she was writhing beneath him, her spine arching into him in a demand for more.

Her eager response set his pulse on fire. Need drummed wildly in his veins, Ashayla's desire calling to the demon in him like no other woman had done before.

On a wordless growl, Sorin tore his mouth away from her breasts to trace a line of kisses down her soft belly, then over each generous flare of her hip bones.

She gasped as he delved lower still, then cried out when he cleaved his tongue into the satiny folds of her sex. "Mmm," he moaned against her tender flesh. "Peaches and cream…I want to lap up every last drop of you, my sweet Asha."

His palms on the tender insides of her thighs, he spread her open to him even more, feasting his eyes on her carnal beauty before lowering his head to her again. Hungrily, mercilessly, he licked her, suckled her, drew her deep into his mouth. She quivered and writhed, then bucked and shuddered as he drove her toward climax.

"Sorin," she moaned, her body tensing under his sensual assault. "Oh, fuck, Sorin…please…I can't hold on much longer."

He wasn't sure he could last long either. The taste of her, the scent of her, the searing, silken feel of her against his mouth as she rode his tongue with erotic abandon…all of it had his heart rate pounding, his cock on fire, ready to explode.

But he wanted her pleasure first, before he buried himself in her and filled her with the full measure of his desire. She sucked in a thready breath as he pushed his tongue inside her tight entrance. Her hands came down on his head, fingers clutching at his hair as she moaned his name and held his mouth to her as the first shock wave of her climax rippled through her and into him.

Sorin drank it down, that pure, potent power of her release.

He was Incubus, and this moment was the thing he lived for. The surge of energy that fed him, sustained him, the way mundane food and drink never fully could.

That it was Ashayla's orgasm pouring into him now only made their connection all the more intense. It felt sacred to him, more priceless than any treasure he could ever hope to possess.

She was sacred to him. In a way he was scarcely prepared to admit, even to himself.

And that fact shook him to his core.

His hands were reverent on her as he stroked her swollen bud, gentling her back down to Earth. When he could wait no longer, he let go of her hips, then slowly rose onto his knees between her parted thighs.

His cock stood proud, the thick staff blood-engorged, ready to burst. She reached down to stroke him and he closed his eyes, a pleasured hiss leaking out of him. Then Ashayla scrambled up from where she lay, moving toward him, her hands still working him, nearly undoing him.

When she bent over him and took him into her mouth, Sorin's head fell back on a curse. Maybe it was a prayer. He didn't know, and didn't much care.

So long as she was fastened to his cock, licking and sucking and driving him mad, he had no control over his words or his thoughts or his body.

Everything belonged to her.

Pleasure knotted at the base of his spine as her mouth covered him, took him in all the way to his root.

Fuck. Her lips were so soft, her tongue so hot and frenzied.

Sensation rocked him, fire licking across all of his nerve endings.

He grabbed a fistful of her long platinum hair, winding it around his hand, a lifeline as her mouth sent him even further adrift with heat and unbearable ecstasy.

She sucked him harder then, deeper, and each time the head of his cock hit the back of her open throat, his climax ratcheted tighter. Christ, he couldn't take it much longer. He was going to burst.

As much as it killed him to drag her sweet lips from his flesh, Sorin ground out a curse and urged her head up.

"I want to be inside you, Asha," he uttered, his voice dry gravel in his throat. "Ah, fuck…I need it. I need it now."

Her answering smile as she reclined back and parted her legs to him was sly, more wicked than he thought a Nephilim's could be. He'd never seen anything sexier in his life.

He wanted to take a moment to admire the gift she was giving him, but there was no time for indulgence. There was only desire. Only the need for this woman.

My woman, a startling voice demanded in the back of his mind.

Asha was his tonight. And the triumph Sorin felt over that had nothing at all to do with their wager or the treasure room prize at stake.

She was his until morning.

For now, that was enough.

He prowled over her, his cock jutting heavy between his legs, aching for her. He stroked her inner thighs, but that was all the patience he could summon. Her slick juices bathed him as he guided himself to her entrance. She was so tight, so hot and wet.

Sorin uttered her name hoarsely as he began to push inside. Then on a roar that sounded more demon than man, he slowly sheathed himself to the hilt.

~ ~ ~

Ashayla clutched Sorin to her as he drove deep, impaling her with the full length and breadth of his passion. His tempo was savage, unbridled...as powerful as a storm.

And she couldn't get enough of him.

"I can't go slowly right now," he ground out tightly against her mouth as he kissed her. "Not this first time."

"No," she agreed, breathless and wanton. "I don't want slow right now either."

His big body pinned her to the mattress, tremendous muscles flexing with every movement, every possessive thrust. She ran her fingertips over his broad back and shoulders, down the narrowed width of his torso. As he slammed into her with wild, relentless abandon, she gripped his ass, reveling in the solid strength of him. The sheer, erotic power of the Incubus in her arms.

She'd already come once, but the beginnings of another intense climax rolled up on her fast and hard. "Oh, God," she whispered breathlessly. "You feel so good inside me. Don't stop, Sorin...I want this too much...I need all of you now..."

He muttered something dark in a language she didn't recognize—Romanian or demon, she didn't know. But the raw, primal sound of it fueled her desire even more. Sorin's strokes took on a fiercer rhythm, an urgent pounding that pushed her higher and higher, toward the crest of a steep, churning wave.

"Sorin!" she gasped as the first quake shook her. "Oh, my God...oh fuck, yes..."

Her orgasm ripped through her, electrifying her senses, shattering her from the inside. She screamed with the pleasure of it, utterly lost. Gloriously adrift with him still riding her, coaxing her toward the next peak. Completely at his mercy and his command.

She'd never known it could be like this. So pure and open, so beautifully intense. The pleasure was so wrenching, hot tears leaked from the corners of her eyes.

Sorin swept them away on his thumbs, cradling her face as he braced himself above her on his elbows. He made a quiet growling noise as he stared into her bleary gaze, his expression smug with masculine pride.

"You're mine, Asha. Mine." He punctuated the command with a deep roll of his hips, one she felt all the way to her womb. All the way to the center of her heart. "Say it."

"Yes," she admitted breathlessly. "Yours. Oh God, Sorin...it's true."

How she would ever move on to anyone else after being with him, she had no idea. The thought alone repulsed her.

There was only him now.

She was his. Body, heart and soul.

And from the wicked gleam in his hooded gaze, the sexy smirk he gave her now, it was clear that her Incubus Master wasn't finished with her just yet.

Rising up onto his fists, he began to move with stronger intent again. He crashed into her, battering her with increasingly harder thrusts of his hips. Ashayla loved his unchecked need. She loved how his cock filled her, stretched her tight as her tiny muscles spasmed around him with the aftershocks of her release.

Sorin gathered her to him, his hands spearing under her shoulders as he thrust again and again and again, deeper and harder and more frenzied—until a coarse shout tore from his lips and he withdrew, bathing her belly with the hot jet of his seed.

He heaved above her for a moment, breathing heavily, then he snarled a vivid curse. "It's not enough yet. Not with you." He took her in a possessive kiss, fucking her mouth with his tongue the way he'd just ruled her body. When he broke away, he was panting, eyes wild with unbanked desire. "I need to have you again, Asha. Now."

He flipped her onto her stomach, at the same time lifting her hips until her ass was in the air before him, her thighs spread, sex throbbing yet still hungry for him. When he speared into her slick cleft, her spine bowed in response, a ripple of pleasure-pain coursing through her like liquid fire. So good. The feel of Sorin inside her, so demanding, so raw and consuming.

She craved this wild part of him and reveled in the fact that it was her who drove him to this mad brink of need.

On a harsh moan, Sorin held her backside in a firm grasp and pumped into her with abandon. Ashayla felt branded, claimed, possessed under his sensual barrage. She felt boneless and melting, more alive than she'd ever felt before.

She surrendered to it fully—and to Sorin as well. She couldn't fight it, even if she tried. Her heart was full to bursting, her body taut and electric, utterly at his mercy.

Her climax broke over her the same time Sorin's tore through him. He shouted a jagged curse and this time he didn't withdraw. Maybe he didn't have time. Maybe he couldn't find the will to leave her body.

God knew, she wanted him there.

She wanted to keep him there for as long as possible...

Forever, came the reckless whisper from her heart. The thought of Sorin being in her life, part of her future, was something she could hardly imagine. So why did it chase a streak of elation into her veins—a sharp ray of hope—to picture herself with him as something more than just another conquest, a wager he'd won as easily as any other he set out to claim?

He'd given her no promises tonight. Only the one that he'd made good on—her, in his bed, begging for him to make love to her.

And despite the bliss of lying naked in his arms now as he pressed her down beneath him and rolled her into his strong embrace, Ashayla struggled to remind herself that all they had was the rest of this night.

In the morning she would be faced with returning to Chicago as the fool who'd not only failed in her promise to bring the pendant back home for Gran, but who'd also left her heart behind at the House of Ebarron too.

CHAPTER TEN

Sorin let her rest a while in his arms before his appetite overcame him again and he had to make love to Ashayla once more. He took things slowly this time, the edge of his need less sharp, yet just as deep and consuming.

More so, now that he'd had a taste of her.

His sweet, responsive, utterly intoxicating Asha.

The energy he'd drunk from her orgasms was still buzzing inside him, a living thing. Her power would sustain him for days. Yet he thirsted again.

Would always thirst for her, a fact that he could hardly begin to deny.

His blood electrified, infused with the carnal energy she'd given him, Sorin extricated himself from her languid embrace and made it his solemn mission to kiss every curve and swell and hollow of her beautiful body. She arched and flexed like a cat under his roving lips and tongue, sighing in pleasure, murmuring his name as he descended down the smooth length of her abdomen.

Pressing his mouth to her sex, he cleaved the wet seam of her pussy and lapped at the swollen bud nestled in her soft folds. She moved her hips shamelessly against him, and the wanton little moan she let out as she climaxed a moment later was the most erotic sound he'd ever heard.

He entered her more slowly than he thought possible, if only to savor the ripples of her orgasm that undulated around his cock as he seated himself, inch by painstaking inch. They came together a few moments later, their cries of release mingled, gazes locked and intimate, as naked and open to each other as two people could be.

Sorin gathered her close as he rolled his weight off her, content to hold her in silence as she drifted into a soft, spent doze in his arms. She was Heaven to him, or as close as a demon like him could ever hope to come to that lofty place. Yet even without the perfect fit of their bodies, without the perfect harmony of the passion they'd found tonight, Asha made his thoughts of any other woman before her fade to utter insignificance.

Where other females, human and Nephilim both, had served to feed him all his life, it was this woman who stoked all of his hungers now. There simply wouldn't be another for him, not like this. Not like her.

How the fuck had he let it happen?

How had he let her get past his defenses? It shouldn't have been her, this Nephilim who'd piqued his curiosity and his ire with her dauntless campaign to reclaim her grandmother's pendant.

The defiant would-be thief who then infiltrated his domain to take her prize by force or cunning. Or by the vial of Nephilim witchery she'd tucked beneath the mattress, assuming he wouldn't notice it was there.

He smirked at the thought. She wasn't the only one with secrets. Sorin reflected on the terms of their deal—one Ashayla had stood no chance of winning, from the moment she'd agreed to stay behind at the roulette table after Korda Marakel was shown the door.

The Master of Ebarron had never been a cheat in anything he'd done in his life. But as he held Asha against him now, after having rocked into her silken heat, reveling at how she had purred with pleasure and sighed his name, he could feel no remorse for what he'd done.

The covert signal he'd given to his croupier at the roulette table.

The one that had ensured he'd have this night with Asha, no matter what.

She thought she was wagering on the pendant, when Sorin would have traded his entire treasury to have her for just one night.

He couldn't hold her to their deal now. In truth, he hadn't intended to hold her to it from the moment she confided in him about her life back home in Chicago, when he'd seen the pain her mother's madness and addiction had caused Asha.

But he couldn't feel sorry for the time he'd stolen with her tonight either.

Now, the hardest part of their bargain for him would be saying goodbye to her in the morning, when dawn and duty called them back to their separate worlds.

As if to remind him of that eventuality, a quiet knock sounded from the door in the other room of his private chambers. Sorin eased out of bed and stepped into a pair of pants before padding out to consult with his Watchman who waited outside.

Milo's grave expression brought Sorin immediately to attention. The captain held a secure phone in his hand. "Devlin Gravori is on the private House line for you. He says it's urgent."

Alarm spiked in Sorin's blood. Although Ebarron had long been on friendly terms with Gravori House, if the other Master was calling in the middle of the night—especially when he had a pretty new mate in his bed back on his Mediterranean island citadel—the news could not be good.

Sorin put the phone to his ear. "Dev. Tell me what's happened."

The news was bad. About as bad as things could get for the Incubi realm, if the report Devlin Gravori had just received from another Master, Jian from the House of Xanthe, proved to be true.

"I understand," Sorin said. "Yes. I'll leave at once."

~ ~ ~

Ashayla peeled one eye open on a sleepy groan, her face buried in a fluffy down pillow.

All around her was the spicy, erotic scent of sex and Sorin, the memory of their lovemaking clinging to her senses and to the tangled sheets on the bed. She was ready for him all over again, a pleasant, wet heat dulling the ache that still lingered from their vigorous night together.

Sighing with a mix of satisfaction and stirring desire, she reached out for him beside her.

Sorin wasn't there.

Asha lifted her head, then sat bolt upright.

He was gone.

The bedroom was quiet. Empty.

"Sorin?" She scrambled out of his bed, wrapping the coverlet around her as she padded into the other room. "Sorin, where are—"

"Master Sorin wanted me to convey his apologies, Miss Palatine." Milo rose from his seat in a chair near the door, politely averting his eyes from her disheveled state.

"Where is he?" Disappointment and confusion made her voice sound small, as raw as she was starting to feel. "Did he...leave?"

"Called away unexpectedly on urgent business." Milo's tone was not unkind, but she could see that he would tell her no more than necessary. No more than he'd been instructed by Sorin, of course. "He did not want you to worry about him. However, as he doesn't know when he might be returning, Master Sorin asked me to see that you made it safely back to Chicago. Travel has been arranged, and we can leave as soon as you're ready, miss."

"Oh," she murmured woodenly. "Of course...okay."

Sorin didn't want her to wait for him. The knowledge stung, but she'd known what morning was going to bring. She'd made a deal with the Master of Ebarron. A deal she'd lost when she gave in to the desire she felt for him.

Even worse, that desire had somehow blossomed into something more.

Something that carved a sharp ache in her breast

at the realization that their time was over, and that he had thought it best to slip away in the middle of the night while she slept, sated and oblivious, in his bed.

Ashayla struggled to suppress the despairing moan that sat lodged in her throat.

She'd have to be a naive fool to expect they would wake up today and...what? Set up house together? Ignore the rest of the world so they could spend another night or twenty making love until neither of them could stand up or catch their breath?

Even if some idiotic part of her had hoped for something close to that, she wouldn't have had the option anyway. Gran was waiting for her. Asha needed to be home, where she belonged. Even she had to return home without Gran's prized heirloom.

In her miserable silence, the Watchman quietly cleared his throat. "Master Sorin asked me to give you this."

He bent to retrieve a white vellum envelope from the cocktail table nearby. She could tell there was something heavy inside. More than one item, by the look of it.

Ashayla took the envelope and lifted the seal.

When she peered inside, her breath caught in her throat.

Gran's pendant...and the vial of Nephilim magic she'd hidden under the mattress.

Oh, God.

Panic raced through her at the sight of the potion she had smuggled into Sorin's home. He knew. Obviously, he knew what it was and what she'd intended to do with it.

And now he was gone.

Gone with instructions for his Watchman to send her home.

Gone without giving her a chance to explain herself.

"Is anything wrong, Miss Palatine?" Milo watched her, and she knew her face must have looked as stricken as she felt.

She gave a numb shake of her head. "I'll just... Will you excuse me now, please? I'll collect my things and get ready to leave."

The Watchman nodded, and turned toward the door.

Ashayla sagged to her knees on a jagged sob the instant he left her in the room alone.

CHAPTER ELEVEN

Chicago
Three days later

Ashayla decided to walk home from Gran's funeral.

The ceremony had been a small, private gathering. A handful of neighbors whose lives Gran had touched with her kindness over the years, and a few Nephilim cousins from the area who'd come to pay their respects.

Although Asha missed her grandmother's company already, she couldn't find it in her to mourn her passing. Gran had lived a long, full life. And in the end, she'd slipped away with grace and calm.

And peace.

Asha had known the return of the pendant would be a relief for her grandmother. The expression on the dying Nephilim's face when she saw the pale blue stone dangling from its silver chain had been nothing short of beatific.

"Oh, my dear child…you've found it!" Gran had exclaimed from her sickbed as Asha had brought the pendant to her when she returned home from Ebarron. Though Gran had been weak and near death, she'd sat up to receive the heirloom with bright eyes and eager hands. "All this time, I feared it was gone forever. I worried that our family had failed Leila in our promise to safeguard Inanna's Tear."

Asha hadn't understood what Gran meant. The names were unfamiliar, something Gran had never mentioned before. She'd suspected the old woman's mind had been fading.

The truth was something far different.

The pendant was an heirloom, an extraordinary one. A priceless one, if Gran's explanation of its history proved to be fact.

Inanna's Tear.

That's what the female who'd created it had called the unusual piece. Her name was Leila, and she had been the last living Succubus.

Before she was slain along with the rest of her Succubus sisters and cousins in the last great war over the Obsidian Throne, Leila entrusted Inanna's Tear to the women of Asha's line, with the promise that they would keep it safe until the time came to use it.

But to use it for what?

Gran didn't know.

And now it was up to Asha to ensure the pendant's safekeeping.

She wore it around her neck now, beneath her blouse as she strolled back home under a sunny afternoon sky. As much as she ached to be away from Sorin and the incredible night they'd shared, as much as it shredded her not to have heard from him in the days since, the familiarity of the old neighborhood she'd grown up in was a welcome balm.

Since she'd been back, she'd drafted a dozen messages to him, only to throw them all away. She didn't know what to say to him. Even worse, she didn't know if there was anything she could say...other than she was sorry. But that was a message she hoped to deliver in person.

If he would ever want to see her again.

That uncertainty made her steps heavy as she approached a farm stand about a block from her house. She would never be as good a cook as Gran, but the lure of fresh produce drew her to the stand to collect a few things for dinner. She put a squash and some bright peppers in her basket, then drifted over to the bins of fresh fruit.

The strawberries smelled amazing, as did the peaches. She lifted one of the velvet-skinned fruits and brought it to her nose. Eyes closed, she breathed in its sweet perfume, recalling all too vividly the sound of Sorin's voice when he had his head buried between her thighs and described the taste of her.

Peaches and cream.

She moaned at the memory, and at the longing she still felt when she thought of him.

A longing she knew would stay with her for the rest of her life. In the days she'd been away from Ebarron, Asha had felt bereft, empty. And as much as she had wanted to deny her desire for him when they first met, what she felt for Sorin now was irrefutable. She cared for him like she had no other man. Like she never would for another.

As impossible as it seemed, she had fallen

halfway in love with him already. Heaven help her, she'd fallen more than halfway.

Asha sighed and started to place the peach in her basket.

That's when her gaze snagged on something unusual in the bin.

A coin with a griffin emblem on it.

No, not a coin. A chip from the Ebarron casino.

She glanced up on a gasp, her heart climbing into her throat. *Sorin?*

She searched all around her, a frantic visual pan of the sidewalk and street as she pivoted where she stood, praying she wasn't hallucinating.

And then...*there he was.*

He stepped out of the entrance alcove of the building next door, dressed in an open-collared, white button-down and charcoal suit pants, his golden hair gleaming in the sunlight as he strode toward her.

"You're here," she whispered, unable to think beyond the fact that he was standing there, in Chicago, his topaz eyes locked on her in that stare that always reached out to her like a physical embrace. "Sorin, I didn't think you would... What are you doing here?"

"My business took longer than anticipated. And I have to leave again soon to meet with the other Masters."

She nodded, unsure why he would feel the need to come all this way just to tell her he was leaving again. He walked toward her, his fluid, powerfully masculine stride making her body come alive with awareness. With desire that had only been banked since she'd been away from him, but not yet extinguished.

He walked closer, until there were only a few scant inches between them. God, he smelled good. And he looked good—even better than the memories she'd been reliving with torturous repetition in the days since she'd left Ebarron.

Hope flared in her, bright and sharp. She didn't dare trust that feeling. Not when he still hadn't said anything to her. Hadn't reached out to her. His handsome face was sober. More solemn than she'd ever seen him.

"I heard about your grandmother's passing, Asha. I'm truly sorry for your loss."

"Thank you," she replied. "Gran died in her sleep the night after I came home. She was happy, at peace in her final moments."

There was so much she wanted to tell Sorin now. That she was sorry for how she'd arrived at Ebarron, what she'd intended to do once she got there. That he'd been right about the pendant—it was something more than just an heirloom. Something much more. Something precious and rare, though she couldn't begin to understand what the true value of Inanna's Tear might be.

And more than anything, she wanted to tell Sorin that she'd cherished every moment she'd spent with him and regretted every one they'd been apart.

She swallowed. "I want you to know that I never would've betrayed you. Not after you and I—not after everything we shared. You have to know that I would've left the pendant behind—"

"I didn't come here for your apology, Asha.

None of that matters to me."

"Why, then?"

He stared at her for a long moment, his gaze intense, contemplative. "Someone once called me a selfish, pompous jackass devoid of compassion. That same someone implied I was a cheat, that I would resort to tricks or games to get what I wanted."

Ashayla shook her head. "No. That was before I knew you—"

"You were right," he said, his deep voice level, unreadable. "I am selfish. Pompous too, though it pains me to admit it. And a jackass? Well...you've seen enough firsthand evidence to attest to that."

She bit her lip, giving him a small shrug. "But you have compassion, Sorin. You proved that to me when you gave me Gran's pendant, even after I lost our wager."

"You didn't lose, Asha."

Her breath caught. "What?"

"You didn't lose, because there was no wager to be won." His mouth lifted at one corner, a wicked smirk. "Which brings me to the charge of cheat."

"What are you talking about? We made a deal. You said if we had sex—"

He moved closer now, and reached out to smooth his hand over her loose platinum hair. "I said, sweet Asha, that I would prove you wanted me as much as I wanted you. I said I'd have you begging for me before the night was through."

"And you did," she admitted, feeling the rush of desire flood her just to be near him again. "You proved your point and I lost. You didn't trick me. I know you didn't use the thrall to seduce me. There was no need for that, Sorin."

He grunted, grinning now. "You did lose that part of our wager. Spectacularly, I might add. You've ruined me for anyone else."

"I have?"

He gave a serious nod. "You ruined me from the moment I first laid eyes on you in my casino. Before that, in fact. From the first letter you wrote to me. And all the ones that followed."

The confession sent her heart into a gallop behind her sternum. Could he possibly feel the same way she did? That the few hours they spent together hadn't been enough—would never be enough?

Could he possibly care about her as deeply as she did about him?

Her excitement nearly diverted her from the other subject at hand. "What do you mean, there was no wager to be won? How did you—" And then it dawned on her. "Back at the roulette table. You rigged the wheel?"

"Not me, but my croupier knew what I needed him to do." Sorin shrugged, unapologetic. Unrepentantly Incubus. "I told you I was a man who liked to win."

She gasped in outrage and smacked her palm on his powerful chest. "You cheated! With Korda Marakel too?"

"No, he lost to the House fair and square. You were the only prize I truly couldn't stand to lose that night." He pulled her against him, their faces less than a breath apart. "Do you forgive me?"

Ashayla looked into his mesmerizing eyes, eyes

that held her with such care and emotion her chest was near to bursting. "I more than forgive you. I love you, Sorin."

His curse was soft, reverent. "Oh, my sweet Asha. I love you too. I want you with me, by my side. Starting right now."

He kissed her, an unhurried joining of their mouths that made her legs weak beneath her. Devotion filled his gaze when he drew back a moment later. His large hands trembled when they came up to cradle her face with utmost tender care.

"You belong to me now," he murmured. "You are more priceless than any treasure Ebarron will ever own."

Elation filled her, flooding every cell in her being. "I'm yours, Sorin. And you are mine. Forever."

He claimed her mouth again, long and slow and deep.

His kiss tasted of passion and tenderness...and the promise of a future she couldn't wait to begin with him.

~ * ~

ABOUT THE AUTHOR

LARA ADRIAN is a New York Times and #1 internationally best-selling author, with nearly 4 million books in print worldwide and translations licensed to more than 20 countries. Her books regularly appear in the top spots of all the major bestseller lists including the *New York Times*, USA Today, *Publishers Weekly*, Indiebound, Amazon.com, Barnes & Noble, etc. Reviewers have called Lara's books "addictively readable" (Chicago Tribune), "extraordinary" (Fresh Fiction), and "one of the best vampire series on the market" (Romantic Times).

With an ancestry stretching back to the Mayflower and the court of King Henry VIII, the author lives with her husband in New England.

Visit the author's website and sign up for new release announcements at **www.LaraAdrian.com**.

BOUNDLESS
House of Drohas

Donna Grant

CHAPTER ONE

Javan Drohas was scrolling on his iPad through pictures of artwork he was considering purchasing for one of his galleries when a file folder sailed across his desk and slid to a stop in front of him.

He lifted his gaze to his Watchman, Elijah. Elijah stood tall with one hand in the pants pocket of his black suit. His crisp white shirt was accented with a crimson and black tie.

Elijah carried the coloring of his ancestors with his mocha skin and inky black hair that tended to curl. He kept his hair short and neat, but it didn't matter whether he was in a tux or jeans—nothing could hide the warrior that he was.

Elijah's unusual teal gaze watched Javan with amused interest. His expression told Javan he was going to have to listen to whatever Elijah said if he wanted to get back to work anytime soon.

"What is this?" Javan asked as he looked askance at the file.

One side of Elijah's lips lifted in a grin. "I found the perfect artist to use at this year's exhibit. We had an empty spot to fill."

"It's a bit late to be adding anyone since the exhibit is in three days." But Javan was intrigued enough to open the file.

His family had been art dealers for generations. They had discovered some of the best artists to ever come out of Australia, and each year their annual exhibit of the Drohas Foundation brought in the wealthiest people from all over the world to look at the latest talent.

Javan studied the first picture. The photographer had an amazing eye. The female model was pretty without being gorgeous, but it was the fractures of light that blurred the model in places, and the pose, that really caught his eye.

The photographer didn't focus on the model's face, but her body. The fluid lines of the model who kept her back to the camera in a deep squat, and her long skirt billowing around her with her arms wide and her head thrown back, was captivating.

"I know," Elijah said.

"The photographer is extraordinary," Javan said as he moved on to the next picture. "How have we not heard of him before?"

"Her," Elijah corrected.

Javan shrugged, mesmerized by the photos. "Has she agreed to be in the exhibit?"

"She's the one who came to us."

Javan set down the photos, concern making him pause. "So late? Why didn't she submit her work a year ago as everyone else did?"

"You can ask her yourself."

"She's here?"

Elijah turned to the side. "She's downstairs."

Javan glanced at his watch. He had a meeting in ten minutes, and the rest of his day was just as full.

There was no time to spare talking to the photographer. "She's talented."

"That she is. If she hadn't come so late, we would've had her in the exhibit. She deserves to be there. She's done a lot on her own, but you know being in the exhibit could propel her career."

"She'll get there on her own," Javan mused as he looked at the photos again. "She's that good. However, I also like the idea of being able to claim we found another talented artist. Add her in."

Elijah gave a nod. "I'll let her know. Do you still intend to go to the meeting?"

"Yes."

The meeting. It grated on Javan's nerves that Marakel had once more leveled claims on the House of Drohas that Javan and his men were trying to dethrone him.

Javan wanted nothing more. Everyone knew it was time for the Sovereign to step down from the Obsidian Throne. His phase was up, and since he had no heirs, the right to rule passed to another House.

Whispers had reached Javan that Canaan Romerac wasn't dead after all. After five hundred years with Canaan's brother running House Romerac, it was now said that Canaan had killed his brother for betraying him.

Javan discovered just an hour earlier that those rumors were true. He was anxious to talk to Canaan and learn what had transpired in those centuries.

Betrayal was a natural part of an Incubus's life. It just wasn't supposed to come from within one's own family. Javan couldn't imagine any of his brothers betraying him.

But Canaan probably said the same thing.

There was upheaval in their world. First, House Akana suddenly dying out, which gave House Marakel the Obsidian Throne. Now, the Sovereign refusing to step down after his allotted centuries on the Throne.

Javan wished that's all there was, but Elijah had given him more news the night before. A few Blades—females who are half human and half angel who were on the Death Squad for the Sovereign— had begun to go rogue.

What the hell else was going to happen?

"Give me five minutes, and I'll be there," Elijah said.

"The Sovereign has demanded I come alone," Javan said as he stood. He went on before Elijah could argue. "That's why I want you in the shadows so he can't see you."

Elijah smiled and pivoted. "Be wary, Javan."

As if he needed to be reminded. Obviously the Sovereign didn't want to give up the Throne, even though it was how the Houses had survived through thousands of millennia.

Just what was the Sovereign up to?

Anyone sitting on the Obsidian Throne had the key to Heaven, Hell, and the prison for the supernatural—the Oubliette.

Family made him think about his own. Javan put his hands on his desk and sighed. Drohas had been a strong House within the Incubus world, and in order for that to continue, Javan needed an heir.

At one time, that hadn't been an issue. The

numbers of their female race, the Succubi, had once been many, but they had since been wiped out.

The only way for an Incubus to continue their line was with a Nephilim—a half human, half angel. The Nephilim were proud of their heritage, and more than willing to birth babies the Incubi needed to continue.

But there was a catch. If an Incubus had sex with a Nephilim more than eight times, they were mated. The Incubus wouldn't be able to have sex with anyone but his mated female. And the Nephilim would become immortal.

It was why many Nephilim had attempted to deceive an Incubus into a long-term relationship. It was also why the Harem had been designed.

Each Nephilim family had a daughter chosen for the Harem. The female was obligated to birth one child for a House. The female would give up all ties to the child.

Each of Javan's three brothers had been to the Harem and conceived children there. Javan was the only one who hadn't seen to his duties.

All that would change in a week's time when he was scheduled for a visit.

It wasn't that Javan didn't want children, because he wanted that very much. But he yearned for what the humans had—a wife, love, a family.

But that wasn't the way for most Incubi.

Javan straightened and walked around his desk. It was time for his meeting.

~ ~ ~

Naomi stared at herself in the mirror of the bathroom. She couldn't remember the last time she had been so nervous, and it had nothing to do with her photographs hanging on the wall for the exhibit outside the bathroom door.

No, it all had to do with Javan Drohas.

She had been following him for several weeks, waiting to get a glimpse of the man. He was cagey, rarely seen. Those times he left the building, she only caught a fleeting look at him. Thankfully there were pictures of him that she was able to look up on the internet.

Of course he would be drop-dead gorgeous. Men like him always were. But that didn't stop her from continuing on her mission. His looks, power, and money were nothing she wanted. No, she was after something else entirely.

The reflection staring back at Naomi looked sophisticated and cultured. Her chic black dress skimmed her body, but was high-necked and sleeveless. The cocktail dress was shorter than she would've liked, allowing much of her legs to be seen. Since she was so tall, she probably shouldn't have chosen the slinky stilettos, but she hadn't been able to resist wearing them.

Her blond hair was pulled away from her face in a low ponytail secured at the base of her neck. The only jewelry that adorned her were gold earrings that hung nearly to her shoulders.

Naomi took a deep breath and slowly released it. "You can do it," she reminded herself.

One last check of her lipstick, and Naomi walked out of the bathroom. The gallery had yet to open to guests. Only the artists who had pieces at the exhibit were in the building.

Naomi glanced around, looking for Javan. She should've guessed he wouldn't arrive until the guests. He was much too important to talk to the lowly artists he wanted to claim he found.

Her stomach rolled violently. She hadn't eaten for fear of tossing up her cookies, and it had been the right thing to do by the way she felt.

"No need to be nervous," Elijah said as he walked up and handed her a glass of champagne.

She put a smile in place and accepted the glass. "There would be something wrong if I wasn't nervous."

"You've had showings before."

Naomi shrugged and took a sip of the golden liquid, feeling the bubbles on her tongue. "Not like this. This is the Drohas Foundation."

"No kidding?" he asked with a wink.

She didn't want to like Elijah, but she couldn't help herself. His jesting eased her riled nerves. Besides, he wasn't the one being blamed for her sister's death.

But he was in Javan's inner circle. That could help her get closer to Javan.

"Javan was sorry he didn't get to talk to you the other day. He had a meeting he needed to attend. I'm sure he'll search you out tonight."

"I'm counting on it," she mumbled beneath her breath before she took another drink.

Their conversation was interrupted by a worker at the exhibit. Naomi turned back to her photos. Though she didn't want to admit it, the fact her work was in the foundation exhibit was a huge boon. It would do great things for her career.

Becky had urged her to submit her pictures for years, but Naomi had always feared being passed over. It was sad that it was Becky's death that had gotten her here.

Naomi's pictures were plastered on the wall in various sizes, the lighting strategically placed to give onlookers the best view.

"What a talent," said a deep male voice behind her. "I can't believe she hasn't been here before."

Naomi gripped the stem of her champagne glass and looked at the largest picture featured, which happened to be her sister as the model. "I'm glad you like them."

"I'm going to buy one."

Naomi turned her head toward him, only giving him a curious glance. She didn't pay him much attention though. He wasn't her mark. "Thank you."

"You're the artist?"

"I am."

He moved so that he stood even with her as they stared at the photos. "You have a gift. You make a story with one photo. Few people can do that."

His praise made her smile, and she was finding she loved hearing his silky voice. He didn't shout. Everything he said was spoken in a soft tone with just enough bass to make her want to lean toward him.

Her skin began to heat, desire rolling through her in thick waves. It was making it impossible for her to think clearly.

"You're very kind," she said and chanced

another look.

He was so tall she had to tilt her head up to see his face. There were few men with that kind of height. His wealth of blond hair was thick and wavy. It was long, hanging to his chin while the front had been shoved back by a careless hand.

She loved it.

The look shouldn't have gone with his ability to pull off a suit that had men and women alike looking his way. Perhaps Naomi should've paid more attention. Wouldn't it be grand if she could find her sister's killer, sell her work, and get a date?

A three-in-one.

She sucked in a breath as her sex throbbed. Her feet shifted as she tried to put a name to the reason as to why her stomach felt as if she was riding a roller coaster.

"It's the truth."

That voice again. Naomi began to take another drink of champagne, then thought better of it as her stomach couldn't decide if it was nauseous or excited.

She turned to face the man, a smile in place when he looked at her. The smile froze, and her stomach soured instantly as she gazed into a face she knew all too well.

"Javan Drohas," she said.

CHAPTER TWO

Naomi tossed back the rest of the champagne at having come face to face with her nemesis. As soon as the alcohol hit her empty stomach, she knew it had been a mistake.

"The detriment of being well known," he said with a charming smile. "People always have me at a disadvantage. It's a pleasure to meet you, Ms. Parker. I've been admiring your work since Elijah brought it to me."

She was going to be sick. Throwing up on him wasn't exactly the kind of revenge she wanted, but it's what he deserved.

Naomi swallowed and took in steady breaths through her nose. By Javan's slight frown, he knew something was wrong. She was going to have to think fast for an excuse.

"Pardon me," she said quickly. "I never do well in these situations. I think it's a little cruel for an artist to stand around while others critique our work."

"You also get to hear the praise."

She forced as much of a chuckle as she could manage.

Javan then gave a slight bow of his head. "If you've no wish to stand here, please feel free to walk around. Perhaps we can talk later."

Naomi watched him walk away. She was finally able to take a deep breath, but whatever had caused her entire body to quiver with raw excitement had begun to ebb.

"Excitement?" She shook her head. "Pull yourself together, Naomi."

Just as Naomi was walking away from her pictures, an older couple strolled up, asking about the photos. For the next half hour she talked to the French couple about her work.

When she next looked up, a businessman from Prague and a woman of Spanish nobility were on either side of her. Her thoughts of Javan, the murder of her sister, and her revenge were forgotten as she spoke about the only thing she loved—photography.

~ ~ ~

Javan couldn't take his eyes off Naomi Parker. The black cocktail dress was understated. It would be called plain on anyone else, but on her, its simple grace only added more mystery.

His gaze went to her hair. It was like spun gold. He'd had a hard time not touching it when he was standing near her. Her artic blue eyes had been direct and searching. He'd become lost in her gaze, drowning in pools of blue.

It had seemed to take him forever to get her to look at him, but once she had, he'd been utterly captivated. She was so stunningly beautiful that his breath had been sucked from his chest.

She had the face of an angel, it was so perfectly

formed. For a moment, he wondered if she was a dream. It seemed impossible for someone like her to exist.

Yet there she was. Sharp cheekbones softened by wide, full lips and a pert nose. Brows of a darker blond arched softly over large eyes.

His gaze lowered down her slim neck to her body. There was a hint of gold tinting her skin, speaking of hours in the sun. He spotted definition in her arm muscles, telling him she worked out.

With his blood pounding in his ears, he took in her breasts, the indent of her waist, and then legs that went on forever.

"What do you think?" Elijah asked from beside him.

Javan finished off his champagne. "When did you know she was Nephilim?"

"As soon as I met her."

"And you didn't think to tell me?"

Elijah chuckled and turned to face him. "I'm your Watchman, Javan. If a Nephilim wants to pay you a visit, who am I to stand in the way?"

"You know I can only have one night with her. What does that do for either of us?" Damn Elijah for interfering. Javan would've been happy never seeing the amazing beauty of Naomi.

"Are you afraid of finding a mate?"

"What I fear is being deceived. You saw what that did to my uncle." Javan put the empty champagne glass down on the tray of a passing waiter and grabbed another.

Elijah held his champagne without taking a drink. "You need an heir."

"What do you know about her?" Javan asked, hoping to turn the topic off the need for him to beget an heir.

"The surname threw me. I didn't recognize it, although she's from Australia, from her birth records."

Javan watched Naomi talk to a good-looking man from Switzerland. He didn't like the spurt of envy that rose at her smiling so easily. She hadn't been quite so welcoming with him.

"I know you, Elijah. You're a damned bloodhound. You know all about her, and for some reason you've waited until now to tell me."

Elijah chuckled, though his humor died quickly. "Parker is not her true surname. It's Williams."

"That sounds familiar," Javan said as he swiveled his head toward Elijah.

"It should. Naomi's sister was Rebecca Williams."

Javan instantly remembered Rebecca and her artistry with clay. "Rebecca was an amazing talent. I hate that we lost her."

"Yes."

Javan's gaze slid back to Naomi. "Tell me the pretty photographer didn't change her name in order to get close to me because she suspects I killed her sister."

"That's exactly my thought," Elijah said with a loud sigh.

"I suppose the police investigation that cleared me means nothing?"

Elijah lifted one shoulder and watched Naomi. "It appears not."

"Well, if Naomi wants to get close, let's give her what she wants."

"Is that wise?"

Javan knew it probably wasn't, but he had to settle this with Naomi soon because his entire family was in danger with the ongoing problems with the Sovereign. "Let's see what move she makes next."

"This should be fun," Elijah mumbled sarcastically beneath his breath.

Javan smiled at his Watchman. Elijah had been with him for centuries. There was no one he trusted more than Elijah with his life or his family.

How Javan longed for the days when the Succubi were still alive. It wasn't that he had a grudge against the Nephilim, even if others blamed them for the annihilation of the Succubi.

Javan mingled around the gallery, stopping to talk to each artist along the way. But his attention shifted back to Naomi again and again.

He'd had a mind to seduce her right up until he learned why she was there. Javan didn't blame her for wanting to know the truth. There were many truths he searched for as well. If he couldn't take her to his bed, he would help her solve her sister's case.

~ ~ ~

Naomi's feet hurt. She could no longer feel her toes, and though she desperately longed to remove her shoes she couldn't for fear her swollen feet wouldn't fit back in them.

It wasn't as if she didn't wear heels often, but there was a difference in donning them for a date and standing in them for hours.

She shifted and tilted one foot back on the heel to give some relief to her poor toes. There had been very few moments to herself since the gallery opened that night.

It helped stroke her self-esteem that so many liked her photos. If that were the only reason she was at the exhibit, it would be an amazing night. But every time she looked at her sister's picture she was reminded of what she had to do.

A waiter passed by her with a tray of food. She snagged one of the shot glasses filled with cocktail sauce and a large shrimp sitting atop it.

She was starving. Naomi had to stop herself from taking the entire tray and sitting on the floor to devour it. It was her own damn fault for not eating. It was backfiring on her. Now she was lightheaded from all the champagne on an empty stomach.

It also didn't help that Javan Drohas was always near. The man oozed power and authority as much as he did sex appeal. But she wasn't going to allow that to affect her. Regardless if he was an Incubus or not.

The first time Naomi had read her sister's diary, she had thought Becky had gone crazy. Naomi had thought nothing more about it until she began to do research on the Drohas family.

Every child mentioned was always male. Then there was the fact that none of the men were ever seen with their supposed wives. Everything about the Drohas family was kept private and out of the public eye.

Naomi had then done her research on the Incubi.

They were supposed to be a legend, like vampires and such. Yet the things Becky wrote about—in detail—were so similar to what Naomi had read about the Incubi that it made her begin to suspect.

For two weeks she trailed Javan Drohas. Or she tried. He was a hard man to track. Rarely was he alone except in his building, and she hadn't been able to get a good shot of him from the building across the street either.

Oddly enough, what she did learn was that Javan looked almost identical to his father, grandfather, and great-grandfather.

Naomi wasn't sure she really believed he was an Incubus, but there was something off about Javan. Incubi were demons who had sex to live. That could be how Becky died. Naomi was going to prove how she died, as well as prove he was Becky's killer.

She quickly smiled, hiding her wince, as a man and woman walked past her. Naomi was going to have to do the unthinkable. She was going to have to remove her shoes if there was even a thought of her making it to her car.

Fifteen minutes later she was handed a list of all her photos that had been purchased. The price was triple what she would have asked for, and the Drohas Foundation only took five percent that went toward helping local artists.

Naomi hated that Javan did something so kind. She wanted to despise him. Not feel that he might have a shred of decency. Then again, what had she read about sociopaths?

"They charmed, lulling their victims," she said.

"Talking about someone I know?"

She whirled around to find Elijah behind her. The sudden movement caused her feet to throb in such a way that she lost her balance.

It was Elijah who righted her. He released her arm and motioned to her feet with his eyes. "I think it's time to take those off."

"That's like asking you to take off your suit jacket."

"Ah, but then my jacket isn't causing me pain. And I can assure you, Ms. Parker, that if I were in pain, the jacket would come off."

Naomi glanced around, noting that most of the patrons had left the gallery. There were only a handful that remained. She spied Javan standing in the back next to a set of overstuffed chairs.

"Please, Ms. Parker," Elijah urged. "Otherwise, I might have to carry you to your car."

She laughed and held up her hands. "All right. I hate to admit this, but it's all I've been able to do to stand here for the last hour."

Naomi kicked off one shoe and put her bare foot on the wooden floor. Her toes were so swollen she couldn't stand to put any weight on them. The second shoe came off in a hurry, and she sighed as most of the pain quieted.

"You've done very well," he said and pointed to the paper in her hands.

"All but two were purchased."

"Actually, Mr. Drohas purchased those before the gallery opened. If you come by the offices tomorrow, you'll find one in the lobby."

Now that was a surprise. "And the other?"

Elijah smiled and turned to look at the picture of

Becky. "In his office."

Did he know it was Becky in the photo? Was she some kind of trophy to display? Anger spiked through her, making her clutch the stem of the champagne glass tightly.

There was no way she was allowing Becky to hang in Javan's office. No matter what she had to do, Becky wouldn't have to suffer that kind of insult.

The stem snapped in her hand, spilling the rest of the champagne. Naomi jumped back in time to keep it off her dress. Elijah was at her side in an instant, taking the broken glass from her hand.

"I have to talk to him," Naomi said.

Elijah lifted a black brow. "He's waiting."

CHAPTER THREE

Javan smiled at the woman talking to him. She was one of the gallery's biggest clients, and she made no secret that she wanted Javan in her bed.

She was attractive, but his attention was on someone else that night.

Out of the corner of his eye, he saw Elijah talking to Naomi. The ecstasy on her face when she removed her shoes immediately made him picture her in his bed as they made love.

The snap of the champagne stem caused him to turn so that he could better see Naomi and Elijah. She didn't even try to hide her anger as she turned and started toward him.

What could she possibly be upset about? The money she made from her photos was more than she had made in the last two years combined. She should be pleased, but there was no denying something had riled her.

"Excuse me, Pamela," Javan said to the patron and turned to Naomi as she walked up.

"You can't have it."

Javan waited for Pamela to get far enough away before he said, "Have what, exactly?"

"The photo." She pointed to the largest of her work. "It's not for sale."

Interesting. "You signed an agreement. Everything you brought to display was for sale."

"I've changed my mind."

"Why?"

She swallowed, a flash of grief coming over her face. "It's special. I thought I could sell it, but I can't."

There was no deception in her words. She meant each of them. Javan had a suspicion that the model was none other than Rebecca. Though the face of the model in the photo was almost impossible to determine.

"Then keep it."

She seemed surprised, by the way her eyes widened and her lips parted. "I didn't expect..." she trailed off, then shrugged.

"Ah. You thought I was devious and uncaring. On the contrary, Ms. Parker, I'm neither. If the photo means that much, then keep it."

She let out a sigh and lowered her gaze to the floor. "No. You're right. I agreed to sell the piece. I can't change my mind now." Her eyes lifted to his. "I had no right to get angry."

"Tell you what. Come to my office tomorrow. If you don't like where I hang it, then you can take it with you."

Her eyes studied him for long, silent moments. "Why are you being so nice?"

"Just because I run such a large company doesn't mean I can't be civil."

"They say you're ruthless when going after something you want."

Javan smiled. Oh, she had no idea. And he had just found something he wanted. "That's a fair assessment."

"Then you must not want my photograph very much."

"Do you say that because I'm not mercilessly refusing to give it up?"

Her blond brows lifted in affirmation. "Yes."

"Perhaps it's not just your artwork I want." Javan let his voice deepen just enough.

He saw the bumps rise on her skin and her chest heave as she tried to draw in a breath. Could she not know she was a Nephilim? How was that even possible?

Javan only needed to close the distance between them to overwhelm her senses. But he kept away. He wanted her to come to him on her own.

Was that a blush that stained her cheeks? She glanced away, but her blue eyes returned to him almost immediately.

"You intrigue me, Naomi," he said and took a step closer. "Not many women do that."

He walked past her, allowing his hand to brush hers as he did. Javan didn't want to leave the gallery, but if he was going to get his quarry where he wanted her, it was his only move.

"Nice," Elijah said as they walked out onto the sidewalk. "She'll be there tomorrow."

"I hope so." Javan fought the urge to look back and see if she watched him.

~ ~ ~

Naomi stood in the lobby of the Drohas building wishing she hated it. From the pale gray walls to the plush rugs to the lettering of the Drohas name above the desk, she liked it all. Her gaze kept returning time and again to the outline of a wolf's head thrown back as it howled. There was something about it that called to her. Then there was stunning artwork everywhere, from paintings, drawings, marble statues, and even large art made up of metal.

She saw one of her pieces above the white leather couches in the seating area. It was both weird and amazing to see her piece in such a place alongside well-known artists.

"Ms. Parker," Elijah said as he walked up. "Nice to see you again."

She tried not to fidget. "He didn't tell me a time."

"Not to worry. Right this way," he said and held out his hand to a private elevator.

Naomi saw the two receptionists eyeing her with envy. It made her glad she had chosen to go with a black pencil skirt and white blouse with the black jacket instead of jeans and a tee.

The elevator doors closed after Elijah pressed his thumb to a scanner. Naomi leaned against the back of the elevator, hating the nervousness that arose within her.

Javan was a killer. She shouldn't be attracted to him. She certainly shouldn't have been thinking about his kind offer. Or dreaming of him kissing her.

They both knew that if she wanted the photograph back, all she had to do was tell him she didn't like it in his office.

And she was prepared to do just that.

She had wanted to get close to him, and when she angrily went to him demanding he return her piece, she hadn't been thinking of her revenge. All she had been thinking about was a picture that was easily one of her best, and also her favorite. How could she have even thought to sell it?

Somehow, Naomi had known Javan would like it. Perhaps that's why she included it.

It wasn't until after he agreed to give it back that she realized how she had just hurt herself. She needed to get close, not push him away. Thankfully, he had given her a way to fix things.

"How are your feet?" Elijah asked.

Naomi looked down at the pair of black-heeled booties. "They hurt like hell."

"I'm a sucker for a woman in heels." He shot her a wink. "Remember that there are men you can bring to their knees, looking the way you do. That should help with the pain."

"What kind of men? Men like your boss?"

Elijah's black gaze narrowed a fraction. "It's no secret he keeps to himself, and as you told him last night, you know he can be ruthless. He's not unfair, however. If he wants something, he'll stop at nothing to have it."

"Including women?" Naomi hoped Elijah thought she referred to herself.

"I've not seen him look at a woman as he did you in a very long time. Give him a chance. You might find that your first impression of him from the media doesn't compare to who he really is."

The elevator doors opened then. Naomi expected grand opulence. What she found was an office with an amazing panorama of Sydney harbor. The office was huge with glass taking up an entire wall with the view.

She stepped out of the elevator and looked around at the office. It was decorated in shades of gray that she found soothing and comforting.

A large desk sat off to the left with bookshelves behind it holding pictures, statues, and books. On the opposite side was a black leather couch with a white and gray shag rug. Two black chairs and a coffee table made it feel more like a living room than an office area.

She turned back to the desk and walked toward it, wanting to see the people in the pictures. It was easy to pick out Javan, and with the other men looking similar to him, they had to be his brothers. There were several with Elijah as well.

Her head turned to the left and she froze. There was her picture. It hung over a long wooden table stained a rustic gray. She paid no attention to what was on the table. All she saw was her photo.

The light pouring in from the glass behind her showered the photograph in natural light that showcased all of the fractures of light she used when taking the picture of her sister.

"I think it looks rather perfect there."

She shivered at the dark, sexy voice behind her. Javan Drohas. Naomi was almost afraid to turn and confront him. Almost.

Slowly, she turned. The sunlight was blinding as she faced the glass. He stood with his back to the sun, causing his face to be in shadow.

Was he smiling? Were his lips, soft and alluring, tilted up at the corners? He stood with his hands at his sides, easy and confident.

He walked toward her and the shadows fell away to reveal his navy suit and the cream dress shirt beneath. He didn't wear a tie, but that seemed to only make him sexier. His chocolate gaze was focused on her intently—and curiously. As if he couldn't figure her out. He was smiling, though it was a half-smile. It made her feel as if he knew a secret that she didn't.

Naomi wanted to see him as a villain after discovering he was linked to her sister, but ever since last night, she couldn't seem to do it.

"Naomi?"

There was a pucker of a frown on his forehead. She mentally shook herself and offered him a smile. "I hope I'm not interrupting."

"Oh, you are, and I thank you for that. There are only so many meetings a man can handle in one day."

His laughter went all the way through her, centering at her sex and making it throb. Good God! What was wrong with her?

"I don't suppose you've changed your mind about me keeping the picture, have you?" he asked hopefully.

Naomi looked behind her. With her sister's arms open wide, she seemed to be taunting Naomi that everything was right within reach.

"I see," he said, disappointment filling his voice. "I'll be happy to return the picture to you if you'll tell me why you really wanted in the exhibit."

Her head whipped around, her heart kicking up a notch. She wouldn't retreat. Not yet. "I don't know what you mean."

"You know exactly what I mean." Javan sighed and leaned back against his desk. His gaze was direct, unflinching. "A trade, yes?"

Naomi was back to feeling like she was going to throw up. This wasn't going at all as she had hoped. And she was with him alone. If he did kill her sister, she was in major trouble.

If? If!

He killed her sister. It had to be him. There was no one else to link to Becky. Javan had enough money and connections to make a little murder indictment go away easily.

"You think you can convince me to leave the picture?" Naomi lifted her chin for good measure. She wanted him to think she was as confident as he was.

She just hoped he couldn't see how her knees were knocking together.

Javan was no longer smiling. He looked...sad. "Take the photograph, Naomi. No one will stop you. But I *will* have your explanation before you do."

"You would force me?"

"No. You want to say it anyway. I'm giving you the chance."

There's no way he could possibly know. She had been so careful. "I wanted to use your connections to further my career."

"Every artist who submits work to us wants that." He inhaled deeply and slowly released it. "Give me the courtesy of the truth. I think you owe me that much."

"Fine. You want the truth?" she asked as she glared at him. "I'm here because you killed my sister. I'm going to prove you murdered her, and I won't rest until you're behind bars."

CHAPTER FOUR

Javan had sensed the fire within Naomi. She held nothing back as she stated her words in a clear voice, advancing on him as she did. She was a warrior and didn't even know it.

How he wanted to yank her against his chest and take her lips savagely.

An image of him doing exactly that flashed in his mind. His body burned to feel her against him, to know the softness of her skin. To touch every inch of her.

He'd fed from a human with sex two nights ago. It should last him several more days, but his body felt as if he hadn't fed in weeks.

"Do you have nothing to say for yourself?" Naomi demanded.

"I was questioned by the police, and then promptly cleared. I only knew Rebecca from interviewing her for inclusion in the exhibit."

"You met with her six times."

Javan saw the anger, the hurt, and the grief in Naomi's blue eyes. She was shaking from her fury, and he wondered how she had held it all in before.

"I did. As I'm sure you know, she was accepted into the exhibit. She was the first artist we admitted.

I liked her work so much that I was meeting with her to create a sculpture for my family for the anniversary of my father's death."

Her head cocked to the side, a lock of golden blond hair falling over her shoulder. "What?"

"That was the extent of my involvement with Rebecca. She was a lovely person. Kind, compassionate. It showed in her art."

"I know," Naomi said in a soft voice, all the steam gone from her words.

Javan watched her carefully. "I wasn't in the country when Rebecca died. I was at a meeting in London to acquire a piece of artwork from a private seller."

"It has to be you. There's no one else." Naomi's eyes slid shut and she shook her head as if she couldn't grasp what was happening.

Javan pushed away from the desk and went to her. Before he thought better of it, he gently turned her to guide her to the couch. Once she sat, he poured her a finger of bourbon and put the glass in her hand. "Drink," he ordered.

As she took a tentative sip, Javan walked to his desk and opened the top left drawer. He took out the file he had given the police with all the documentation to prove where he had been.

Javan set it on the coffee table and opened it. Then he took the seat across from Naomi as she thumbed through the papers.

After a moment she dropped her head. "You were all I had."

"Let me help you find the killer."

Javan didn't know why he offered. There were all kinds of turmoil happening in his world, but he had no choice but to help Naomi. He wouldn't be able to focus until she had her answers.

Blue eyes the color of the ocean out his window met his. "Why?"

"Because there's something about you. I saw it in your work, which pulled me in. But you...you, Naomi. I'm drawn to you without thought or reason."

She didn't say a word, merely looked at him as if she wasn't sure what to make of his statement. Javan knew he could've been more suave about it all, but the words had come out of him in a rush.

He rose and walked to the windows to look out. It was either that or reach across the table and pull her into his lap. Javan was fairly certain Naomi wouldn't have appreciated that.

"How did you find out about me?" she asked.

"Elijah is very thorough."

The sound of her setting the glass on the table reached him. "I know what kind of killer we're looking for."

"Do you?"

He could see her reflection in the glass. She was debating on whether to say anything more.

"An Incubus."

Javan wasn't sure she could've said anything else that would've shocked him more. He turned to her. Did she know she was Nephilim, then? He'd have bet millions last night that she didn't.

"How do you know that?"

She looked at him askance. "You accept what I said that easily?"

"Tell me how you know that?"

Naomi rubbed her hands together as she rested her arms on her knees. "Becky's diary."

Shit. Javan looked back out the window. If it was an Incubus, that meant the odds of it being someone in his family were strong. There were other Incubi running around the city, but for Rebecca to stumble across one?

"What?" Naomi asked as she stood and strode to him. "What aren't you telling me?"

She was so close he could feel the warmth of her body. Heat flooded him, his cock twitching with need. "I'm not sure you really want to know."

"I do," she insisted.

Javan felt her hand on his arm. It burned through his jacket and shirt to the skin beneath. He made the mistake of letting her turn him to face her.

He looked into her face, and was once more drowning in her magnificent eyes. His body demanded to feel her, to sink into her wet folds and let pleasure take them.

Her lips parted as she lowered her gaze to his mouth. When her eyes returned to meet his, there was no denying the desire he saw there. He could see it in the way she breathed, in how she was attuned to his every movement.

"I can help you find the killer." His head lowered a fraction as he ached to kiss her.

She moved a fraction closer. "How?"

"Because Incubi are real." Her mouth was mere inches away. She was like a drug and he the junkie. And he hadn't even kissed her yet.

Javan knew he would put himself to the ultimate test when it came to Naomi, and yet he couldn't turn away. She focused him. She cleared away the world until only she existed.

Her hand moved from his arm to his chest. "You're one."

"Yes," he said and took her mouth.

For a moment, he held still, his breath locked in his lungs as he put the instant to memory. Then he pulled away and looked at her.

Naomi blinked up at him, a small frown furrowing her forehead. "Is that why I can't think of anything but ripping your clothes off?"

He groaned. She had no idea how close he was to taking her right there. "Yes. And no."

"I can't think." She grabbed her head and took a few steps back. When she looked at him, there was doubt and fear in her blue eyes.

Javan leaned his hands against the glass and let his chin fall to his chest. "It's just as I thought. You have no idea who you are, do you?"

"I'm Naomi Williams."

"Not your name, Naomi. Your bloodline. You're a Nephilim."

"A what?" she asked in shock.

He pushed away from the glass. "Half human. Half angel."

"Riiiiiight. Because that makes sense."

Javan strode to the bookshelf behind his desk and pulled out the heavy leather-bound tome. He then walked to the coffee table and set it down, opening it to the title page. "Read," he ordered Naomi.

She hesitated for a moment, but it was her curiosity that won. Naomi moved back to the sofa and sat.

Javan knew she would be there for a while. If she truly didn't know her heritage, she had a lot of reading to do. He returned to the windows as the phone on his desk beeped.

Work was done for the day. He had something else to focus on – Naomi.

And the Incubus who killed her sister.

CHAPTER FIVE

Naomi couldn't stop reading. The words flew past her as she flipped page after page, soaking it all in. Occasionally, she heard voices in the office, but she was too absorbed to look up.

At one point, Javan had stuck a bottle of water in one of her hands and a hamburger in the other. Naomi hadn't even bothered to look up. She ate without tasting anything.

Her mind was blown. That was the only way to describe what was happening to her. Incubi, extinct Succubi, angels, demons, and Nephilim.

It was all so much to take in. And yet, from what she had read, all those unanswered questions she and Becky had about the odd things they suspected, and the strange feelings and such, were answered. Finally.

Naomi finished the book and leaned back on the sofa and closed her eyes. Her head rolled back to rest against the cushion. It took her a moment to realize how quiet the office was.

She cracked open her eyes. The first thing she noticed was the inky black sky outside the windows. Had she really spent the entire day reading?

A glance at the three-inch-thick volume confirmed it. Naomi glanced at her watch and saw that it was nearing midnight. Her gaze then swung to the desk where Javan was intently looking through a stack of papers.

As if feeling her eyes, his head lifted. Slowly he set down the papers and rested his elbows on the desk. "You look exhausted."

"How did you know that I am a Nephilim?"

He rolled back his chair and stood. Javan came around the desk to the chairs and stopped behind one. "It's a sense that all Incubi have. With the Succubi all gone, the only way to continue our race is with yours."

"Yeah," she said and swallowed. "I read that. I just don't understand how Becky and I didn't know. I read all the family names of the Nephilim. We're not on there."

"Elijah is...proficient at discovering all there is to know about a person. It's how we found out you were Rebecca's sister. He also learned that you and Becky were adopted."

Naomi barked with laughter. "You know, I believed everything in that book," she said, pointing at the tome lying before her. "But you've crossed the line."

"Becky was eighteen months old and you were just days old when the Williams family adopted you. I have the paperwork to prove it."

She shook her head, not wanting to believe it. But why would he lie? What did Javan have to gain? "They never told us. Adoptive parents end up telling their children."

"Not if you were adopted to be saved." Javan's dark eyes held hers. "Your family is the Martins.

There had been a feud between them and the Ryans. It was the Ryans who wiped out your family. Your parents kept your birth secret. They employed a human nurse who took you and Rebecca away before the attack."

Naomi put a hand over her stomach. This couldn't be happening. It all sounded so farfetched, like it was out of some sci-fi movie.

"A female child about your sister's age who had been delivered to the morgue was put in the house so when the Ryans attacked, they believed your entire family was killed."

Naomi jumped to her feet and began to pace. "How do you know all of this?"

"I told you. Elijah can find out anything. I'm glad you're finished reading. I know you have many more questions, but I'd like to ask you if Rebecca described her lover?"

Naomi stopped and stared. "Have you found something?"

"Possibly." He started back to his desk and motioned for her to follow. "As you learned from the book, there are ten Incubus families. Mine controls Australia. It doesn't stop other Incubi from traveling and such. However, I've had Elijah find out the whereabouts of each of those I'm responsible for on the night your sister died."

She leaned over his shoulder after he sat and looked at the papers. Naomi couldn't believe he had gone to all this trouble just for her. If she hadn't told him she knew he was an Incubus, she wondered if he would be helping her now.

Javan looked up at her. Naomi realized how close

they were. She thought of the quick, hard kiss he had given her. And how she wished it had lasted longer.

Her breath left her lungs in a whoosh when Javan's gaze lowered to her mouth. The man had a serious way of making her forget everything but wanting to be in his arms.

No. Wanting was too weak of a word. She yearned. She craved.

She *hungered.*

"Yes," Naomi said, her voice sounding breathless and needy even to her own ears.

Javan's lips lifted in a half-smile. "Yes?"

It took a moment for his question to sink in. Naomi shook her head to pull herself back from the brink of the overwhelming passion. "Yes, Becky described him. He was tall with dark hair and dark eyes."

"You've just described a number of men in my employ, including Elijah."

Naomi straightened and crossed her arms over her chest. "So we're not any closer?"

"I didn't say that. There are a handful of men who don't have an alibi for that night. Elijah is looking into them now."

"Aren't you worried it might be Elijah?"

Javan smiled and turned his chair to face her. "He was with me in London. He's my Watchman."

That's right. Naomi remembered reading about the men whose job it was to look after the head of each Incubus House and lead the under-Watchmen. Elijah would go anywhere that Javan went.

"Good," she said. "I like Elijah. I'd have been upset if it was him."

Javan stood then. "It's been a long day for both of us. Let me take you to dinner."

Dinner? Alone with one of the hunkiest men she had ever encountered? Did she even attempt such a thing?

"All right. Should I go home and change?"

He put his hand on her back and guided her across the office to the elevator. "You're perfect."

The man knew exactly what to say, Naomi would give him that. Perfect? She was hardly that, but it was nice to hear that he thought so.

Their shoulders were touching in the elevator. Naomi could feel his gaze on her. He was like a magnet, enticing her closer the longer they were together.

The elevator went past the lobby of the building to the basement where it opened and a car was parked, waiting. Javan's hand was once more on her lower back. She found she liked the feel of his hand there.

Naomi felt protected, sheltered.

It was...nice.

She slid into the passenger seat of the white Jaguar XK. As Javan shut the door after she was inside, Naomi spotted Elijah getting into another car. Javan got behind the wheel and drove away.

"I admit, I was offended that you thought I murdered Rebecca," Javan said. He glanced at her. "But it brought you to me."

"I have to know what happened to her."

"And you will. I'm going to make sure of that."

She watched the city lights pass in a blur. "Is that what money and position can do?"

"Yes. I'll not apologize for what my family began."

"Nor should you. I've just never had that kind of privilege."

He flashed her a smile. "Have you seen your work? Naomi, you're extremely talented. You're going to make a lot of money because of it."

"Only because I was in the exhibit."

The car slowed as he prepared to turn into a drive. "You sell yourself short. Being in the exhibit will get you there faster, but trust me, you were going to get there regardless."

Naomi smiled, beyond pleased at his words. They stopped in front of a garage door. Javan rolled down his window and punched in a few numbers. A moment later the door opened.

It wasn't until they drove into the garage that she realized he'd brought her to his house.

"I thought you might want to talk privately instead of trying to hide our words from a waiter," Javan said after he put the car in park. "If you'd rather, we can go to a restaurant."

Naomi shook her head. "This is fine. And you're right, I don't want to watch what I have to say."

She got out of the car and was met by Javan who walked her to a thick wooden door. There wasn't time to look long as Javan ushered her inside the house.

As soon as she entered, she felt at ease. It could have something to do with the same soothing grays as his office, or the fact that the artwork everywhere was awe-inspiring.

The next thing she knew, they were ascending a

set of switchback stairs. Javan then stood at a large entrance and smiled, waiting for her to enter.

Naomi stepped through and gasped at another spectacular view of the harbor. The clinking of crystal pulled her attention from the lights reflecting off the water.

She turned to find they were in a library. Tall walls held hundreds of books on black bookshelves. A large fireplace sat in the middle of a wall with a cozy set of chairs and a couch. There was no fire roaring. Instead, there were dozens of small candles sitting among the logs, giving off a golden hue as their tiny flames flickered.

"It's one of my favorite rooms," Javan said. He held up a bottle of wine.

"Please," Naomi said in regard to the wine. "This place is amazing. I didn't think anything could beat your office view, but I think I've found it."

He handed her the glass of wine as he stood beside her. "I'm glad you came into my life."

"I have a hard time believing that." She took a drink to try and calm her nerves.

Javan took her wine glass from her hand and set it next to his on a table beside him. He then turned her to face him. His gaze was intense, holding hers so she couldn't look away.

"I want you, Naomi."

His words were like a match to her desires. They roared to life, burning her with need.

"Your artwork drew me to you. I didn't know why until I saw you at the gallery. I knew then that I'd be a fool to let you walk out of my life."

"I just met you," she said, her mind whirling

from his words.

Javan touched her face tenderly. "You're a Nephilim. You feel desire anytime I'm near because I'm an Incubus."

"So it's not real?"

"Oh, it's real."

"But I'd feel it with any Incubus. Say, like Elijah?"

One blond brow lifted. "You've been around Elijah. Did you feel desire?"

Naomi thought about the times she was with Elijah and shook her head.

"You have your answer, then."

Unable to help herself, Naomi reached up and ran her hands through his blond locks. Then she rose up on her toes and put her lips to his.

She had barely begun to pull back when his arms went around her, pulling her against his hard chest. He slanted his lips over hers and took her mouth in a kiss that stole her breath.

Flames of passion licked at them, pulling them deeper into the fire. Naomi shoved his suit jacket over his shoulders. He let it slide down his arms before he unzipped her skirt. In moments, they each had the other devoid of clothes.

Naomi was then gathered in his arms. She wrapped her legs around his waist as he walked to the fireplace and knelt. He was kissing her as he laid her back on the fur rug, covering her body with his.

She sighed at the feel of his arousal pressing against her sex. His hips rocked against her. Naomi couldn't get close enough to him.

A moan fell from her lips when he shifted and

took a nipple in his mouth. Her lids fell shut, pleasure rushing through her.

Naomi ran her hands over his back, feeling the hard muscle moving beneath her hand. His suit belied the toned body beneath. His barely restrained hunger only pushed her closer to the edge.

The blunt head of his arousal was at her entrance. With one thrust, he entered her.

CHAPTER SIX

Javan now knew what Heaven was. He held it in his arms, her soft cries filling the room. She was so tight, her walls slick as he filled her.

He lifted his head to watch her. With her lips parted and her eyes closed, her chest rose and fell quickly. Her golden locks were scattered around her, the light from the candles in the hearth making her appear as if she had been dipped in gold.

Javan swore he would only take her once. It's all he would allow himself. He had planned to go slow, to tease and torment them both for hours before he buried himself within her tight sheath.

With one electrifying, soul-stealing kiss, he hadn't been able to control himself.

Her legs held him firmly as he began to move his hips, slowly at first. He fisted one hand in her hair and struggled to get ahold of himself.

Then her lids lifted and she speared him with her blue eyes. The passion, the desire he saw there wiped away the last shreds of his control.

He pulled out of her and then thrust hard. In answer, her nails dug deep into his back. Again and again he plunged inside her while her hips rose to meet him.

Javan was consumed with her. He heard her shout as she clamped around his cock with an orgasm, but he didn't stop. He continued thrusting, taking her higher.

Naomi had never had such an intense orgasm before, and just as she was coming down from one, another slammed into her. Was this what it was like to make love to an Incubus?

Their bodies slid against each other as he ruthlessly drove within her. Her back arched as yet another climax ripped through her.

He groaned before he claimed her nipple in his mouth once more. He suckled deep, and lightly bit down on the turgid peak. Naomi bucked, a scream of ecstasy lodged in her throat.

Her body should be mush after three such mind-blowing orgasms, but all she wanted was more of Javan.

Suddenly, he pulled out of her and flipped her onto her stomach. He raised her up on her knees and entered her once more. With his fingers clutching her hips tightly, he began to thrust.

Naomi closed her eyes, the fire within her only growing higher instead of diminishing. The only thing that existed for her was Javan. She only felt his touch, his kisses. She only heard his breathing and his moans.

He leaned over her, cupping a breast and nipping at the lobe of her ear. She reached back and around to touch his face as he kissed down her neck, all the while his hips pumping into her.

To her surprise, another climax was building fast. His hand caressed down her stomach to her sex to run his thumb over her clit. Naomi whispered his name right before she was swept away on another tide of bliss.

This time, he came with her. He thrust deep as his body shuddered.

They collapsed to the side, their bodies still joined. Naomi liked being nestled against his chest with Javan's arms around her. Her eyes closed, drifting in that place between wake and sleep.

She didn't remember dozing off, but she woke on her back with Javan sliding inside her. Their gazes met, held. The inferno that took them earlier grasped them once more.

It refused to release its hold, and Naomi wasn't sure she wanted to.

Again and again they made love. She adored the hard sinew of his body, the penetrating way he held her gaze as he dared her to follow him on the path of passion.

She touched, licked, and kissed every part of him. Only after he had touched, licked, and kissed every inch of her. There was no talking. There was no need.

Their bodies spoke a language as old as time itself. Several times as she drifted off to sleep she felt Javan rise, but he always returned, making love to her more wildly than the time before.

There was no concept of time, no thought of the morrow. Or the consequences to their night of passion.

~ ~ ~

Javan held Naomi in his arms as he watched the sun rise through the window. Whether she knew it or not, Naomi had changed his life.

His course was set. Despite his valiant attempt to walk away from her and her exquisite body, Javan had made love to her well past eight times.

He was now tied to her. His life depended on whether they had sex or not. No other would he be able to touch. Only Naomi.

Javan kissed the top of her head and tightened his arm. She was new to their world. It had been reckless of him to take her last night. He should've known he wouldn't be able to stop after just one time. He'd known it the moment they kissed.

And yet he didn't stop it.

He'd given it a half-hearted try, which had done nothing.

The door to the library cracked open. Elijah came in carrying a tray without looking at Javan. After Elijah set the tray down, he retrieved the one that was untouched from the night before. Elijah left without a word, the door closing softly behind him.

"Do I smell food?" Naomi asked with her eyes still closed.

Javan smiled. "I suppose that means you're hungry?"

"Starving, actually." Her eyes opened and she smiled up at him.

Javan's heart was seized. This woman was his. All he could de was pray she gave him a chance to earn her love. "Morning."

"Morning." She turned her head and yawned before she sat up. "How did we get on the couch?"

Javan loved how the morning sun filtered through her golden locks. "I put us here."

Naomi's blue eyes slid to him. "It was quite a night."

"Yes, it was."

"I've never experienced anything like that before."

Javan felt his chest expand. "Neither have I."

A blond brow rose as she looked at him skeptically. "Really?"

"Really." Javan sat up and smoothed a lock of hair away from her face. "Naomi, there's something I must talk to you about."

"Can you talk and eat at the same time? Because if I sit here any longer, I'm going to start gnawing on the couch."

Javan laughed and nodded. They rose from the sofa with Naomi wrapping a blanket under her arms and tucking the end. She didn't wait on him as she hurried to the food and grabbed a piece of sausage to stuff in her mouth.

He put on his pants, but didn't fasten them. Naomi had already taken a seat at the table when Javan reached it. He dished food onto his plate, wondering how to broach the subject of their joining.

Javan moved his plate and saw an envelope. He pulled it out and opened it to find Elijah's handwriting with a single name written on the sheet of paper.

"What's that?" Naomi asked.

He handed it to her. "The name of your sister's killer."

She took it from him and read the name as she finished chewing and swallowing her food. "Are you sure?"

"Elijah is never wrong. After breakfast, you can shower and change, and we'll go pay him a visit."

"Is he is part of your family?"

Javan shook his head, relieved that the murderer was from another House.

"Will you turn him over to the police?"

"No. We have our own brand of justice."

She wiped her mouth with the napkin and drank some orange juice. "Would you mind if we go now?"

"Not at all. I'll show you to the room you can use."

They walked from the library. Javan decided it would be better not to bring up their bond now. Naomi needed closure regarding her sister. Perhaps after, he could bring it up.

He was prepared to do whatever it took to woo her. All he had thought about was holding Naomi in his arms.

He stopped next to a door and opened it. "I asked Elijah to pick up a few things for you."

"Did you know I was going to be spending the night?" she asked with a little smile.

"I'd hoped, but I asked it of Elijah a few hours ago."

Her blue eyes grew round. "Did you sleep at all?"

"Not really." Javan closed the distance and drew her against him. He gave her a soft kiss. "I was too busy making love to you."

"You've thought of everything, it seems."

Not even close, but she didn't need to know that.

"Take your time. When you're ready, you'll find Elijah waiting for you out here."

Javan walked away from her with difficulty. His strides lengthened as he focused on the one thing he could control—bringing Rebecca's killer to justice.

CHAPTER SEVEN

Naomi stood in front of the full-length mirror looking over herself. Everything she could possibly need, from scented soap to makeup to clothes, was available.

She couldn't decide if she should be offended that he had everything there for his female guests, or flattered that the makeup was all new and the clothes—also new—fit to perfection.

The thick-heeled brown booties looked great with the faded denim, but it was the light pink short-sleeved tee beneath the thin charcoal gray cardigan that hung to her hips that she loved the most.

It was one of those T-shirts that women searched their entire lives for. It had a semi-fitted shape, but was fluid enough to appear sexy. Now if only she had one of every color.

Naomi's smile faded as she remembered where she was going. She walked from the room and found Elijah standing in the hallway just as Javan had said he would be.

"Ready?" he asked and started down the hall.

She followed him for several steps. "Thank you for the clothes and other things."

"It was my pleasure."

"Is it something you do often? You know, buying clothes for women?" She really wished she hadn't asked that, especially when Elijah halted and turned to look at her.

His dark eyes held no censure or anger. Merely...curiosity. "You have no idea, do you?"

Naomi wasn't sure what to make of his statement. "I guess not. What are you talking about?"

"He's never brought a woman here. You read about us yesterday, so you know how long Javan has been alive."

She did, thanks to the book she had read that listed the birthdates of him and his brothers. Javan was over seven hundred and thirty-two years old.

"As for the items purchased for you, Javan was very specific as to what he wanted. I simply procured the items on his list."

Naomi had no words. What did one say in a situation like this? She was taken aback, shocked, dazed, and a hundred other feelings at the news.

But she was also beyond pleased. A kernel of joy had blossomed into a field of delight. Javan had done all of it for her. Not other women, but her.

"Oh."

Elijah smiled, his eyes crinkling in the corners. "I take it by the look on your face that this pleases you?"

"Definitely."

"Good. Javan deserves happiness. He's waiting for you."

Naomi followed Elijah once more. As she recalled the text she read, a frown grew. "Elijah, if a

Nephilim is the only way for your kind to continue, why aren't more of you married? Why is there a need for the Harem?"

"Because Nephilim began to trick us into taking them as ours, and then refusing to share our beds."

She was sickened by what Elijah said. "But a mated Incubus can only have sex with his woman. Without it, he dies."

"Precisely. However, the Nephilim still has immortality."

Well, no wonder the Harem was set up. If she was an Incubus she certainly wouldn't trust any Nephilim. How would she ever know if she could trust one?

"It's why you looked into my past, isn't it?" Naomi asked.

Elijah nodded his head of dark curls. "My job is to protect Javan as the Master of House Drohas. Many Nephilim have tried to get close to him over the years."

"Then why let me?"

"Because of Rebecca," Elijah said as he reached a door and put his hand on the knob. He stopped and waited for her to reach him. "She didn't deserve her fate, and you were only seeking information on her killer."

"Did you foresee last night?"

"I see the way Javan looks at you. You intrigued him, but you also made him want to help you. I knew eventually the two of you would end up together."

Naomi looked down at her shoes. "Only for a night. I'm really not ready for it to end."

Without another word, Elijah opened the door.

Naomi looked up and saw Javan leaning back against his Jaguar. He wore dark slacks and a pale yellow dress shirt that was opened at the neck, showing her the bronze skin of his throat.

She had kissed that throat, felt his pulse against her tongue. In an instant, she was transported back to their night of inconceivable passion.

A night where no protection was used and they had sex more times than she could remember. Naomi was going to have to make Javan understand that she hadn't done that in an attempt to trick him. In truth, she had been so wrapped up in their desire that rational thought had vanished.

Naomi walked toward Javan as he pushed off the car and shot a smile at her. Her knees wobbled at the sight of him. He was gorgeous, but it wasn't just his looks. It was the way he made her feel. The way he made love to her.

Javan opened the car door for her. Only after she was getting into the backseat did she realize Elijah was driving. Javan walked around and climbed in beside her.

Naomi clasped her hands together in her lap as the car drove away from the house. So much for having some time to talk to Javan. She didn't know how much time she had left with Javan, but it was important that he understand she hadn't attempted to trick him.

She listened as Javan spoke of the prisoner. He was from the House Marakel, which had control of the Obsidian Throne. Politics never interested her, but whether she liked it or not, the Incubi were now part of her world. She needed to know the ins and outs of things.

"The fact Marakel won't give up the Throne is a worry to all of us. We just learned that Canaan Romerac, who we thought had been dead for half a millennium, had actually been imprisoned the entire time. More and more secrets are coming to the surface," Javan said with a shake of his head. "I suspect the Incubus who killed your sister wasn't here by accident."

Naomi whipped her head around to him, fear tightening her stomach. "You think he was after you?"

"We're about to find out," Elijah said as he stopped the car.

Naomi looked out the window to find they were parked in front of a warehouse at the docks. She opened the door, and before she could step out, Javan was at her side. She took his offered hand, liking the warmth that surrounded her when his fingers closed around hers.

As they walked toward the door, Naomi spotted several other men stationed around the warehouse.

"A precaution," Javan said. "My men are everywhere. Some you can see, and some you can't."

"All for one man?" she asked.

Javan was the first to enter the warehouse. He stepped over the threshold and moved to the side to await her. "Rebecca isn't the only woman he's killed during his year in Sydney."

Naomi saw the man sitting in the middle of the empty warehouse on a chair. He wasn't tied, which made her wary. At any moment he could get up and run. What was keeping him there?

Then she saw the dozens of men above them watching him. Ah. Well, that would certainly keep her in the chair as well.

Elijah put his hand on her shoulder to halt her in the shadows as Javan continued on. Naomi looked at Elijah, but his gaze was on Javan.

"Go to him," she told Elijah. "I'll stay here."

"Javan has ordered me to protect you. That's what I'm doing."

She flattened her lips at his tone. Then her eyes returned to Javan. He strode with long, sure strides to the man before he halted in front of the chair.

Naomi saw Javan in profile, and even from that angle she could see the cold fury in Javan's face. In that moment she was reminded that he wasn't human, but a sex demon. He had wealth and power in degrees she couldn't fathom. With one word he could stamp out someone's life.

And still she wanted to be with him.

"Well, Frank," Javan said, his voice holding just the right amount of seething rage. "You have one chance to tell me what you're doing in Australia."

"I don't have to answer to you." Frank snorted, a cocky smile upon his handsome face.

Javan's smile held no mirth. "You're in my territory, and you've been killing humans."

"Not humans," Frank stated.

So he had known Becky was a Nephilim. Had the others he'd killed also been half angel? Naomi hated that her sister had been duped by an attractive face and pretty words. Becky hadn't known what they were. She couldn't have been prepared for the seductive urgings being so near an Incubus caused.

161

Javan put his hands in his pants pockets. "So you're after Nephilim. Why? You kill them and we can't carry on our line."

Naomi saw Javan jerk slightly. She glanced at Elijah to see his jaw clenched tightly.

Javan gave a bark of laughter. "So that's your angle. You wipe out the Nephilim in Australia to prevent my line from carrying on. Do you forget about the Harem?"

"Marakel is the only one capable of ruling. He'll remain on the Obsidian Throne for eternity."

"Without an heir, himself?" Javan asked. Then his eyes widened. "I see. You intend that the only one to use the Harem is Marakel. Nice play."

Frank's smile widened. "Everything was working perfectly except that Elijah was supposed to take the fall for the killings."

Naomi felt Elijah's fury, but he didn't make a move.

Javan walked slowly around Frank. "You made several mistakes. First, in thinking you could come to my land and not be discovered. Second, in believing you could frame Elijah. You really should know your adversaries before you wage war on them. Third, in taking the lives of the Nephilim."

"You know the Nephilim can't be trusted," Frank said with a sneer. "All they want is immortality. They offer one daughter to the Harem in the hopes that one of their other offspring will catch the eye of an Incubus for immortality."

Naomi winced. Did all Incubi think this way of her kind? No wonder the Incubi turned to the Harem as a way to continue their line.

She was really going to have her work cut out for her in regards to Javan. He didn't say anything to oppose Frank's views. Naomi knew she couldn't be a part of Javan's life, but she really didn't want him thinking ill of her.

Not when she thought so highly of him.

"I would have given you the opportunity to leave Australia and return to Marakel with what transpired here," Javan said. He stopped in front of Frank. "But you murdered. That's punishable by death."

Frank's face went slack. "It's not for you to decide."

"It is." Javan took a deep breath. "Australia is Drohas domain, you idiot. You knew to be caught meant death."

Naomi suspected it was coming, but she still jumped when Javan took two steps and snapped Frank's neck.

Without so much as a backward glance at Frank, Javan released him and walked to her. He stopped in front of her, his dark eyes searching hers.

"Rebecca has been avenged."

She swallowed, glancing around him to Frank's dead body. "And the other girls he killed?"

"We're notifying their families," Elijah said.

Naomi turned at Javan's urging. They walked side by side from the warehouse. "What happens to Frank now?"

"He'll be sent to Marakel."

"Aren't you afraid of Marakel's retribution?"

Javan halted next to the car and opened the door for her. "It's past time for him to give up the Throne. He's attacking Houses in an attempt to weaken us, but what he doesn't know is that a meeting has been called. Marakel won't be the Sovereign for much longer."

CHAPTER EIGHT

Javan had hoped killing Frank would give him some measure of relief, but all it did was prove that he would go to great lengths for Naomi.

Sure, he killed Frank because the bastard had come to Australia with the sole purpose of trying to harm the House of Drohas, not to mention all the Nephilim he had murdered. But it paled in comparison to Javan's need to hurt Frank as he had hurt Naomi.

Javan felt Elijah's eyes on him through the rearview mirror. He ignored his Watchman and tried to find some way of telling Naomi that they were mated.

She hadn't said much since he left her to shower. It was obvious by the way she fiddled with her nails that something was on her mind. Was she trying to find a way to cut clean of him?

He hoped to hell that wasn't what was going through her mind, but Javan had already planned for that, should it happen. He would give her space. But he wasn't going to give up on her. He would do whatever it took to convince her they were meant to be together.

The silence in the car as they drove back to his

house was deafening. Many times he wanted to ask what she was thinking. In all his years with Elijah, there was little he kept from his friend, but this was a conversation Javan didn't want others to overhear.

By the time they reached the house, his gut felt as if it was held within an iron fist. He climbed out of the car and walked around to Naomi's side. Javan opened the door and helped her out. Her gaze met his briefly before she looked away.

His chest constricted painfully.

It wasn't until they were inside the house that Naomi asked, "So that's it? It's over?"

It was far from over, but he didn't want to tell her about the war he knew was coming. She had just been introduced to their world. It was better if she slowly learned of the conflict instead of tossing it at her like a bucket of water.

"For now." Javan saw Elijah's quick look in his direction. He put his hand on Naomi's back and gave a little pressure so she would walk with him.

"You're not telling me everything," she said.

Javan smiled at her perception. "No, I'm not. Though I'm not keeping it from you because I don't want you to know. You need to know, but you don't have to learn everything right now."

Her feet halted as she turned to face him. "You killed the Sovereign's man. He's not just going to let that go."

"Then he shouldn't have sent his man here."

"Don't make light of the situation," she admonished. "I'm worried."

Javan walked ahead of her to the door on the right and entered the library. He returned to the room because he wanted to remind her how great they had been together.

As he expected, she followed him. "Did you hear me?"

"I'm not making light of anything. I know what my actions mean for myself and my family." Javan motioned for her to sit, which she promptly ignored. "I appreciate your worry."

Naomi's blue eyes were fastened on him. Her head tilted slightly to the side. "I don't want to worry about you. I'll leave here and never see you again. I'll never know if you're all right or not."

Javan briefly looked at the floor. Her words hurt him far more than he wanted her to know. "I can have Elijah visit."

For long moments they simply looked at each other. Then Naomi crossed her arms over her chest. Her chin lifted stubbornly, and some of the light went out of her eyes. "I can't ever repay you for the justice you brought for Becky and all those other women killed."

"Your thanks is enough." That wasn't true. An eternity in his arms was what he wanted to demand as payment. Javan paused. Her words had said one thing while her voice, laced with a hint of anger, said quite another. "We've been honest with each other since yesterday in my office. Let's continue that way."

"Sounds like a plan," she stated. "You start."

Javan hadn't expected that. Instead of Naomi getting whatever it was off her chest, she had quite succinctly turned it on him. He opened his mouth, but nothing came out.

He wasn't sure how to tell her anything. Javan had spent his life around women—human and Nephilim alike—doing his damnedest to keep their greedy paws off him.

But the tables had been turned. Now he wanted Naomi more than anything else, and he had no idea how to tell her.

She raised a brow in question, waiting for him to talk.

Javan cleared his throat and ran a hand through his hair. "I've never been in this place before."

"Elijah told me you've never brought a woman back to your house." Her arms dropped and her shoulders sagged. "You don't have to worry, Javan. I'll not be returning here. I know we only had the one night."

Her words were just penetrating the fog in his brain when she turned around. "Wait," he called.

"I'm not angry. I wanted you to know that I'm not like some Nephilim," she said, continuing toward the door.

Javan rushed to her, grabbing her arm and turning her to face him. "I never said you were."

"You don't have to. I heard Frank today, and I know what I read in that book yesterday. The Nephilim have that reputation because of the actions of a few. That's not me."

"I know."

Her lips lifted in a small smile. "I...um...I should probably remind you that we didn't use any sort of protection."

The idea of her belly swelling with his child made the room spin. Javan wanted it so badly he could taste it. Never before had he cared about having a child of his own. But that was before Naomi entered his life.

"It was just one night," she said with a forced laugh. "I'm sure it'll all be fine. The odds of me getting pregnant after one night are slim."

Javan's hand on her arm tightened as he pulled her even closer. "I was scheduled to go to the Harem soon."

"Oh." Her gaze darted away.

"I didn't tell you that to hurt you, Naomi. I tell you so you'll understand that when I say you came as a surprise to me that I truly mean it." He smiled when her blue eyes returned to his face. "Last night was heaven. I would like to say that I was strong enough to stop touching you, but the truth is I can't get enough of you. Even now, it's all I can do not to tear those clothes off you and carry you to my bed."

Her confused and wary look let him know he was going about this badly.

Javan grasped both of her arms in his hands and drew in a steadying breath. "I don't know how and I don't know why, but I can't keep my hands off you. Even as I made love to you for the ninth and tenth and eleventh times, I couldn't stop."

Naomi's mouth parted in surprise.

"I can see from your expression that you know exactly what that means." Javan forced himself to drop his arms to his sides. "There is something between us. I know you feel it. No one can make love as we did and not feel something strong and deep."

She brought her hand to her forehead and closed

her eyes.

Javan hurried to finish speaking. "I ask nothing of you except to allow me to win your heart. You're good for me, Naomi, and I'd like to think I'm good for you. We could have something special."

"Incubi don't take a Nephilim as theirs."

"It's done. Not often, but it's done. I want you as my mate, my wife. I want us to bring children into this world together. I want to share everything with you."

Naomi was shaking. Javan's words echoed through her head. Was it all real? Did she want him so badly that she was creating all of this in her mind?

"I love you."

Her head lifted, her eyes swinging to him. "You...can't."

"I can." He smiled, his lips curving upward. "I've loved you from the moment Elijah showed me your portfolio. Give me a chance, Naomi. Please. I need you."

"I have to know. Is it because I might be carrying your child?"

"It has nothing to do with that and everything to do with you. Can't you see I'm crazy about you?" he implored.

Naomi had been too afraid to hope. But how would she ever know what could be if she didn't take a chance?

"There is something between us," she admitted. "Something strong and steady. Ever since I woke up this morning I've dreaded the time I was going to have to walk out of here and leave you behind."

"What are you saying?"

She laughed and put her hand on his chest. "I'm saying that I want to stay. That I want to be yours."

"You understand that you're immortal now, right?"

Naomi waved away his words. "It's nice because I'll get to be with you, but it's nothing I knew could be mine before yesterday."

"You do realize that you hold my life in your hands? If you don't allow me in your bed, I die."

She smiled and reached down to cup his cock that quickly grew hard in her hand. "Then I suppose you better take me to bed."

Naomi let out a shriek of laughter as he lifted her in his arms and carried her out of the library. They passed Elijah in the hall, grinning at them.

She gave Elijah a thumbs up as she realized she had somehow found happiness from looking into her sister's murder. Fate worked in mysterious ways.

~ * ~

ABOUT THE AUTHOR

New York Times and USA Today bestselling author **DONNA GRANT** has been praised for her "totally addictive" and "unique and sensual" stories. She's the author of more than twenty novels spanning multiple genres of romance.

Her latest acclaimed series, Dark Warriors, features a thrilling combination of Druids, primeval gods, and immortal Highlanders who are dark, dangerous, and irresistible.

She lives with her two children, a dog, and three cats in Texas.

Visit Donna at **www.DonnaGrant.com**.

DAUNTLESS
House of Trevanion

Laura Wright

CHAPTER ONE

Casworon Trevanion would've preferred to remain in Hong Kong for the meeting with Jian, Devil and the other Masters, discussing the pendant Sorin had recently discovered and its possible significance to their cause. But instead he was aboard his private jet, returning home to Cornwall. Tonight the fate of Akana would give way to the fate of Casworon himself. It was the Trevanions' annual Seafarers Ball, and as newly 'crowned' Master of Trevanion it was Casworon's duty to not only attend and preside over what he deemed was an outdated celebration, but to accept the mate chosen by his mother.

An ocean of black water beneath him, Cas leaned back in his leather club chair and flipped through the newspapers one of his staff had placed on the granite table before him. True, there had been a few Masters taking mates as of late, but for an Incubus it was a rather unusual pursuit. An Incubus who didn't carry the name Trevanion, that is.

"Shall we start the celebration now, my lord?"

Cas glanced up. The short, stout Watchman with dark eyes stood before him with two frosty mugs, full near to the lip with dark, amber liquid. "I believe it is a last meal before execution, Pennice," he replied dryly.

A grin curved the man's lips. "Come on, then," he chided, dropping into the cream leather chair opposite and setting the mugs down on the table between them. "A good pint or two will smooth the way."

"The way to what?" Cas returned bitterly. "Misery? Shackles? Being forever coupled to a Nephilim of my family's choosing? To bed her, whatever she may look like, and to rely on her and her alone for my sustenance?" A flash of fury rippled through him and he squashed the Times in his fist.

After a healthy swallow of beer, the Watchman shrugged. "It is your House's legacy, my lord."

Cas despised that answer. "We live in the twenty-first century, Pennice." He sniffed and turned to stare out the window. The night was exceptionally black. "And I am a Master. I should make the choice about who I mate, who I feed from—who I fuck!"

Several of the flight crew turned his way, but he paid them no attention. Each one had seen him bare-assed and rutting on this very plane more times than he could count.

"Yes," Pennice agreed. "You should have that choice. But it is not the tradition—"

Cas cut him off with a sneer. "Of the grand Trevanions."

"Have you spoken to your mother, your family?" the Watchman asked, taking another swallow of ale. "Perhaps you could persuade—"

Cas's dark laughter echoed through the cabin. "Does one attempt to persuade a feral cat not to consume its prey?"

The man's brows lifted. "Yes, I see what you mean. Lady Kayna is both determined and ruthless."

"Even more so now that my father has ascended to the afterlife. She is finally in charge. After all those years of sacrifice, mating a male she didn't know or love, a male who was forced on her for the sake of tradition. She wants her position to mean more than it ever has. She wants our family's connection to the monarchy to grow and flourish."

That last bit interested Pennice very much. He sat forward. "Will the royals be at your mating, my lord?"

"That is what I hear," Cas said dryly.

"They haven't been to a ball in many years."

"My imprisonment is guaranteed entertainment." Cas reached for his ale.

"Dare I say," Pennice began over a rumble of turbulence, "that as with the males who came before you, there is no requirement to lie with only your mate? She will have to feed you, true. But your pleasure can be found elsewhere...in many beds..." The man grinned over his own near-empty glass. "Against many walls."

Cas rolled his eyes. "I think you get far too much enjoyment from watching me, Pennice."

The man didn't deny it. Instead he drained the cup. "You do what I cannot. Make another near implode with desire."

"I have told you, there is no issue with you finding a male of your own."

"Yes," Pennice agreed. "You have told me. But others..." He sighed. "I would be harassed."

"If you are, my friend, I shall be notified. Swift action will be taken." A growl exited his lips. "Once again, this is the twenty-first century. Though some things must remain the same, others can and will be changed."

His dark eyes shadowed somewhat, Pennice granted him a half smile. "I appreciate that, my lord. More than you know. But in the meantime, how can I help you?"

"I will be mated. There is no help for that." He drained his ale and set it down on the granite with a bit too much force. "But as you said, I can continue to play. Tonight, after I receive my new mate and she returns home to plan our ceremony, ready the cottage."

The man nodded. "How many females do you require?"

It wasn't unusual for Cas to entertain up to three or four females when he was home. However, tonight he wished for something outrageous. He needed something outrageous. If only to remind him that although duty and tradition compelled him to concede in this one thing, he was still very much an Incubus Master.

"I require ten females," Cas commanded, snatching up the remaining newspaper. "Have them waiting for me at midnight—bathed, naked, wet and ready."

Pennice's eyes glowed. "As you wish, my lord."

~ ~ ~

The household's palpable excitement flickered

through Lia as she rested on her knees and scrubbed the beautiful, dusty ballroom floor. She'd come to work at Trevanion Castle only five months ago, so tonight's grand Cornish party was to be her first.

To witness, of course. Not to attend.

She glanced up, took in the three other maids who were dotted about the room, one washing the floor like her, the two others polishing fixtures. They would be watching as well. Staff did not co-mingle with the family, or their guests. The Trevanions had blood ties to the royals, for goodness sake, and did things differently than most Incubi households. Formality was key. And anonymity. The latter being why Lia had applied for the position in the first place.

Just as Lia was wringing out her rag, a sudden burst of energy and sound erupted outside the ballroom doors, in the gardens. In seconds, Ms. Gilly, the housekeeper, rushed in.

"Stand up, you silly girls," she called, clapping her hands three times as she scurried over to the doors. "It's Master Trevanion. He's home."

A thrill went through Lia as she pushed to her feet. Smoothing down her pale green work dress, she watched as a party entered the ballroom. It was a group of six or seven, and they were moving fast. Master Trevanion was among them. Surrounded by them. But she couldn't yet catch a good look at him.

Ms. Gilly dropped into a curtsy and said grandly, "My lord." As did the other maids.

But Lia remained standing. As a Temple Blade she would have never genuflected to anyone—including Masters or royalty—unless under threat of death. And even then, she was not so sure. But that wasn't the reason for her blatant insolence. She'd finally caught a true glimpse of the Master—her Master—as he moved, deep in conversation with his Watchman, and her body wasn't listening to her mind. It was an unfortunate pattern with her. Lack of mind/body connection when it came to this man. And staring. That, she did far too often as well. Granted, she'd seen plenty of Masters in her time, and with every one her body reacted as any Nephilim's would: with hunger, heat, need. But her reaction to Casworon Trevanion was something altogether different. Otherworldly. Fearsome. Problematic. When he was around, the air seemed to bloom with scent, the light seemed to dim proactively, the energy thrummed with life.

And her muscles and bone and skin no longer felt imprisoned by scars and ugliness and pain.

As those around her remained in a respectful curtsy, Lia dragged her teeth across her upper lip, fighting to keep her ragged breathing under control. Her eyes clung to him. Watching, admiring, coveting. Intimidatingly tall, his heavy muscles straining beneath the crisp gray suit and black tie he wore, he was truly a formidable sight to behold. And as he walked—no…that was too gentle a word for what he did. Stalked was far better. He moved with intention and an air of animal rage.

For a moment, he turned and glanced about the room. Lia's breath caught in her throat at the full view of his face. His thick ebony hair was cut shorter than usual, and his light caramel skin gleamed like the sex demon he was. But it was those sharp, overtly sexual violet eyes that made her insides turn to liquid fire, made her tremble with fear and longing and something she'd tried so desperately to tamp down.

Hope.

When she had been a Blade, high-ranking and respected, she might've offered herself to him. Her strength and ferocity would've matched well with his sensual power and hunger. He would've noticed her. He would've wanted her, craved her. But now...she was a small, inconsequential bug. Squashable only because she was in the way, not because she posed a threat.

The moment of curious perusal passed and the party of seven continued on, filtering out of the ballroom. And as the doors closed decidedly behind them, the atmosphere of excitement, of anticipation for the night ahead, dimmed.

Tonight, she would watch from the balcony with the other maids. Watch as Master and Lord, Casworon Trevanion was presented with his mate. The one who would sleep in his bed, feed him—the one who would bear his young.

"You three," the housekeeper called, yanking Lia out of her thoughts. "Back to work. We have but ten hours until the ball. There is no time to dawdle."

Slowly lowering herself to the ground, Lia grabbed her rag from the bucket of cold water and started washing a fresh circle of floor. No doubt the highly sought-after Nephilim would be beautiful and graceful, ready to please, and thrilled beyond words to claim such a male. And Lia would go back to her room, to her work—to a life of being unnoticed. Never noticed. Not that she truly wished to be. Not anymore. Besides her limp, she had a scar that ran from her lip to her temple. Both courtesy of the rogue Blade who had murdered all four of her sisters—all highly decorated Blades, and all that remained of her family.

Her lips curved into a rare smile. As it always did when she thought of that Blade. Lia had made sure the female never took another breath. But, in turn, the Blade had made sure Lia would live out the rest of her days in weakness and obscurity, an object of pity.

A female who could look at a male like Casworon Trevanion, and wish, desire, hope.

But never touch.

CHAPTER TWO

Cas leaned into the salty wind as he rode the Cleveland Bay stallion he'd purchased three months ago along the cliff's edge. It was a daunting path he'd regularly traversed since he was a very young male. While his father had always found the risk, the flash of fire and impulse inside of Cas impressive, his mother had felt the opposite. There was not a day that went by where she didn't follow him to the stables and beg him not to go or to please take a groom—or even better, stay to the far gentler terrain of the moors. He would smile and assure her of his abilities. He was an Incubus, after all. But that didn't sway her in the least. For years, Cas believed her worry stemmed from the deep and abiding love of a mother. Then one morning when he was twelve, just as he'd been ready to ride out, she'd allowed him to see her true nature.

"You may be an Incubus, my son," she'd said, her lip curling as if that was the most detestable of fates. And he would learn later that to her, it was. "Close to immortal. But you are not fully grown. At this tender age, you cannot escape all injury." Her eyes had moved over him. "Who will want you if you are a scarred male? Broken?" Those eyes had risen to meet his own. "Not one of the royal females, that is certain."

"What do I care for royal females?" he'd returned hotly, giving his dancing mare a couple of strokes to her long neck.

"How selfish you are, Casworon," she'd scolded. "Your father almost made such a mistake when I was presented to him, and it near cost him this castle. I won't let you be so foolish. Your fate is already secured."

"What does that mean?" he'd demanded, feeling strange and confused as a child does when he starts to understand his parents' union might not be what he believed it to be.

"Never mind," his mother had said. "I want you to get down from that animal and come inside."

But Cas had not been one to obey. Strong-willed, his Incubus blood revving in his veins, he'd ignored her—kicked his mare into a run and headed for the cliffs. The next morning he'd found his mare in her stall, her throat cut. His mother's wordless punishment, and future threat.

Do as I say, or the things you love will die.

Whatever love he'd had for his mother before that day, it was gone by sundown. Granted, he didn't stop pushing back, or even disobeying her. But never again did he underestimate her. She wanted her connection to the royals solidified—no matter the cost—and she knew Cas would never put his people, his staff or his animals at risk.

His duty would be done.

The bay picked up speed as he neared a small chasm in the rock. Inexperienced though the stallion might be, he had instinct and drive, and a hunger to soar. Cas leaned forward, his insides tightening up as his outsides relaxed. The bay flew over the gulf, then came thundering down on the other side. Sea spray hit Cas's face and neck and he growled at the sensation, then licked his upper lip. He loved the salty taste. It reminded him of a female's heated skin, slick with sweat.

His body stirred. He could hardly wait for tonight. Ten females beneath him, atop him, against him. They would steal the memories of the mating introduction, remind him of what he was. Would continue to be.

An Incubus.

A sex demon.

A male who was not bred, born or destined for something as weak and trivial as love.

His lip lifted to form a sneer just as the cell phone in his pocket started to vibrate. He jerked the stallion to a halt only feet from the cliff's edge. The sea crashed against the rocks below.

"Trevanion," he nearly growled into the receiver.

A rumble of deep laughter greeted him. "You sound tense, *amico mio*?"

Scarus Vipera, Master of the House of Vipera, was a friend, a partner in the unshakable quest to rid their world of Marakel, and a male who had strangely—willingly—given himself over to a female he'd met in the Harem. Cas would never understand the latter move. Unlike himself, Vipera had the choice to remain a solo sex demon and yet... Perhaps something had tainted the water in Italy...

"Shouldn't you be dreaming of your *bella* mate-to-be?" Scarus continued, a smile in his tone. "Shouldn't you sound excited?"

"Why would I be excited?" Cas retorted, wanting to reach through the phone and throttle the male. "Would a hawk be excited to have his wings clipped?"

"I am mated, and I let my Rosamund clip my wings all day and night. It brings a satisfaction I've never known before."

"I cannot imagine this." Cas's jaw went tight. "But then again, she is a female of your choosing, is she not?"

There was a moment of silence on the other end, then Scarus amended, "Yes. I apologize, my friend. I forget that your House has this tradition."

"No apology is necessary," Cas said on a slight growl. "Now. The sun is descending here. Did you call only to wish me well?"

"I had question. Your mate? She will be Nephilim, *si*?"

"Yes." Cas sensed the sudden unspoken tension in Vipera's voice. "Why?"

Scarus released a weighty breath. "There have been...how you say...rumblings at the temple, about the Nephilim. The Three are unhappy with us, with the Masters, so I wished to see how far their tentacles spread."

"What does that mean?"

"I—and others—wondered about your ball this evening. If the Nephilim, even those connected to royalty, would still be in attendance."

Understanding dawned, and a dark frown spread over Cas's features. Below him the sea grew wilder, hitting the rocks with such force he felt the spray dampen his clothing. "As you have somewhat gathered by now, it is a different world here in Cornwall. The Nephilim in attendance and the one I will be introduced to tonight care naught for the Three. All were raised to respect only the decrees of their mothers, and their Sovereign. And I don't mean the one we keep asleep and protected."

"I see," Scarus said, sounding pensive. "You will inform me if that is not the case?"

"Of course."

"Then I bid you good luck, *amico mio.*"

"I appreciate that, my friend."

Cas ended the call, replaced his phone back in his pocket, and after one brief glance at the wild and unrelenting sea below, kicked the bay into a run toward the castle.

~ ~ ~

The sea's salty water had, over the many years, found its way to the edges of Trevanion Castle property, creating two large pools. They were deep and lush with greenery and flora. In the summer months, each was frequented by the staff and even some members of the household. But in spring, fall and winter, most stayed away, as the water was far too cold.

Not for Lia, however.

For Lia, it was perfect.

Not just because it offered her privacy, but because it quelled the ache in her damaged leg like nothing else. After her leg was crushed so thoroughly in the fierce attack of the rogue Blade, the cold salt water both soothed and numbed her muscles and skin. Truly, she could stay in for hours. Today, unfortunately, she didn't have that option. The sun was setting, and she didn't want to be traveling the road as the guests arrived for the ball.

His ball.

The Master's ball.

Her mind started to wander as she swam toward the edge of the pool. *I wonder what he's doing right now. Getting ready? Is he in his private bath, naked, the shower spray pummeling his muscular body? Is he excited? Ready to meet his mate? Watch her descend into the ballroom, his eyes taking in every graceful step?*

"The way Casworon Trevanion will never see you," she said to herself as she stepped slowly out of the water, her limp not nearly as pronounced as it had been two hours ago. Nude and drenched, she came to stand at the rock that had her robe draped across it.

"Is that what you want?" came a voice. "For the Master to see you?"

On a gasp, Lia whirled. Despite the pain that would surely follow, she crouched, ready for battle. Looking around, eyes narrowed, she searched the brush and trees. But saw nothing. "Who's there?" she demanded caustically. "Who are you? Show yourself."

"Please," came the voice again. Then a man stepped out of the shadow of a large Eldertree. He wasn't wearing the traditional garb of a Trevanion House laborer, but she knew he worked for the Master. She'd seen him before. He was a Watchman called Pennice.

"I mean you no harm," he stated, hands in the air as if she held a gun in her hands and not a thick, white robe.

Pain lanced through her thigh and shot downward. She hissed through her teeth. "It is you who should be worried. State your business here, Watchman, or I will be doing the harm."

Dark eyes flickered with sudden satisfaction and the male lowered his hands. "I knew you were no ordinary servant." One brow lifted in question. "Blade or Temple Blade?"

A thread of unease moved through her. Had this male been watching her? Having others watch her? For how long? And why? Since coming here, she'd made it a point not to be noticed. Head down, work focused, no friends, no interactions.

Only fantasies.

Her eyes were fierce as she stared at him, and slipped on her robe. "What do you want from me?"

"I'd like to help," he said simply.

Lia smiled darkly. "In what exactly? Bathing? Dressing? Both are already taken care of, I assure you."

His face paled as if this idea appalled him. "You misunderstand me."

It was amazing. For a few seconds, she'd actually forgotten about how she appeared to others. The limp, the scar. Of course this male was not interested in accosting her. "Then what is it that has you lurking around my bathing pool, Watchman?"

"I have been tasked to gather ten females for the Master tonight." He let this information sink in, then locked eyes with her and added, "I have only nine."

"What does that have to do with me?" she asked, trying not to imagine Master Casworon entangled in eighteen sets of long, smooth, eager limbs. "Are you looking for someone to round up suitable candidates for you?"

The male actually smiled. "No."

"Then I don't know what—"

"I believe the tenth female is standing right before me. In white robe and fierce expression." He inclined his head. "It is you I wish to bring to the Master."

Lia stared at the male. Unblinking. Stunned. She couldn't have heard him correctly. Either that, or he was playing a very hideous joke.

As if sensing her disbelief, Pennice quickly stated, "I am very much serious."

She sniffed, nearly laughed.

But the male didn't. He held her gaze, his eyes clear and true.

"But…" she began, shaking her head. "Why?"

"What do you mean?"

"Why me? There are females in town or in his own household who would be more than honored—"

"You are strong and intelligent and I think he would be very pleased with you," the Watchman said. "And I wish only to please the Master."

Warning bells were going off inside her. What he suggested was madness. Strong and intelligent didn't attract an Incubi. She knew it, and she believed this male knew it too. Whatever he was doing, playing at, she wanted no part of it. "You saw me come out of

190

the water—brazen and disrespectful as it was."

He nodded. "I apologize for that."

She continued undaunted, "You saw how I moved. Or rather how I *limped*." She fairly growled the last word. She pointed to her face. "You see the scar that runs from my mouth to my temple. I am no female to enter his bedchamber."

No matter how much I wish it. No matter how many times I have dreamt of it.

Pennice stared at her, his eyes like shining obsidian in the reigning dusk. "I don't agree. You have a rare beauty that comes from more than appearance. More than intelligence and strength even." His brow lifted. "Shall I prove it to you?"

Lia swallowed hard. What did that mean? What was he saying? Prove it to her? This was a joke. It had to be. And yet she couldn't stop herself from asking. "How?"

A slow smile spread across his features. "Do you wish to go to the ball tonight?"

She started to laugh. Such a suggestion—

He cut her off with a look. "I mean what I say."

She gave him a look. "Even if that were possible, I would never allow him or anyone else in attendance to see me as I am. Now, stop making fun of a poor house worker and be on your way." She started past him, wishing she'd brought a stick to help her. Her leg was paining her again, stinging her, and she would have to travel the moors instead of the road.

"I'm not making fun of you, Lia," the Watchman called after her.

She stopped at that and glanced over her shoulder. "How do you know my name?"

Eyes bright, soft smile on his lips, the Watchman reached into his coat and took out what appeared to be a wand. It was cherry wood and highly polished. "You will go to the ball tonight, dance and laugh and have a wonderful time with the Master—then at midnight you will retire to his cottage and join the other females."

Breath stalled inside her lungs, Lia could only stare blankly at him. This male was insane. Had to be—

Her thoughts were abruptly cut off as the male circled his wand slowly and green sparks of light exited the tip.

"You…" she breathed. "You have magic?"

He smiled. "My Cornish family's legacy. Quite useful on everything but human hearts." His eyes connected with hers. "If you wish it, if you say yes, you will go to the ball, and to the Master's bed, as the female you once were. No limp. No scar."

The wind of the sea whipped her wet hair about her face, cooling her hot cheeks. How did she answer this, answer him? *No* and she would return to the house, to her work—her dreams, her pain, her anonymity—without knowing, and possibly with regret. *Yes* and she was engaging with someone who would never see her after this night. Would never care for her. Would never truly know her.

And yet…what an experience.

Her gaze slid to the wand. Every few seconds, green sparks erupted from the tip. If Master Trevanion wouldn't even know it was her, a mere servant in his household, then what was truly the harm?

In jumping?

She turned around, faced the Watchman. "I don't know why you offer this, Pennice. Not really. But I will take it. I fear I must take it."

The Watchman's smile was broad as he nodded. Up went his wand, and as Lia stood there in the salty air and coming night, the male started to speak, low and quickly, chanting, eyes opening and closing. At first, she felt nothing at all. She nearly laughed at the sight before her. Not in a cruel way, but bitterly, because she wished it so much now. Was too hopeful.

And then...

Something happened. Started to happen. Within her. A warm, liquid feeling, moving through her veins like a snake. Healing her, piecing her back together, it seemed.

Before her, Pennice wielded his wand; flashes of green fire erupted and crackled. Lia gasped, her breath suddenly gone from her lungs. Fear blasted through her and she dropped to the ground.

Then everything stopped. The air, the sound of sea—the heart beating in her chest. And just as quickly started back up again. For several seconds, Lia wasn't sure where she was or what had happened to her. Then the past fifteen minutes came rushing back and she started to rise. Every inch of her felt whole and strong and light. She touched her face. Smooth. She waited for the pain as she stood. None. She glanced down at her robe.

Gone.

She gasped. Yards of the most beautiful white and green and gold fabric met her gaze. And shoes…extraordinary shoes. Glass and gold. She glanced up. Pennice was staring at her like he couldn't believe his eyes.

"You're perfect," he breathed. "The Master will not be able to resist you. In fact, I'll wager he won't even see the other nine."

Her waist was drawn in, her breasts jutted out. What a dress. And her hair…her curls…loose and flowing and glossy. Besides the absence of pain and her scar, she felt so different. So alive. Hungry as she hadn't been in years. Tears pricked at her eyes for the loss, but she swiped them away. She'd made this bargain. She wasn't going to waste it in grief.

"You need one last thing," Pennice said before whipping up his wand once again.

Lia watched as this time golden sparks erupted from the wand tip. And in seconds, a beautiful white mare in golden tack stood before her.

She laughed, then turned back to the Watchman. "This can't be real."

"I assure you it is," he said, placing his wand back inside his jacket pocket. "But Lia, please note that this spell will last only until dawn."

A sobering feeling moved through her. Of course it wouldn't last. She nodded. "I understand."

He helped her mount, then gestured toward the road in the distance. "Go now," he urged. "Enter with the other guests."

She found his gaze and for the first time, smiled with true and genuine warmth. "Thank you."

He nodded. "Go."

And with that, she turned the mare around and headed for the road that led to the castle.

CHAPTER THREE

Music trilled through the ballroom, drinks on silver platters were being offered to the beautiful people milling about, gold banners with the Trevanion House sigil of two crossed swords swayed in the breeze from the open windows, and the lights from the seven ancient chandeliers burned bright. It was a glorious, sumptuous, sensuous sight. And yet Casworon Trevanion could barely force a smile as he sat back on his father's black velvet throne and surveyed the room. This was no party to be savored and enjoyed. This was his end. The only thing getting him through it being the promise of ten naked, wet and ready females awaiting him in the cottage.

The demon inside him expanded at the thought, would've been allowed to roam free if Cas's mother hadn't come to stand at his side.

"Your boredom is showing, my son," she said in a strained, singsong voice.

"Good."

"It will not do to have your mate see you this way." She leaned in, close to his ear. "Don't push me, Casworon. You know better than to push me."

He turned to look at her. She was still a very beautiful female: dark hair like his own, green cat's eyes. But the soul is seen on the skin whether it wants to be or not. In an expression. A gesture. And Lady Kayna's soul was an ugly, tortured one.

"Don't worry, Mother," he said evenly. "You will have your alliance. I only ask that this charade be done swiftly. I have plans for the rest of the evening."

She sneered at him. "Retiring to your cottage?"

"I am."

Her lip curled. "Like father, like son."

Cas hadn't taken much time to understand his parents' relationship over the years. Like most children, he was consumed with himself. But clearly, the union had not only been an arranged one, but a contemptuous one. It was curious then, he mused, turning back to face the ballroom and his guests, that Lady Kayna would want the same misery for her son.

The orchestra conductor caught his eye then and raised a brow. With his father gone, it was Casworon's duty to open the ball. He was Master. He was Lord. He nodded, then sat back and watched the stream of males and females move onto the floor. The first dance was a waltz, each couple more or less performing for his pleasure. But Cas's attention had already been diverted to the small parade of females and their escorts coming toward him. It was time. The shackles already felt too tight. His gaze moved over them. Which one was she? This mate who would no doubt end up hating him, as his mother hated his father.

One was dressed in pink and pale yellow, while another was white like a bride, and yet another in red to tempt his Incubus, no doubt. The first stepped forward, and introductions were made to the lilt of the waltz.

"Master Trevanion," the page to his left called out. "May I present the Lady Beatrice of London."

Lady Beatrice was small with fine curves and a wide smile. She dipped low into a curtsey before him, then glanced up through thick lashes. Her eyes were a beautiful dark brown, and deep as he imagined his own to be. He inclined his head, then waited for her to move off and another to take her place.

"My lord, Lady Neda of Wales."

This was the Nephilim in the red dress. Perfect height, perfect figure, sharp eyes and a sharper smile. She hated him, hated this. He didn't blame her.

"Master Trevanion," the page continued. "The sisters, Brachia and Ornathe of Edinburgh."

Pink Dress and White Dress respectively, both trying to win his attention. But too caught up in their competition, neither managed to truly connect with him at all.

"My lord," came the page's call. "The Lady Gemma of Manchester."

A female stepped forward, and instantly Cas knew this was his mate to be. She was his physical type exactly. What he'd always requested: dark hair to the waist, dark eyes, full mouth, small, high breasts, and an air of reverence. His mother had done her due diligence. He could most certainly fuck the Lady Gemma into oblivion tonight and for many nights to come. His demon was more than game. He looked her over darkly, inspecting her, and she didn't wilt. Instead, she gave him a hungry, compliant smile. She was ready. She was perfect. She was exactly what her position required her to be.

So why was his cock already bored?

The waltz ended then, and a round of applause sounded.

Get it over with. The sooner you agree, the sooner you can get the bloody hell out of here. Perhaps the Lady Gemma would like to join you. Be your number eleven.

The applause slowly died down, and a hush fell over the crowd. Cas lifted his gaze, passed the lovely yet perhaps too eager Gemma, and surveyed the dance floor. What was happening? Only a few guests were chatting in small groups dotting the perimeter, but everyone else was staring up at the top of the stairs.

"The Lady Gemma would like to dance, Casworon," his mother was saying at his side.

Cas ignored her. His demon had pulled his attention to the top of the stairs where a tall female with long, blond curls stood. She was alone, yet comfortably, confidently so. She had a small waist and large breasts, and her dress was no doubt as pretty and as enticing as all the other dresses in the room. But Cas hardly noticed what she was wearing. His gaze—and that of his demon—was focused entirely on her face. Her expression, actually. What was it? Raw, almost innocent excitement coupled with the fearlessness of someone who needed nothing from anyone? Who was here for her own enjoyment alone?

And then the scent hit him—her scent—and everything and everyone around him ceased to exist.

Like a predator, a wolf on the moors, a drained Incubus, he jerked to his feet and headed for the stairs. As he went, he heard rumblings behind him.

"Who is that?" his mother asked.

"I don't know, my lady."

She clicked her tongue. "Find out."

"Yes, my lady."

The female with the face and the scent was descending now. Coming toward him. But why was everyone else staring? Why was everyone else captivated? Did they not know to whom she belonged? He sneered. They were in his castle, after all. Everything that stepped foot inside these walls was his to take, consume, fuck, feed from...

His demon was emerging with each breath he took—each step closer. That scent. *Bloody hell.* That strange, erotic, addictive scent that belonged under him, inside him, on his tongue.

But what of the agreement? something ancient whispered into his brain.

The Trevanion tradition?

Your mate is waiting, Casworon.

"Fuck them all," his demon growled as he neared the staircase, neared her.

And then. Green eyes lifted. Locked on him.

Those eyes. They were strong and deep and alive. So alive it made every cell in his body quake with longing. He reached for her—

Just in time to watch her being swept away onto the dance floor by one of his cousins.

~ ~ ~

What was that?

God in Heaven, what was that?

Lia forced a smile and tipped her face up to the Incubus male who gently moved and circled and turned her around the dance floor. He was good-looking, thick dark blond hair with eyes the color of the sea at night. And he most certainly carried that Incubus aura of pleasure and desire within his blood.

And yet he did nothing for her.

Her mind, her entire focus, was on the...she couldn't call him a male or the Master, Lord Trevanion or even an Incubus, because that...*thing* that had come stalking toward her was not of this world. That thing was a fire-breathing demon with eyes that both warned and promised sex with him would be the best she'd ever had.

Don't look, Lia.

Just don't.

If you look, you'll lose your breath first and then your footing, and once again you'll be that limping, scarred servant who cleans these floors, not dances on them.

And tonight you will dance.

Tonight you may even answer that demon's silent call.

The music wrapped around her and she gave in to it, letting her very capable partner lead her around the floor and in and out of the other couples. It was incredible. Thanks to Pennice, she felt no pain, only strength and excitement and wonder. She was here. She was admired. She was that fearsome Temple Blade once again. No...she was better, harder, sexier. And though she didn't dare look, she knew the eyes of Casworon Trevanion and his demon were on her.

"What is your name?" the male asked, pulling her from her thoughts.

"Lady Elia," she answered with absolute confidence.

"And where do you come from, Lady Elia?" His eyes moved over her face. "I have never seen you before. And I would have remembered if I had."

She smiled. "I believe that is what all males say when they are making polite ballroom conversation."

His brows lifted. "You are sharp-tongued."

"I am."

His grin widened. "I like it."

She laughed. But her laughter didn't rest on the blond male for long. Halfway through the waltz another male cut in, his eyes Incubus-bright and hungry, his hand wrapping her waist possessively. Lia had seen him at the castle before. Some type of business titan who'd once worked with the late Master Trevanion and wanted to court the new one. She wanted to inquire about his work now with Casworon, but before she was able, yet another male broke into their dance and swept her away. It was strange and wonderful and breathless, and she wondered what was coming next. Or who.

She really should've known it would be the demon of all demons.

The song ended with a flourish and the crowd parted. Where Lia's partner had only moments before been confident and domineering, it took only one look from Master Casworon Trevanion and his death stare, to have the male backing off and returning to the crowd.

Lia held her breath as the demon in black tie strode toward her like he owned the room. Which of course, he did.

He looked gorgeous. Tall, muscular and intimidating. His thick black hair a little mussed, his hard jaw shaven smooth. And those eyes, amethyst in color, were locked to hers.

When he reached her he bowed. "My lady."

She inclined her head. "My lord."

"It is time," he said, his tone threaded with lust.

It made her shiver. "For what?"

His eyes flashed fire. "You have had your fill of males on the dance floor." He reached for her and eased her into his arms. "Now you will only dance with me."

CHAPTER FOUR

Her scent was his drug.

And he wanted to smoke it all night long.

As the music began again and the couples started to dance around them, Cas stared down into the eyes of the female who captivated him.

"Are we to dance, my lord?" she asked boldly, though Cas saw her pulse beating furiously against the pale skin of her throat.

Would it slow or quicken further if he leaned down and ran his tongue over the soft band of muscle?

"Lady Elia, is it?" he said, tightening his hold on her as he began to move.

She looked both impressed and concerned. "You have discovered my name already. Well done."

"Unfortunately that is all I have discovered. I want more."

"Do you?"

His lips curved into a smile. "Yes. I want everything."

He heard her breath catch and he released her for a moment, twirled her, then scooped her back up again and continued a slow rotation with the other couples on the floor.

She stared up into his eyes. "Perhaps I'm not very keen to give it."

"Why would that be?" he asked, leading her to the center of the floor. "Do you have something to hide, Elia?"

"Yes I do, my lord," she answered daringly.

A low growl rumbled in Cas's throat. "I demand to know what it is."

Her eyes flashed green fire. "I don't respond to demands."

His body hummed with awareness. "Even from an Incubus Master?"

"Even then."

Heat surged into him, tightened his skin around his muscles—sent blood to his cock. This female had no fear of him, no wish to please him. Only a delight in challenging him. It was a characteristic he had never admired before. Or tolerated, for that matter.

Until this moment.

"What perfume do you wear on your skin?" he demanded.

"Why?" She smiled slowly. "Does it offend you?"

His nostrils flared and he took her into his lungs. "It does not," he nearly groaned.

What was happening to him? Was this female an apparition? A cruel ruse? Sent by an enemy who wished to drive the new Lord and Master of Trevanion to his knees?

"I wear nothing," she told him. "What you scent, my lord, is only my bare skin."

Cas slowed to a side sway and drew her closer. His cock was hard and his mind was nearly taken over by his demon. The demon that wanted nothing more than to—

"The song has ended," she said, her eyes on his.

So it had. But he didn't care, didn't let her go. He wondered in that moment if he ever would or could. "Do you wish to dance with another male, Elia?" He knew his tone was excessively harsh. "And I caution you against saying yes."

"Because you wouldn't like it."

"That, and I would have to rip his arms from his body."

Her lips twitched. Such full, rose-colored, edible lips. "That isn't very nice, Master Trevanion."

He sniffed. "I'm. Not. Nice. Elia."

Guests moved around them almost silently. Or perhaps he had tuned them out in favor of this female's voice.

"Would you want me to decline another's request to dance out of fear?" she asked him. "Or because you're forcing me to comply with your wishes? Is that how you like your females, Master Trevanion? Subservient and timid?"

"Sometimes," he answered honestly.

Her eyes searched his. "I don't think you'll like me that way."

His cock hardened further and the blood in his veins coursed hot and thick. His demon was an irrational taskmaster inside him. It wanted this female like it had never wanted anything before, and it didn't care how or where. Skirts up, panties ripped off, and fucked hard right here for all to see.

But though his hands shook with hunger, Casworon still held the reins. He couldn't allow the creature inside him nor the crowd around him such feral, voyeuristic pleasure.

"May I tell you how I would like you?" he uttered blackly.

Her pupils dilated, her lips parted and the scent of her arousal drifted up into his nostrils. "I'd rather you showed me, my lord."

A gasp was ripped from Cas's lungs. Who was this female? What did she have over him? Her scent, her eyes, her bold nature. He had never wanted anything or anyone more than he wanted her. And though he'd never admit to it aloud, he would've dropped to his knees, as his enemies might enjoy, and begged for her hand, her touch, her mouth and her climax.

"Come with me, Elia," he breathed, taking her hand.

"Where?" she asked.

"Does it matter?"

A soft smile on her lips, she shook her head as he led her out of the ballroom. "No."

~ ~ ~

The royal carriage that had whisked them away to the cottage had a glossy black exterior, steel gray leather seating, and a silent driver who handled the two white horses glistening beneath the moonlight with precision and ease. Lia sat very straight, her gaze traveling between the moors and the male sitting beside her.

Was this truth or dream? She actually wasn't sure anymore. She had no pain, no scar. She was what she'd been before the attack. Beautiful and strong, a fighter, and a very sexual being who had no compunction in asking for or taking what she desired. And here was what she desired. Right beside her. His hand covering her own in an ongoing display of possession.

As they headed for the cottage.

Her gut twisted just slightly. She was no prude. She knew what was coming and didn't fear it. Nine other females waiting for them. Nine naked and ready females. For Casworon, a typical Saturday night. But she would be in the middle of it. Sharing him. Perhaps even being instructed by him to touch someone besides himself. It wasn't what she wanted. And yet, it was all she'd been offered.

"You are quiet, Elia?"

She turned to look at him, and inwardly sighed when she did. He was breathtakingly handsome in the moon's light. Dark, foreboding, sensual and mythic. "I am only thinking."

"About what?"

"You," she said, then smiled when his brow lifted provocatively. "How you left the ball without a word to anyone."

He looked confused. "I am Master. I don't need to inform anyone of anything."

"I know, but...wasn't this ball to announce your mating?"

A muscle in his jaw tensed. "It was."

"I heard no announcement. Saw no mate."

"That's because all I wanted you to see was me."

A frustrating, evasive and deliciously wonderful answer. "But you saw her?" she pushed, unsure why

207

she was pushing. "Were introduced to her?"

"Yes," he ground out.

"Did you find her beautiful?"

"She was acceptable." He reached out then and cupped her face. "Stop asking these questions. I don't like speaking of her to you."

"Why?" she asked breathlessly. His fingers on her skin...his warm touch...

"She means nothing."

"How can you say that?" she countered. "She's going to be your mate. Isn't that everything?"

"Not to me," he said flatly, jerking away.

What was she doing? Why was she trying to ruin this? *One night, Lia. For heaven's sake.* "I'm sorry."

"Don't apologize."

"It's not any of my business. You owe me no explanation. And yet I..." She trailed off. *Just stop talking. Stop right now if you want this night to end well. If you want this night to end with his touch, his kiss, him inside you.*

But Casworon Trevanion was trying to read her expression. "What, Elia? What is it?"

She shook her head. She couldn't tell him that all she wanted was him alone. No other females. Just one night. And then he could and would go back to his full bed.

The carriage came to a slow halt, and Cas announced with husky intensity, "We're here."

Lia turned, expecting to see the massive cottage alight with lamp glow and the faces of beautiful, eager females in the windows. But that wasn't at all what met her gaze. In fact, she wasn't sure where on the massive estate they were. She hadn't been paying attention as they drove along.

"This isn't—" she started, then stopped.

Cas had stepped down from the carriage and was offering her his hand. "Isn't what?"

"Well..." she stumbled, stepping down. "I...it isn't what I expected." Why weren't they at the cottage? Were the females here instead? Had plans changed?

"If it's not pleasing..." Cas began tightly.

"No," she said at once. Her eyes moved over every inch of the converted greenhouse that was expertly concealed by blooms and trees and lit by torches and firelight. "It's incredible." She turned to him, her eyes brilliant with pleasure. "It's perfect."

The grin that broke on Master Casworon Trevanion's face was contented and dynamic, and stunningly rare.

CHAPTER FIVE

Cas knew that his about-face, his abrupt change of plans, would no doubt strip him of the title of Incubus Master. To abandon ten ready females for one? Unheard of. Almost human-like.

His lip curled at the thought as he led Elia inside the small greenhouse he'd frequented as a young male, then had converted to living quarters just a few years ago. Up until this moment, it had been his refuge. Where he'd gone to think and relax and mourn. Never had he brought a female here. It was near-sacred space. And yet he had texted Pennice as the carriage was being ordered, canceled the night at the cottage and ordered his greenhouse readied.

The Watchman should've been confused by the command, but Pennice hadn't sounded the least bit surprised. In fact, he'd been downright pleased.

What the hell was that about? Cas wondered.

"This place is so beautiful," Elia remarked as he led her through the sumptuous living area with its comfortable furnishings, lush plants, roaring fireplace, and walls and ceilings of glass. "I had no idea it was even here."

"That's exactly how I wanted it," he said. "Absolute privacy. This is the kitchen." He pointed out the small, functional space with a brick oven and stainless appliances. "Not all that grand, but it does the job."

She turned to stare at him. "Do you cook?"

He laughed. "Is that such a strange concept?"

"Yes," she returned, picking up on his laughter. "Because I was always under the impression that Incubi don't eat."

Heat rumbled through him. "Oh. We eat, my lady."

Her cheeks instantly flushed pink and Cas laughed again, then gestured for her to follow him down the hall. "This is my bedroom. The only one. And beyond that is the bathroom. It was something I added to the existing structure. All glass, and the panels in the roof open to let in light and air."

She gasped. "Really?"

Cas's heart—or what he assumed that working muscle was called—squeezed. What was it about this female? She drew him like a moth to light. Her smile, her enthusiasm. It was as though everything was new, to be savored. Combined with her fiery, dauntless tongue, and the raw need she had for him, he was well and truly captivated.

Was this what the other Masters felt? Was this what drove them to mating? Not the forced kind of mating with no care or thought for the other being. But the kind that inspired a male to cancel an orgy just for the chance to not only taste the female at his side, but talk with her...laugh with her...

Show her the one thing about him that was truly private.

He turned to her and noticed she was glancing

around, slightly agitated. "What's wrong?"

"Are we alone?" she asked.

"Yes. Were you expecting a crowd?"

Her eyes lifted to meet his. "Kind of. You do have a reputation, my lord."

"I am Incubus," he said, his arm slipping around her waist. "But the idea of sharing you doesn't appeal to me."

She wrapped her own arm around his waist. It was very strange. This intimacy. Strange, yet...good.

"I thought it would be more likely that I'd be sharing you," she joked.

His jaw tightened imperceptibly. "Do you wish for that?"

"Hmmm," she said thoughtfully. "I think I'd like that about as much as I'd like to roll around with a hornets' nest."

Cas laughed and pulled her even closer. This madness he was feeling, that was running through him... Never had he wanted to be alone with a female. Never had he been furious at the thought of not only another male touching her—but a female's hands on her as well.

"Are you hungry?" he asked her.

"No," she said. "Maybe later?"

"Anything you want, I can make."

She smiled softly, sweetly, dangerously. "Master Casworon...what I want, all that I want right now, is you."

The words were like little explosions inside his chest. Each one made him want to do something— scale something, slay something, all in her name, then come back and kneel at her feet.

It was a feeling, a sensation, he didn't like.

It made him feel vulnerable.

He eased his arm from her.

"There is something I must see to," he said, his tone still lingering with warmth. "But I had a bath prepared for you. If you would like."

Disappointment flickered in those stark green eyes. She was wondering what had just happened—what would keep him from taking what she'd been so gracious to offer to him.

And Cas wasn't about to explain it to her. This reaction to a sudden loss of control. Vulnerability where it had never existed before. These *feelings*.

He needed a moment. To pull himself back together. Return to the power of the demon.

"That would be lovely," she finally answered, her tone a little tight. She pointed to the door. "Just in there?"

He nodded, his body warring with his mind, the former wishing to go with her—show her the bathtub, undress her. "You'll find a robe, soaps, salts, anything you could want."

She gave him a half smile as if to say, *I told you what I want*, then turned and headed for the bathroom.

When the door closed, Cas stalked into the kitchen and poured himself a drink. Anger raged through him. She was in there, stripping down to that skin he could scent even now, and he was out here thinking and drinking, and trying to regain his control. Why?

Why?

Who cared for control when there was so much

pleasure to be had? And yet, the pleasure came from such a female. Never had he thought about the females he bedded before. Truly, he shouldn't start now. No matter what virginal feelings were arising from her presence.

Feelings...

Christ, those feelings.

That was the bloody problem, wasn't it? Not control. He couldn't process the—

"Casworon?" Elia call out. "Could you help me?"

Her voice was like ice water to his brain and he forgot all about his drink and his *feelings* and headed straight for the bathroom door, sending it flying back as he entered.

"What's wrong?" he demanded, surprised at the level of his concern. "What is it?" His eyes shifted about the candlelit room.

Her ball gown was laid out on the brown leather chaise in one corner, while the female herself was standing near the tub in only her corset.

Cas nearly lost his mind in that moment, his hands forming fists as he struggled with reaching for her. *Mine. Mine to take. To consume.* The demon wanted skin, wanted to be fed.

"I'm sorry," she said, gesturing over her shoulder. "I can't reach the laces in the back."

It took everything inside of Cas to tamp down the demon's desires. The beast didn't like it. It was used to getting what it wanted—whenever it wanted it.

Without a word, Cas moved to stand behind her. Trying not to take her scent into his nostrils, he worked the laces, one by one, until she was free. His eyes pinned to the creamy skin of her back, he let the corset drop to the ground. Then, without thought, reached out and ran his fingers over the marks the tight material had placed on her skin.

Her perfect skin.

Her warm skin.

Take. Take her.

She stepped away then, and beneath his dark, hungry gaze she removed her stockings and panties. Cas hissed out a breath. If her sharp mind and dauntless tongue weren't temptation enough... She had an exquisite body. Long legs, full hips, small waist, heavy breasts with tight nipples and a nearly shaved pussy.

His mouth watered.

As he stared like the rabid demon he was, his body humming with a need like no other, his cock so hard it pained him, she stepped into the steaming water.

Envy enveloped him.

For a bloody bathtub.

"Thank you for the help," she said, looking up at him. "I'm not used to wearing a corset."

His nostrils flared and he nodded. She looked irresistible beneath the water, her head resting on the edge, blond curls falling over the side.

"You can go now," she said, then smiled. "Or not. This is a very large bathtub." Her brow lifted in question.

"Are you asking me to join you, Elia?" His tone was as hard and unyielding as his body.

"Yes." Her smile widened. "Unless you have something else you need to attend to."

Fuck him. Fuck his demon. Fuck his feelings. Nothing was keeping him from this female.

His eyes locked to hers, he removed his jacket, then his tie. Lia watched him every step of the way. Her eyes skimming over his naked chest, his shoulders...then dropping and widening as she took in his cock.

All your doing, female.

A soft growl exited his lips as he stepped into the bath and settled in across from her. Perhaps later she would oblige him and stand under the rain shower with him.

"First time in a tub?" she teased, her eyes alight with mischief.

He growled again. Louder and more aggressive this time. "How can you tell?"

"You're normally not an awkward male."

A small, strange twinge went through Cas, and he locked eyes with her. "How would you know that? We have never met before. Have we?"

It was only a second, but Cas saw her brow furrow and heard her breath quicken. Then she smiled and shrugged. "No. I...just assumed."

"The truth is I've always preferred showers."

"Oh," she replied, mildly thwarted.

He settled deeper into the water. "Until now, anyway."

She face broke with a lovely smile. "Well, my lord, I'm glad my naked presence has changed your opinion."

"It has," he confirmed, stretching out his legs. "I am committed to doing it again."

"With your mate?" she asked, then instantly

looked as though she wanted to take it back.

A thread of irritation moved through him. "Why do you speak of her? Especially now. Like this." *With me.*

She shook her head. "I don't know. I'm sorry."

"You should not feel threatened by her, Elia."

"I don't," she insisted. "I—"

"She will be a food source only," he continued, feeling the urgent need to explain so they could return to the ease and sensual play of a moment ago. "And of course mother to the young that may come." He smiled knowingly at her. "But everything else my life affords now will stay the same."

But instead of looking reassured, understanding that he meant he would wish to see her after this night, her face went ashen. "That sounds..." She shook her head.

"What? Realistic?"

"No. Heartless."

He breathed. Perhaps she was not informed of his duty, his future as Master of Trevanion, or how his kind existed in this world. "It is how things are, Elia. For me. My family. And for Incubi. Our kind must have sex to survive."

"I know."

"We don't have it within us to forge deep, long-lasting connections. Incubi do not love."

She cocked her head and asked, "Is that really all Incubi? Or just you?"

Cas paused. He didn't like this line of questioning. It delved into a subject that both irritated and confused him. Especially lately...

"Yes, there have been some Incubi who have

taken mates out of what they believe is love."

"But you don't believe it," she prodded.

"I cannot fathom it," he admitted. "Have not seen it. Not in my family. We are forced to mate for the good of our line, our name, our tradition. Perhaps that is a sort of love. I don't know."

Her eyes were probing his, trying to dig deeper into his soul. "What would happen if you broke with tradition?"

He smiled darkly. He wouldn't have guessed she was a romantic. He felt her foot against his thigh and claimed it. "My life is not the one that matters, Elia. It is everyone I'm responsible for. From those who live on my land to the ones who work in the castle. I care about their welfare."

Her eyes softened measurably.

"What I said pleases you." He started to massage her foot.

"Getting to know you pleases me," she said on a smile.

"I can't believe I've said as much as I have. It is not my usual way."

"Does it make you uncomfortable?"

"I'm not sure." It was an honest answer. All he had. "What of you? Tell me about you."

A sudden shadow moved across her features, and her gaze dropped to the water. "You didn't bring me here to talk, did you?"

Her abrupt change confused him. No, he hadn't brought her here to sit in a bathtub, naked, and talk. Most assuredly because before this moment he'd wouldn't have conceived of it. But he would be lying if he said he hadn't found the whole thing strangely enjoyable. Even though some subjects were difficult to discuss.

"I have told you much about me," he said, pushing her a little. "I want to know you, Elia. Where are you from? Do you have family? Is there—"

She didn't let him finish. She eased her foot from his grip and scrambled to her feet. Bathwater spilled over the sides of the tub. "I think I'm done with the bath, my lord."

Cas sat up, and for one brief moment, he wondered why she had become so agitated. Why she didn't want to share anything about herself. But the thoughts quickly died. She stood before him, dripping bathwater, her pussy just inches from his face.

His nostrils flared. "Don't move," he said on a growl.

"But I'm done. I'm soaking wet."

"Not nearly wet enough. Now, spread your legs for me, Elia."

~ ~ ~

Her back to the soft down comforter and Casworon Trevanion looming over her, moving in and out of her body.

That was what she'd imagined would happen this night.

And it had been a good fantasy. One that had gotten her through many a lonely, tired night as she found a moment of privacy curled up next to the kitchen's fireplace in the castle.

"Legs apart, Elia," he commanded, more fiercely

this time.

But this… She shuffled her feet out until they touched the sides of the tub. This she couldn't have fathomed. This was the stuff of novels or things the Temple Blades would speak of in hushed tones at night as they shared their latest conquests and secret assignations.

She glanced down. In the warm, soothing light of the many candles situated about the room, Casworon looked terrifyingly handsome. Naked and aroused, he sat there, eyes pinned to her sex, the demon that rumbled inside him near to his thickly muscled skin.

Her insides clenched with longing. To have this male even once…it would be a dream come true. One only her heart had made.

"You are very beautiful, Elia," he said, his breath fanning her heated skin. "Pink, wet…but not wet enough to please me." He glanced up, his amethyst eyes a blaze of predatory hunger. "Do you want to please me?"

She nodded, breathless. Was she really to stand here? Let him look at her? Let him…

A grin split his features and he said in a hard voice, "I want you to touch yourself, my lady."

Shock barreled through her. She couldn't possibly have heard him right. She'd been deep in thought, struggling with questions. But then he said it again.

"You wish to please me, yes?" he asked. "Do it. Touch yourself."

"But I thought—"

"That I would be touching you?" he asked, brow

arched. "Oh, I will be. But first I want to see…I want to know what you like…how your body responds…"

Was it possible for a person to feel both embarrassment and shattering lust? Lia forced out a bleak, "But…I…I can't—"

"You can and you will," he growled, then dropped back to recline against the tub. His arms went behind his head, which made his already wide and heavily muscled chest expand. "If you want my hands on you tonight, yours must come first."

Her cheeks flamed, and her breath was coming in shallow pants. Could she? *The old Lia would,* her mind whispered. *The old Lia would take this challenge and run. Moan. Cry out. Jump.*

So be the Blade you once were. She's still in there, still inside you.

Brave.

Raw.

Pushing away her nerves and embarrassment, she placed her hands on her breasts. Eyes locked to Casworon's, she slowly began to massage herself. First gentle and easy, then slightly more rough, aggressive. It felt good; it had always felt good. But it was this male's ravenous gaze, and his cock, which was standing up proud in the water, that truly made her heart beat wildly in her chest and her insides go liquid.

With a hiss, she squeezed each nipple, then moaned as she rolled them between her thumb and forefinger. The muscles of her sex clenched. She knew how wet she was becoming. Not with the bathwater anymore, but with her body's cream. Cas's eyes were growing heavy-lidded as he watched, and she wondered if he wanted to touch himself too. She would like to see that. But he didn't. He only stared, his nostrils flaring as he growled softly.

Slowly, languidly, Lia let her hands drift down. Over her ribcage and belly. Her sex ached for her touch, his touch. Cas inhaled sharply just as she reached the top of her nearly shaved pussy.

"That's right," he snarled through gritted teeth. "That's what I want. Show me."

Her breath coming hard and fast now, she opened herself with the middle and index finger of her left hand, then gave her clit a soft, quick pinch. A moan escaped her throat, and her knees softened. How would she keep herself vertical for any true length of time?

"Bloody hell, female," Cas ground out. "I'm going to come right here in this bathtub."

Eyes drifting closed, Lia started to circle her clit. Two fingers pressing against her tight, hot bud. Arousal coated her fingers with every rotation, while a few drops trailed down her inner thigh.

"I smell that," Cas ground out blackly. "Fuck, I want to taste you."

Then do it. Do it now. Stop making me wait. You don't need my tutorial. You're a bloody Incubus.

She moaned softly as she continued to work herself over. In the past several years, she'd pleasured herself many times in the privacy of her small attic room. But nothing had ever felt like this. She was on the verge of exploding, but inside and out—both in body and in mind.

"Stop, Elia."

The command was deep and lust-filled, and had her freezing mid-rotation. Her eyes opened.

Casworon's face was a mask of hard angles, demon heat and fury. Before she could ask him what was the matter, he commanded her to please him further.

"I want your fingers inside your pussy now," he demanded roughly. "I want you to show me how deep they can go. How deep I can go."

"My lord," she breathed.

"And you will call me Cas from now on."

Her gaze held his. She nodded, her heart squeezing with pleasure as her body roared with unquenched need. "You will call me Lia."

For a moment, it seemed the wheels inside his mind were churning, thinking...

No. No... She couldn't have that. Abandoning her clit, Lia slid her fingers down and thrust them up inside the slick, hot channel of her body.

A gasp of pleasure broke from her lips. "Oh, yes. God, yes."

A growl rent the steamy air. It was otherworldly, pained, yet predatory. His demon was back. In control. She was safe.

As she slowly rode her fingers, her moans grew more and more anxious. She wanted deeper. Needed to get deeper. She couldn't believe she was doing this.

"It's my turn now," Cas announced, sitting up. "My demon's turn." His eyes were pinned to her pussy, watching intently as her fingers thrust in and out of her body. Then a frighteningly sexual snarl escaped his lips and he reached out, grabbed her hips and licked her from top to bottom.

The feeling was so shockingly wonderful, Lia thought she would lose her footing right there.

"I will hold you," he whispered against her soft pussy lips. "Put one foot on the edge of the bathtub. I want to watch you fuck yourself while I eat you." His eyes lifted. "Lia."

Her hips jerked in response, but she quickly did as he instructed. Instantly, Cas was on her, his tongue slashing through her lips to taste the swollen clit beneath. Lia groaned at the exquisite feeling, and started thrusting once again.

This was madness. The best kind, she thought. The only kind she would ever need. Cas's mouth on her, his large hands gripping her as he swirled and stroked her. Nipped at her clit, then flicked it back and forth until she cried out. There were even times when his tongue made contact with her fingers, and he would groan with hunger as he lapped at her arousal.

Lia knew she wasn't long for this moment in time. It was all too much, too perfect. Moaning, trembling, she squeezed the inner muscles around her fingers as Cas drew her clit into his mouth and sucked. She wasn't ready. Not for it to end. She wanted more...she needed him...

But a dam can only hold so much water before it breaks.

Wide open.

A cry rent the air. Her cry. It ripped from her throat as her sex exploded with heat and the pulse of deepest pleasure. Cas was all over her, licking, sucking, groaning with hunger and desire as she rode his mouth to the most intense climax of her life.

Time fell away in those moments. Her mind was a cloud, her body, heat and blood, raw nerve endings. Her heart so full and happy it wanted to burst through her chest and offer itself to the male beneath her.

Beneath…

She wasn't sure how she stayed standing on one leg, but she had to assume Cas was holding her. Though she didn't feel it. And her eyes refused to open.

Then she was being lifted out of the tub and set on the rug. Cool air washed over her skin before a towel was wrapped around her. Then she was being lifted again.

"Cas?" she uttered, hoarse. "Where…am I going back?"

His laughter was highly charged and lethally erotic. "I'm taking you to bed, Lia. Where I'll dry you off, then get you wet all over again."

CHAPTER SIX

He cared nothing for his own hunger.

The pain of having no release shuddered through him, and yet all Cas wanted was to taste her again. Her scent, her climax, it had filled him with such pleasure. Unlike anything he'd ever felt before. He didn't understand why this female captivated him the way she did, the way she had. But he knew, as he placed her on his bed and gently dried her legs and feet, that when dawn came tomorrow morning he wasn't letting her go.

She would belong to him.

Perhaps not as Vipera's female or Jian's or Devil Gravori's. He couldn't have that. His name belonged to another—had since he'd been born. But he could give her...

What? What, Master Trevanion? What can you give her?

"I need you." Lady Elia—Lia, as she wanted him to call her—was gazing up at him with eyes so liquid and heavy, his cock leaked at the tip.

Never had he wanted anything more than to be inside this amazing female. And when she reached for him, opened her arms to him, he melted into her. Covered her body with his own. And kissed her.

Oh. Bloody. Hell.

Kissing was another amusement he usually denied himself, and the females in his company. It had seemed trivial, pointless. Too personal for a hot, impersonal fuck. But with her, with Lia, it felt vital. Sacrosanct.

Her arms went around his neck and he groaned as he tasted her. Her lips were so soft and full, and just like the lips he'd devoured not five minutes ago.

Irresistible.

"Lia," he breathed against her mouth.

She smiled. "Yes?"

"You make me feel…" He growled.

"What?" she asked him. "I make you feel what?"

He brushed his nose across her nose. "That's it. You make me feel."

For one brief moment their eyes locked, and something unspoken passed between them. An understanding, perhaps? A hope? A wonder? And then she wrapped her legs around his waist, pressed herself against him and kissed him once more.

Hot, wet pussy riding the base of his shaft. *Now*, the demon inside him roared. *Take. Feed.* The beast had been impatiently waiting, so hungry.

It was time.

His mouth plundering hers, his tongue playing with hers, Cas reached between their bodies and fisted his cock. The thing was like steel. Fuck, he couldn't wait. Tight, hot, sugary-sweet walls milking him. He positioned himself at the slick entrance to her sex, nearly howling with longing.

"Please," Lia begged, canting her hips.

Without another word, Cas drove up inside her

and held.

Lia gasped, cried out, gripped him tighter and bit his lower lip.

Fuck, he snarled. Pulling out, he waited a moment, then drove back in—this time to the hilt, until his scrotum was flush against her backside.

Heaven. Pure paradise.

She pulled her mouth from his then, her eyes opening and finding him. "Don't stop. Don't play with me. Don't go slow. Just...please..."

"Tell me, Lia," he commanded. "Tell me exactly what you want."

"I want you to fuck me, Cas," she said, circling her hips, then thrusting upward. "Hard."

Cas laughed at her audacity, but the sound came out as more of a snarl. She was hot as summer, tight like a fist, and moving like a temptress, and he was past emotion and feeling now. He wanted to claim her, send her into climax and feed from her sweet, erotic, addictive energy.

Teeth gritted, he started to move, deep, slow strokes to her womb. Her legs tightened around him and her nails dug into his back. Every thrust made him growl. Every feminine, throaty moan made his cock weep. He could feel her walls pulsing against him as they prepared for orgasm.

Not without me, female.

Not without the beast.

He took her mouth again, plunged his tongue inside to taste her, while his hips ground against her and his cock pistoned over and over. The rush of blinding pleasure was rising, rising, nearly overtaking him. And then she ripped her mouth from his and screamed, her walls vibrating and fisting and milking his cock until he couldn't bear it another second.

Pounding into her, he came in an explosion of heat and electricity. He was nothing and everything. He was filled, overcome. He knew emotion through fucking and he would never want anything else.

And it was all because of her.

Her.

With sudden concern, he rolled to the side, taking her with him. He held her tightly against him, protectively, forehead to forehead. For long seconds, their breathing was interlocked, then Cas lifted his head and found her gaze.

Warm, satiated green eyes stared back at him.

"I have no words, Lia," he began. "That was…"

She nodded, understanding at once. "For me too," she managed.

"I am so glad you came here with me."

"I'm so glad you asked."

"This night has been surprising to me. I will remember it always."

A flash of something moved across her face. Discomfort. Or was it unease? He asked, "What is it? What's wrong?"

"Maybe I should go…?" she began.

"No." The word sounded gruff and absolute. To further make his point, he wrapped his body around her and held her tight.

She laughed and snuggled into him. "Okay. Not right now, then."

He kissed her ear and whispered into the soft shell, "No. Not now."

Then to himself, he added: *Not ever.*

~ ~ ~

Lia woke with a start, her eyes seeing only the white pillow in front of her. At first she wasn't sure where she was, but then she felt it all around her—the magic of the Incubi. Her Incubus. It was heady and luscious, yet grave and problematic. Her gaze shifted to the windows. The many windows that made up one entire wall. The sky was no longer pitch. And she was in Master Casworon Trevanion's bed. In his arms...

Oh God.

Her heart lurched. She'd slept for hours. Too many hours. Momentarily alarmed, she reached up and touched her face. No scar. And no pain in her leg. She still had time. But by the look of the gunmetal sky, not much.

But how exactly did she manage this? Disentangling herself from him without waking him up? And she couldn't wake him up. That would be the ultimate disaster. What if he asked her to stay—*demanded* she stay? Dawn would break as she was convincing him she had to go, and the truth would be revealed.

Just the thought of Cas seeing the real her had Lia moving. Swallowing hard, she slowly eased one heavy, muscular arm off her waist, then sort of crab-crawled the rest of the way off the bed.

The moment she stood up, her feet to the wood floor, she felt cold. Wrapped in Cas's massive body, she'd been perfect. The male gave off so much delicious heat. He gave so much everything...and she would never feel it again after today. A lump formed in her throat. She pushed it away. There wasn't time for that. Or a point to it. Days, weeks, months—that wasn't what she had wished for. Just a night. One night to know him, to experience him— to hold on to him.

The ball gown was a bear to get on and fasten, but she managed, sans corset. Lord, if she had her way, she'd never wear one of those again. Or the shoes. Her feet were desperately sore and tired. Slipping on a pair of riding boots that had been outside the closet door, she gave the male in the bed one last look. He was so beautiful in the gray light, his strong features softened by his sleep. She had an urge to run her fingers through his hair one last time, but cursed her foolishness and left the room.

As she stole out of the greenhouse and hurried down what she hoped was the path to the castle, she wondered how far she would get before the spell would be broken. It was cold, and there were strange sounds all around her. She had traveled maybe a quarter of a mile before another sound—a male voice—met her ears.

"Lia!" he called.

Oh, God. She stopped and glanced around. *Cas. Where is he? He sounds far away. He must be far away.* Panic surged into her and she turned and started running. Toward the coming light. Toward the moors. Toward something she recognized. Something that would get her—

"Lia!" he shouted again, his voice a demon's call, fierce and demanding. "Lia!"

But she didn't stop. She couldn't. He wouldn't

see her.

She ran. Hard and fast until she could barely catch her breath. Onto the moors and deep into the gorse where she hid.

Until dawn broke.

And the spell with it.

CHAPTER SEVEN

"Shoes and a corset, my lord?" Pennice stood over Cas's desk in his private office in Trevanion Castle. "That is very little to go on."

Cas glared at the Watchman. He'd been up since dawn, riding the moors, looking for Lia, wondering why she would leave his bed—leave him. "You have her description," he ground out, setting down his pen. "What she was wearing. That she was traveling from here. Are you opposed to a little detective work, Pennice? Because I would be happy to find your replacement, if that is the case."

The Watchman didn't answer. In fact, he was devoid of all panic or fear over losing his job. Instead, wonder glazed his expression. "Was everything to your liking at the greenhouse? Barring the fact that the female left...on the early side."

Growling, Cas returned to the paperwork on his desk. "It was fine."

"I'm glad, sir," the male said, a grin in his tone. "Though I have to say I was surprised to get your message last evening. I don't recall you ever...*entertaining* at the greenhouse."

"Pennice," Cas ground out. "You are forgetting your place."

"My lord, I never forget it, I assure you."

"Then stop fishing for details I will not be sharing with you and do your job." The command was punctuated with a frustrated, worried heave of breath. Where was she? Why had she gone? Stolen away before the sun was even up? It had not been something he'd ever considered. That she would walk out on him while he slept. Had he been too rough with her? Too demanding? Or was it something worse...like not wanting to be with him? Or... His nostrils flared and he groaned softly. Was she already claimed by another?

"You will find her, Master."

Cas's eyes flipped up to his Watchman. "You're still here?"

The male continued, "That won't be the problem, however."

"What the devil are you talking about?" Cas narrowed his eyes, leaned forward. "Do you know something, Pennice? About this female? Who she is?" A snarl erupted from his throat and he jerked to his feet. "If you do and you are not revealing—"

"What I know is that you care for her deeply," Pennice stated, stepping back a foot. "More deeply than you ever believed you could. And I hope that if you find her, you will share that with her. Let her see your heart."

His heart. That muscle he'd believe dead. Or at the very least, inactive. Cas's quick ferocity waned.

"I only wish to see you happy, my lord," Pennice said gently.

Bloody hell... The male was a thorn in his side. But a loyal, true and good thorn. And a thorn he

234

would never remove. His gaze held the Watchman's. "If I find her, my friend," he began in a thoughtful tone. "I will make certain that both of us have—"

"A happily ever after?" Pennice finished.

A smile touched Cas's lips. "Inasmuch as that's possible for an Incubus."

"And for a Watchman such as myself," he added with a touch of melancholy.

Cas waved away the suggestion that because Pennice cared for males instead of females, he wouldn't find happiness. And love. "Go," he ordered. "Send the messages to everyone we know. Report back at day's end."

"Yes, Master." He turned to leave, then paused. "If I may ask, what of the Lady Gemma?" He glanced over his shoulder, one brow raised. "And worse, what of the Lady Kayna?"

Cas sat back down and laced his fingers, looked past Pennice to the open door. "I said it once upon a time. Things will and have changed. I am Lord and Master. I don't think I quite understood what that meant until now. I will govern as I see fit. And I will choose who governs beside me." His eyes shifted to the Watchman. "Now off with you, my friend. I have much work to see to."

~ ~ ~

Exhausted, yet strangely keyed up, Lia smoothed down the comforter on the bed, gave the room a once-over and left the blue guest chamber. It wasn't standard for her to be given chambermaid duties. Ms. Gilly normally used her in the kitchens, ballroom and sitting rooms. But today when she'd clocked in, the housekeeper had informed her that one of the maids was ill and Lia would be standing in for her.

Pushing her cart down the hall, she paused at the door of the next chamber she was scheduled to clean. The cruel irony of it was not lost on her—or her heart. Not four hours ago, she was in his bed. Not this one of course, but his bed nonetheless.

Inhaling sharply, she gave the heavy door a solid knock, and when she got no response entered. Of course he wouldn't be in here. It was day. He worked on the estate and the business of the Incubi Masters in his offices on the main floor. Closing the door behind her, she allowed herself to take in the massive and very rustic space. Brown leather dominated, as it had at the greenhouse. And wood, many different kinds, made up a desk facing the window, a table in front of the couch—and the bed.

She went over to it and stared down at the rumpled sheets. Was this how the bed at the greenhouse looked right now? Her skin warmed, and the muscles between her legs flexed. Without thinking, she reached for one of the pillows and brought the thick, white mass to her nose. She inhaled deeply, and as his scent rushed into her nostrils, every inch of her went liquid.

How was she to manage this? Her feelings? Her desires?

Would it subside in time, or grow like a beautiful cancer on her heart?

She didn't know, but it hardly mattered. Her one night of exquisite pleasure was over now. The magic gone. She would have to be thankful for what she'd been given.

She was just inhaling his scent one final time when the bedchamber door suddenly burst open. Lia gasped and instantly dropped the pillow on the bed. Her eyes closed and she prayed that it was only Ms. Gilly behind her. Or one of the maids. Or—

"Please continue," came a deep male voice. A very familiar voice. Achingly familiar. One that had demanded wicked things of her in the bathtub last night, then whispered sweet and tender things while he held her close. "The bed must be seen to, of course..." he said.

She didn't dare turn around. Not because Cas would recognize her—that was impossible—but because she couldn't bear to look at him and see that cold, impersonal stare. Not after how he'd looked at her last night. With such fire, such desire, such knowing.

Magic was both wondrous and cruel.

"Yes, my lord." She said the words softly, carefully, trying to hide her voice. He would not recognize her scarred face, but her voice... That could be the one thing to rouse suspicion.

"But first, see to my closet," he commanded.

Was this going to be her punishment? An hour or more of Casworon Trevanion ordering her about—his maid...

Without a word, she started across the room, her limp as pronounced as ever. Maybe more so. Stress was not kind to ailments. Aware of his eyes on her, she straightened her spine as she moved. She despised the tears that threatened. She would not give in to emotion. This was as it should be. As it was meant to be.

"You hesitate," he observed in a firm tone.

"No, my lord." Chin lifted, she gripped the double doors and opened them wide.

The first thing she saw had her gasping, had her backing up a foot. "Oh…" There, on the floor, surrounded by several pairs of handsome Italian loafers, were her shoes from last night. Gold and glass slippers. She stared, her heart beating a frantic, confused, hopeful tattoo. If he'd not only kept them, but placed them with his own—

"Was it in battle?" he asked, his voice no longer edged with authority

Her heart lurched. *No. No. No.* She shook her head imperceptibly. "I'm sorry, my lord, I—"

"How you were injured?"

Her eyes closed on a sigh. This wasn't happening. She had to do something…come up with something. He couldn't know… "There was an accident on my family's farm, my lord." Was her voice high enough?

"Where is this farm?" he inquired. "And pray turn around to face your Master, female."

Lia's heart dropped into her belly. The very belly that had, only hours ago, thrummed with heat and climax. Lord Trevanion had just commanded her. She had no choice. She couldn't disobey him. Breath caught in her lungs, she slowly turned, but kept her eyes on the rug.

"You won't look at me?" he asked.

"I think it's better if I don't, my lord."

She heard a sniff of irritation, then without warning, an object came flying at her. Time slowed. Born out of instinct long held and honed, Lia's hand shot out and easily caught the object before it hit the wall.

Candlestick.

Her breath came out in a rush as she realized what had just happened, and that Casworon Trevanion knew exactly who and what she was.

Her lip curled. Pennice had given—and he had taken away.

No doubt, she would be out of this house before lunchtime.

Her eyes lifted to connect with those of the Master and Lord of the castle she'd called home for the past five months now. It hadn't been a perfect existence, but it had suited her.

Where would she go now?

His gaze moved over her, from her maid's uniform to her face. "It is you," he said. The words were neither accusatory nor blissful.

"Yes," she admitted.

For long seconds, Lia stood there under his scrutiny. *Yes, Master Trevanion. That is a hideous, repulsive scar. And yes, I stand lopsided and damaged. And no, I didn't tell you of it last night. What you had in the bathtub and your bed was an illusion. Now say what you must and release me.*

"You were a Blade?" he said, his voice accusatory. "A Temple Blade?"

"Yes," she confirmed, trying to hold back her tears.

"And a servant in my own home?"

His gaze moved over her again as if he was seeing her for the first time. She despised it. Despised herself. She wanted to run.

"Oh, Lia," he breathed and crossed the room. Had her in his arms in seconds. "My Lia."

Lia stood there, frozen, confused.

"Bloody hell, female," he uttered, running his hands up her back. "I am so relieved to find you, to see you.

Her heart was pinging and paining, and she didn't know which one to listen to. "And yet, you didn't see me before," she whispered back, tears pricking her eyes.

He was quiet for a moment, still. Then released her. "No," he admitted, looking down into her face. Her scarred face. "I didn't see a great many things. I'm afraid I've been feeling rather sorry for myself lately. Do you know anything about that?"

Her chin quivered. What was he doing? Why was he toying with her? Had he seen his mate today? Would he take *her* to the greenhouse tonight?

His eyes softened to liquid lavender. "Did you even want to be seen, Lia?"

The question startled her. "What?"

He took her in his arms again, forced her to look up at him. "You have been hiding here, haven't you? My Temple Blade?"

Tears pricked her eyes and one started down her face in a casual path to her upper lip. Cas reached out and wiped it away.

"Last night," he began. But she interrupted.

"Was a fantasy. An illusion, my lord."

His grip on her tightened. "Don't call me that. I'm Cas. To you, I'm Cas."

She cried out. Not from any physical pain, but the pain in her heart. "I'm not the female you bedded last eve, goddammit! Look at me."

"I am looking at you," he insisted with ripe passion. "I see you, Lia. Perhaps you don't see yourself. Your worth. Your beauty."

"Beauty." She laughed bitterly.

He held her still with one hand and reached up with the other, ran his index finger over the scar on her face.

"No," she groaned, trying to fight him.

"Don't you understand? This makes you even more beautiful than you were last night. This demonstrates your bravery, your skill, your perseverance." His eyes penetrated her very soul in their ferocity.

Tears spilled down her cheeks. "My leg...you can't possibly want—"

He had her in his arms in seconds and was carrying her to the bed.

"What are you doing?" she cried.

"Showing you how inconsequential that is." He placed her on her back and started removing her clothing. "Unless it pains you. You must always tell me."

Lia's heart was beating a mile a minute. She glanced at the door. Closed. "My work," she started.

"Is done. Over." Once he had her naked, he started on himself. "You left my bed and my life once already. I will not allow it to happen again." Gloriously naked, he came to rest over her, careful not to put too much weight on her. "Does this pain you, my sweet Lia?"

She shook her head, speechless, breathless. How was this happening? Was she still in the greenhouse, dreaming?

Cas leaned down and kissed her softly on the mouth. "You are mine now, do you understand? My one and only. And I am yours."

She gasped, then he kissed her again, and gently splayed her thighs.

"But your mate—" she uttered when he came up for air.

He lapped at her lower lip. "Yes. My mate." Then kissed a path up her scar and back down again. "My Temple Blade. My warrior. My lover." He grinned, his eyes locking with hers. "You are my mate."

She felt him at the opening to her body and inhaled sharply. All that he'd said, all that it meant...

One black eyebrow shot up. "If you'll have me?"

As she cried out her happiness, her acceptance, and the true happily ever after to an impossible hope, Cas pushed inside her. He felt so warm, so right. It was like coming home. They belonged like this, together. One.

Mates.

Minutes expanded to hours, and as daylight turned to sunset, and another climax was taken, Lia knew true happiness for the first time in years. She had the male of her dreams. Her Master. Her lord. Her prince. And she was never letting him go.

Tired and sweaty and smiling, she curled up against him and prepared to sleep. And she must have, for when she woke it was dark except for one candle burning on the bedside table, and Cas's cell phone was buzzing beside it.

She felt him reach for it, turn off the sound. Then his body stiffened. She looked up. Cas had the phone in his hand and was reading the screen intently. Where he'd been relaxed and languid and hungry and sexual for the past several hours, he now appeared strained.

She came up on one elbow. "Is everything all right?" she asked, then leaned in and kissed his shoulder.

He turned to her and his eyes warmed as he took in her face. "It's Tiege, Master of Furia. My love, there is much I must tell you about my dealings with the other Masters."

She raised a brow at him. "Is this good news, or...?"

A slow grin touched his features. "Very good, I believe. We can finally figure out how to rid ourselves of Marakel. Once and for all."

Lia's Blade radar went off. She knew Marakel, and what this could mean for both Incubi and Nephilim.

"I must leave to deal with my Incubi brothers as soon as possible," he said. "But first..." He was moving down her body in seconds, eyes flashing with hunger and desire as he settled himself between her already trembling thighs. "I must have your cream on my tongue once again, Lady Trevanion."

She laughed softly and canted her hips. "Oh, my lord, I will always feed my mate."

His possessive growl rent the air.

"And his demon, of course," she added, then gasped as Cas's tongue slipped through her pussy lips and found the swollen bud beneath.

The next day...

"It is only fair," Lia exclaimed from her spot outside the carriage.

From inside, Pennice gave her a weak smile. "I can't do this."

Her hands went to her hips. The Trevanion apothecary was giving her some herbs to help with the pain in her leg. And so far it was doing wonders. "Of course you can," she told him, sticking out her hand. "And you will."

He ignored it, but climbed out of the carriage anyway. "You're far too cocky," he said, looking pale and nervous. "I knew putting you and the Master together was going to be trouble."

Lia warmed at the mention of her mate. He'd been gone only a few hours, and she already missed him desperately. "Then why did you?"

"To piss off his mother?" Pennice suggested.

Lia started walking up the cobblestone steps. "Try again."

"All right, that's not it, but you should watch your back, dear. Lady Kayna can be vicious when she doesn't get her way. And in this, in you, she most assuredly did not."

Lia felt no fear. She was a Blade, after all. "When

Cas gets back he's escorting her to London. For good. If she puts up a fuss, I have his back." She grinned. "Now, why did you put us together?"

They had reached the door of the cottage. The cottage that had once welcomed Cas's many lovers, but would now grant Pennice privacy and a fresh beginning.

If he would only take it.

The male stopped on the stoop and exhaled heavily. His eyes locked with hers and a sweet smile touched his mouth. "It was destined."

Yes. She felt that too. Lia reached out and took his hand. "Well so is this."

Pennice shook his head. "I don't know—"

"You deserve to find happiness. Cas and I are partners in this mission." She shrugged. "Let us perform a little magic for you."

Those words were the Watchman's undoing. After a moment, he released a breath and nodded.

For the second time in two days, Lia opened a door to a grand and wondrous surprise. She led Pennice inside, and into the living area.

"Pennice, Watchman of Trevanion," she said, gesturing toward the leather couch. "Let me introduce you. This is Raphael, George and Bram. They look forward to getting to know you."

~ * ~

ABOUT THE AUTHOR

New York Times and USA Today Bestselling Author **LAURA WRIGHT** is passionate about romantic fiction. Though she has spent most of her life immersed in acting, singing and competitive ballroom dancing, when she found the world of writing and books and endless cups of coffee she knew she was home. To Laura, writing is much like motherhood – tough, grueling, surprising, delicious, and a dream come true. Born and raised in Minnesota, she has a deep love of all things green, wet and grown in the ground.

Laura is the author of the bestselling Mark of the Vampire series, the USA Today bestselling series, Bayou Heat, which she co-authors with Alexandra Ivy, and the *New York Times* bestselling Wicked Ink Chronicles series. Laura lives in Los Angeles with her husband, two young children and two loveable dogs.

She loves hearing from her readers, and can be reached by email at laura@laurawright.com or visit her website at **www.LauraWright.com**.

RECKLESS
House of Furia

Alexandra Ivy

CHAPTER ONE

Jian, Master of the House Xanthe, and his captain of Watchmen, Taka, stood in the private lounge of the Hong Kong airport. This quiet oasis was thankfully shut off from the thousands of anxious travelers who rushed from one gate to another in an effort to be shoved onto a waiting plane.

In here, there were no screaming children or angry passengers demanding constant attention.

Instead there was quiet music piped through the speakers, and beautiful women who offered chilled beverages as the handful of males waited for their private flights. Overhead, the ceiling was constructed to mimic the undulating, shimmering waves of the ocean that was visible through the glass wall, and the plush seats were built for comfort.

Not that Jian was interested in their surroundings. Or the female gazes that lingered on his lean face that was framed by long, blue-black hair and eyes that were faintly tilted and glowed like melted gold. He barely noticed the slender fingers that slid over his black Gucci suit in silent invitation.

He was an Incubus. A sex demon. Just standing in the room was enough to make the females tremble with need.

At the moment, his entire focus was on his companion. Unlike him, Taka was wearing his usual leather pants and black T-shirt. He was a large male with bluntly carved features, and his head was smoothly shaven. Currently his massive arms were folded over his chest, blatantly revealing the tattoo that marked him as a warrior for Xanthe House.

"You have the coordinates?" he demanded.

Taka nodded. Although it'd been less than an hour since the Masters of the Incubi Houses had gathered in their secret location, they'd already formulated a dozen different plans to bring down Marakel, the current Sovereign who sat on the Obsidian Throne.

Jian's task was simple. He was to protect the bodies of the Master of Akana House and his two servants that Jian had found hidden in the Oubliette. They weren't entirely certain what Marakel had done to them to put them into such a deep sleep, or how to awaken them. Hell, they didn't even know what the bastard intended to do with them.

But the Masters all agreed they had to keep the unconscious males out of the hands of the Sovereign.

Jian's first thought had been to stash them at one of his estates. He possessed a dozen homes spread across Asia, but he wasn't a fool. He didn't doubt for a second that Marakel had spies everywhere. And that even now they were being watched.

So instead, he'd commanded his servants to spread out in different directions, while he'd concealed the bodies on his private helicopter that was to take Taka to a boat waiting in the middle of the Pacific Ocean. From there the Watchman would travel to a small, uninhabited island that had a dormant volcano where Akana and his men could be protected by a small contingent of guards.

"Yep." Taka held up his phone. "I'll download them into my GPS once we're out to sea."

"Once you're in the helicopter I'll send out three planes at the same time. With the additional cars, trucks, and vans that are already heading across Asia, that should distract anyone who's keeping an eye on our activities, but you still need to stay off the radar," he warned his companion. "And make sure the bodies are stashed deep enough in the volcano that they can't be—"

"Did you intend to tie my shoes and wipe my ass before I leave?" Taka abruptly interrupted.

Jian cocked a brow. "They weren't on my list of things to do."

Taka snorted. "Good, because I've been the captain of your Watchmen for a long time. I don't need to be told how to do my job."

Jian grimaced. No question he was fussing like a mother hen.

Not really an image he wanted for himself. Unless it involved his lovely mate...

"Sorry. We're all a little on edge," he said, his voice raspy with weariness. He couldn't remember the last time he'd slept. "The future of our people is hanging in the balance."

Taka nodded, his gaze covertly sliding toward the male Incubus who was slouched in a chair next to the bar.

Tiege, Master of House Furia.

The Incubus was a tall male with a sculpted face that was more forceful than handsome. He had an arrogant thrust of a nose, high, chiseled cheekbones, and eyes the color of polished copper surrounded by thick lashes. His lips were thin and were framed by a well-groomed goatee. They could be cruel or sensual, depending on his mood. His black hair was just long enough to curl at his nape and fall in a silky swath across his broad brow.

Currently he was wearing a designer charcoal suit with a brilliant crimson shirt and gold tie that matched his House emblem of a phoenix.

A decadently beautiful male who seethed with sexual energy.

And, unlike Jian, he didn't hesitate to take advantage of what was being offered in the exclusive lounge—plates of food, an open bottle of wine, and an enthralled female who was currently perched on his lap.

"Some of us are more on edge than others," Taka muttered.

Jian's lips twitched. Tiege looked like he was waiting for an orgy to start, not preparing to travel to the Mojave Desert so he could raise the dead. Of course, he was fairly certain that there would be at least one or two orgies once the male arrived. The Incubus would be staying in Vegas, after all. Sin City was the ultimate destination spot for an Incubus.

"True," Jian murmured. "Although there's no one better to discover the truth behind the pendant."

During the meeting of the Masters it was decided that someone had to discover the meaning of the pendant recently discovered by Sorin. The magic that was contained inside was clearly powerful. The Masters needed to know what it was, and if it posed a danger to them.

Since the magic was clearly Succubus, and there hadn't been a female sex demon around for centuries, they had no choice but to call on the voices of the past to guide them.

"How did you convince him to help?" Taka demanded.

Jian studied the male across the lounge, an ancient regret twisting his heart. "He claimed his brother, Petros, insisted that he represent the House of Furia."

Taka narrowed his gaze. "You think there's more to it?"

Jian nodded. "My House suffered deeply when my grandfather stood against Marakel and his claim to the Obsidian Throne, but nothing could compare to Tiege's loss."

"You mean Portia?" Taka asked, referring to the betrothed mate of Tiege's brother. The gentle young female had disappeared over a century ago and was never seen again. After his loss, Petros had stepped aside as Master of his House, handing the reins to Tiege and going into deep seclusion. "I know she disappeared, but no one really speaks of what happened."

Yeah. No one wanted to discuss the fact that they'd all turned a blind eye to murder rather than openly confront the Obsidian Throne.

"I'm not sure anyone knows the precise details," Jian said in a low voice, "but Tiege has always claimed that Marakel had chosen her before she fell in love with Tiege's brother. Supposedly the bastard kidnapped her and then beat her to death when she refused to warm his bed."

Taka's jaw clenched. The hardened warrior had a soft spot for vulnerable females and children.

"What do you think?"

"There's no proof, but I don't doubt that Marakel is capable of killing a female in a fit of rage," Jian said without hesitation. "Unfortunately, there was no proof he took her, and his servants refused to say if they'd seen her, let alone if they'd disposed of her body. We didn't have enough evidence to have him brought to justice."

"A damn shame."

"Beneath his pretense of not giving a damn about anything, I don't think Tiege ever forgave the rest of us for not doing more to prove Portia was murdered." Jian heaved a sigh. Now that he had his own mate, he truly understood the pain that Petros must have endured, and why he'd turned his back on his life, handing his responsibilities to Tiege. "And I don't blame him. If we hadn't been so damned self-centered and consumed with our own petty issues, we could have worked together and realized there was something wrong with the Sovereign and his dysfunctional reign."

Taka jerked his head toward Tiege. "So he's only helping because his brother forced him to?"

"That's what he says, but I would guess that he hopes the pendant will offer him the opportunity to destroy Marakel."

Taka made a sound of surprise. "Why would he

think they're connected?"

"To have the pendant found just when we've discovered the connection between Marakel and the angels, not to mention the treachery of the Nephilim priestesses…" Jian gave a lift of his hands. "It has to be more than a coincidence."

Taka grimaced, but he didn't argue. Magical creatures possessed a healthy respect for fate.

"Have you ever seen him…"

Jian chuckled as his ruthless, outrageously courageous friend shuddered at the mere mention of Tiege's powers. "Talk to the dead?" he finished for him.

"Yeah."

Jian shook his head. "No one is allowed to witness the ceremony."

"Let's hope he's as good as he claims to be."

~ ~ ~

Tiege strolled onto the private jet with a small yawn. He'd been on a three-day binge when Petros had called him home on a matter of 'utmost urgency.' He'd almost ignored the command. Wasn't it enough that he was expected to devote endless hours to the family real estate business? Now he had to deal with the Masters on his days off?

It really was too much to ask of a genuine hedonist.

Then he'd realized that the bastards had at last come to their senses and accepted that the current Sovereign was truly a psychopathic monster. About fucking time.

Yeah, it was too damned late to help Portia or Petros, but it at least offered him the opportunity to destroy the male who'd caused so much damage.

Settling in the deeply cushioned leather seat, he accepted the drink that was handed to him by the exquisite young stewardess and watched as the thin, silver-haired man dressed in a somber black suit moved through the streamlined aircraft to take a seat opposite him.

The male looked like a traditional English butler with his narrow face and haughty expression, but in truth he was a highly skilled Watchman who'd been Tiege's personal guard since he was just a child.

"Jacob," Tiege murmured.

The elder guard offered a dip of his head. "Master."

"You've made all the arrangements for my arrival in Vegas?"

"I have." The male carefully tugged at the cuffs of his crisp white shirt. "I've reserved your favorite suite and a limo will be waiting at the airport to take us to the hotel."

"And you made sure that the bar is stocked?" Tiege demanded. Just because he had a duty to perform didn't mean he couldn't enjoy himself.

Hell, it was all the more reason to party.

He'd discovered after his father's death and his brother's retreat into his stoic depression that he could follow them into the darkness or he could plunge headfirst into pleasure.

And plot the day he would have his revenge.

"Of course," Jacob assured him. "By the time we arrive it will be filled with your favorite selection of wine, cognac, cigars, and several cheese plates."

Tiege sipped his whiskey, smiling at the stewardess who hovered near the end of the cabin. Even at a distance he could catch the scent of her arousal. One lift of his finger and she'd be crawling all over him.

"You sent out the invitations?"

"I did," the guard assured him in dry tones. "Not that they were needed. Once word of your arrival spreads through Vegas we'll be turning away potential guests."

It was true. The last time he'd been in Vegas he'd caused a near riot when the hotel manager had tried to limit the number of guests who could enter his suite.

"And the female?" he asked.

He'd requested that a Nephilim be procured so he could feed before he performed the ancient ceremony. He would have to be at his maximum strength to call on the dead owner of the pendant. And then he would need to feed again when he was finished to help him regain his powers.

Jacob nodded his head. "I spoke to your brother before I left for the airport. One of the House guards was sent to collect her. They should arrive at your private suite before nightfall."

"As efficient as ever, Jacob," Tiege murmured.

Jacob shrugged. "That's why I get paid the big bucks."

"I thought it was because you had to deal with me," Tiege drawled.

"There is that."

Tiege gave a sharp burst of laughter. When he

was a youth, he'd gone through a dozen different guards who'd all sworn he was a reckless hellion who was destined for an early grave. Only Jacob possessed the necessary nerve to accept Tiege's love for danger.

Tiege polished off his drink and set the glass on the nearby table. The jet had already made a smooth takeoff, which meant he had nothing to do until they reached the States.

"If everything is in order, then I intend to get some rest," he said, nodding his head in the direction of the stewardess who instantly turned to hurry toward the bedroom at the back of the plane. Tiege was confident he would find her stretched out naked on his bed. "Once I arrive, I plan on enjoying myself."

"When don't you?" Jacob demanded in sardonic tones.

Tiege smiled. "What's the point of being an immortal demon if you don't savor the pleasures this life has to offer?"

Jacob arched a silver brow. "Your brother would say the continuation of the family line."

A vicious pain sliced through Tiege.

He understood his duty. Now that Petros had lost his betrothed, the House of Furia depended on him to continue the family line. But he wasn't prepared to face that ugly truth.

Not yet.

Once he did he would have no choice but to accept that the golden days when his father was the ruthless Master of the House of Furia, and Petros and Portia were giddy with happiness, was at an end.

That was...unacceptable.

"Have you truly considered the horror of a posse of little Tieges running around?" he instead mocked.

"The mind boggles at the possibility." As always, Jacob's expression was unreadable. Yep. He truly would have made a perfect butler. "Of course, we can always hope they take after their mother."

Tiege rolled his eyes as he headed to his bedroom and the waiting stewardess.

"Wake me before we land."

~ ~ ~

Sloane entered the elegant Vegas hotel and edged her way around the twirling carousel. All around her, tourists scurried to reach the nearby casino or hit the streets to join the endless crowd that surged from one end of the Strip to the other.

Thankfully, her connection to the House of Furia meant that she didn't have to fight her way to the reception desk. Instead she headed directly to the private office of the manager and pushed open the door.

There had to be some compensation for having to deal with Tiege, she silently acknowledged, stepping into the large office.

Instantly a middle-aged human rose to her feet. Dressed in a tailored jacket and pencil skirt, she perfectly fit the office.

Elegant, but subdued.

"Ah, Ms. Bellator, welcome," the manager murmured. The two had met the year before when Sloane had been forced to travel to Vegas with a large amount of cash to pay for the damage done by one of her Master's outrageous parties.

Most people in Vegas assumed that Tiege was some eccentric European royal who devoted his life to fast cars, fast women and expensive wine.

They weren't entirely wrong.

They just didn't know the whole "lethal Incubus" part.

"Has Mr. Furia arrived?" she asked.

The manager gave a dip of her head. "He has."

"Is he in his suite?"

There was a brief hesitation before the woman managed to pin a smile to her lips. "I believe so."

Sloane resisted the urge to roll her eyes. Obviously the party had already started. Dammit.

"I presume he's not alone?" she said in dry tones.

The manager cleared her throat. "I believe he's hosting a small gathering."

Better known as a drunken orgy.

"I see."

"Would you like me to call up and let him know that you're here?"

Sloane shook her head. "Actually, I prefer to surprise him."

The woman gave a nod of her head. "Very well."

Sloane turned toward the door. She needed to speak with Tiege before he became too preoccupied with his...amusements.

"Have my bags taken to my rooms," she commanded.

"At once," the manager promised.

Crossing through the casino, Sloane headed to the elevators at the back of the hotel. She was exhausted after her long flight, and in dire need of supper and a hot bath, but she wasn't going waste time freshening up. Not until after she'd spoken with Tiege.

The sooner he learned the truth, the sooner she could crawl into bed and sleep.

Besides, she wasn't going to let the bastard think that she cared about his opinion.

When she'd become a guard in the House of Furia six months ago, she'd been hyper-sensitive to any hint of disapproval. After training from the age of eighteen to become a Nephilim Blade, she'd been tossed out of the temple when she questioned the need to kill the children conceived between an Incubus and human female. She didn't regret her refusal to perform that duty, but she'd been acutely aware that others would consider her honor tarnished.

Perhaps she shouldn't have been so eager to leap at Petros's offer to become a guard in the House of Furia. She'd known the male was only giving her the opportunity because she was a cousin to his dead betrothed, Portia. But she'd been so relieved to have a respectable position that she hadn't realized she would be working directly with Tiege, or that she would be so annoyingly sensitive to his mocking amusement.

He thought she was a priggish, inflexible bore who had forgotten how to be a female.

She thought he was a pain in the ass.

They clashed every time they were in the same space.

With a grimace, she resisted the urge to glance in

the mirror on the elevator wall. She knew exactly what Tiege would see.

A slender woman who barely topped five feet, with shoulder-length honey brown hair that was pulled into a high ponytail. Her tiny face was heart-shaped and dominated by a pair of hazel eyes. With a slender, tip-tilted nose and wide lips, she looked more like a Dresden doll than a trained killer.

Currently she was dressed in a pair of faded jeans and T-shirt, with a leather motorcycle jacket despite the sweltering Vegas heat. She had to hide the two handguns and obsidian blade she had strapped to various parts of her body.

Hardly the type of female to impress a jaded Incubus Master.

Not that she wanted to impress him. Of course she didn't.

Not. At. All.

There was a shudder beneath her feet as the elevator came to a halt and the doors slid open. Jerked out of her ridiculous thoughts, she forced herself to walk the short distance to the door. There were only four suites on this particular floor. All of them large, and elegant, and obscenely expensive.

Tiege always chose the corner suite that overlooked the Strip. It was, of course, the largest and most expensive.

God forbid he not have the very best.

She didn't bother to knock. She could already hear the heavy rap music and the shrill giggles of the bimbos who flocked around him like clucking hens around a crowing rooster. Instead she pushed the door open and battled her way through the half-dressed women and drunken males who filled the large room.

She had a vague impression of paneled walls and marble floors, with velvet furnishings that were in various shades of brown and tan. There was a bar at one end of the room and a hot tub at the other, but Sloane headed toward the attached suite.

There was only one place to find a sex demon in the middle of a party...

Stiffening her spine, she stepped into the bedroom, her heart slamming against her ribs at the sight of Tiege leaning against center of the massive headboard.

Dammit. It didn't matter how she braced herself, the first sight of the male was always like a punch to the gut.

He was just so...outrageously beautiful.

It was unfair.

At the moment, he was framed by four naked females who were busily kissing and fondling his perfectly chiseled body that had been stripped down to a pair of black boxers. His dark hair was rumpled and his eyes glowed with a rich copper heat.

As she watched, he allowed his slender, artistic fingers to glide down the bare back of a gorgeous brunette who was kissing a path over his shoulder. Even from a distance she could see the sparks of energy that leaped over his fingers and trailed up his arms in a shimmer of energy. It wasn't a full Incubus feeding. More like a pre-dinner snack.

Her lips pressed together, and she told herself that her stab of annoyance had nothing to do with the naked bimbos and everything to do with her personal sense of responsibility. Petros had sworn that Tiege's presence in Vegas was a matter of life and death. And that she had to be willing to do whatever necessary to assist him in his duties.

Instead of preparing for his solemn ceremony, he was wasting time with yet another orgy.

Was it any wonder she felt like pulling out her gun and shooting the collection of drunken fools who filled the suite?

"Hello, Master," she managed to force past her stiff lips.

Lifting his head, Tiege studied her with something close to horror.

"Sloane," he breathed her name like a curse. "What the hell are you doing here?"

She tilted her chin. Okay, so there wasn't any love lost between them. Still, he didn't have to look at her as if she was something he'd found stuck to the bottom of his shoe.

Prick.

"I was sent by your brother," she said in wooden tones, ignoring the females who continued to crawl over his half-naked body with nauseating gusto.

Tiege narrowed his gaze. "Petros always did have a peculiar sense of humor," he muttered. "Are you here to be my babysitter?"

Her lip curled. "There isn't enough money in the world to entice me to become your babysitter."

His gaze lowered to her heavy leather jacket, easily sensing the weapons that she'd strapped to her body.

"I have Jacob as my guard," he drawled.

"I was sent to retrieve your..." She deliberately

allowed her gaze to move toward his slender fingers that continued to draw lazy energy from the unsuspecting humans. "Dinner."

He arched a brow, lifting an arm to tuck it behind his head as he studied her with an intensity that made her shiver.

"You?"

She planted her hands on her hips and forced herself to meet him glare for glare.

So what if he was gloriously sensual? So was Beelzebub.

In fact the two closely resembled one another.

The dark, smoldering beauty. The lean, sculpted features. The thin lips framed by the trimmed goatee.

Demons who preyed on the weaknesses of females.

"Trust me, I was equally surprised," she muttered.

He smiled with mocking amusement. "But you obeyed."

She could feel her face tightening. It didn't matter how many times she told herself she didn't give a damn about this male's opinion, he always managed to make her feel like uptight ass-kisser for doing what was right.

"I understand duty."

"Implying that I don't?"

She refused to rise to the challenge. The aggravating, intoxicating creature was just waiting for the opportunity to mock her rigid devotion to her position.

Instead she shrugged aside his question. "We need to speak."

"Then speak." He lowered his gaze to watch the brunette kiss her way down his washboard stomach.

Sloane rolled her eyes as the blonde on the other side of Tiege tried to dislodge the brunette.

"In private," she snapped.

"Later." He didn't bother to glance at her. "In case you didn't notice, we're having a party."

Sloane was fairly certain that there was no one in Vegas who wasn't aware there was a party in the elegant suite. The sounds of a hundred voices shouting over the throbbing music had swelled to a deafening level despite the fact that it was still early in the evening. And that didn't include the crash of expensive bottles of champagne and the person who was throwing up in a nearby bathroom.

"This is important," she insisted.

"What could be more important than this?" He waved a languid hand around the vast room that looked like it could have been plucked from an English mansion. "Good food, good wine, and exceptional company."

"I don't know," she said in dry tones. "Maybe the reason we're here."

He flashed his wicked smile, threading his fingers in the brunette's hair as she inched ever closer to the massive erection that was disturbingly obvious beneath the silk boxers. "There's only one reason to be in Vegas."

She took an instinctive step back as an odd pain twisted her heart.

"Fine," she hissed. "You don't want to listen, then don't blame me when there's no ceremony."

She turned on her heel and marched toward the

door. Enough was enough. Let the bastard deal with the mess.

"Christ, you're a pain," Tiege growled from behind her. Then, without warning, he gave a sharp clap of his hands. "Everyone out."

CHAPTER TWO

Tiege folded his arms over his chest as he watched the human females scurry from the room.

He should have been furious.

The fun was just getting started when Sloane had forced her way into his room and disrupted his plans for a few hours of mindless pleasure.

But he could barely work up a vague sense of disappointment as the giggling gaggle disappeared into the drunken revelry that still raged in the outer suite. If he were completely honest, he'd admit that he'd been going through the motions since his arrival in Vegas. The expensive suite, the cases of expensive hooch, the females...

He told himself it was because he was focused on the upcoming ceremony and the potential hope the pendant might help them rid the Obsidian Throne of its current Sovereign.

What was more important than revenge?

Nothing, that was what.

But that didn't explain the sudden sparks of excitement that buzzed through his body the second Sloane had entered the room.

It was crazy.

She was dressed like a biker, her glorious honey

hair was scraped into a ponytail and her delicate features were scrubbed clean of any hint of makeup. Not at all his style. But that hadn't kept his cock from stiffening as she'd halted at the end of the bed, her expression so pinched she looked like she'd just eaten a lemon.

Every time it happened, he told himself it was nothing more than a basic reaction to the female's blatant disapproval. There was something highly erotic in the thought of melting that brittle censure off her pretty face and teaching her exactly what she was missing.

What male didn't enjoy a female who played hard to get?

Something all too rare for an Incubus.

And the only reason he hadn't already had her in his bed was out of respect for his brother. This female was a cousin to his beloved Portia. It made the entire situation...complicated.

So instead he took out his sexual frustration by mocking her rigid devotion to duty and lack of anything approaching humor.

Hey, a man had to have some pleasure.

The door closed and Tiege turned to send his companion a humorless smile. "Are you happy?"

Her lips thinned. "Why should I be happy?"

"You managed to ruin the party," he pointed out, inanely wondering if there was anything that made this woman happy. "Wasn't that what you wanted?"

Her chin tilted. "All I want is a quiet dinner, a glass of wine, and a comfortable bed."

He couldn't resist. Hell, he didn't *want* to resist.

Deliberately advancing, he crowded her toward

the nearby mattress. "Why didn't you say so?"

Predictably, Sloane was swift to back away. For six months she'd acted like his touch was something that might contaminate her. Hell, she could barely be in the same room without inching along the wall until she was as far away from him as possible.

It pissed him off.

"What do you mean?" she demanded.

"If you're looking for a bed—"

"I have my own," she interrupted in sharp tones.

"Does it ever get lonely?" he taunted, lifting his arm to trail his fingers along the side of her pale face. "Or does your duty keep you heated during the long nights?"

She jerked away, sending him a glare that could strip the paint off the walls. "Why do you have to be so obnoxious to me?"

He unconsciously rubbed his fingers together, savoring the potent charge that shuddered through him.

Christ. Beneath all that starch and vinegar, the female was seething with sexual energy. Temptation curled through the pit of his stomach, taunting him with what he couldn't have.

"Because you make it irresistible," he informed her.

"Of course it's my fault," she muttered, pretending that her cheeks weren't heating with an arousal she couldn't entirely disguise. She might want to stick him with her obsidian blade, but she still desired him. "Would you like to hear my report?"

Did he? Nope. Not at all. What he wanted was to tumble her back onto the mattress and strip off that leather jacket and…

He sucked in a deep breath, shivering at the sweet scent of honeysuckle. "Not particularly, but you've made it clear you're not going to leave me in peace until you've had your say."

Her jaw clenched. "I traveled to pick up the Nephilim who'd agreed to be your companion during the ceremony only to discover that word has gone out from the priestesses that the Houses are rising up against the Obsidian Throne and can't be trusted."

Tiege stiffened, his hand lifting as he used his power to lock the door.

Any thoughts of parties or getting Sloane naked on his bed were forgotten as released his breath in a frustrated hiss.

He should have been prepared.

The Masters had suspected the Three had been assisting Marakel in maintaining his control of the Obsidian Throne. Not to mention the fact that they'd refused to step down and allow their successors to replace them.

And then Sloane had revealed that they'd been using their Blades to kill human females who became impregnated by their Incubi lovers.

It was a flashing red light that the Three would do everything in their power to prevent the Houses from rising up to destroy the Sovereign.

"Treacherous bitches," he growled. "They're afraid their own sins will be revealed."

Sloane nodded. "That would be my guess."

He lifted a hand to shove his fingers through his hair. "When you came to Petros you said they could

ALEXANDRA IVY

no longer be trusted."

"I couldn't accept that their method of destroying helpless innocents was a holy duty." She shuddered, her glorious hazel eyes flecked with gold darkening with pain. "Even if they did brand me a traitor."

For the first time since meeting his aggravating female, Tiege truly considered the price she'd paid for leaving the temple.

Only a select few Nephilim were chosen to train as Blades. It was a position of honor that very few would have been willing to abandon, no matter the cost of staying. And now she was a lowly House guard, knowing that her job had been given to her out of a sense of pity.

Maybe it wasn't any wonder she was so prickly.

He grimaced, a rare sense of regret tightening his chest. "We should have paid closer attention."

"I…" She licked her lips, regarding him with a wary suspicion. It was the first time he'd offered her the respect she deserved for her painful decision. "Anyway, most Nephilim accept the priestesses' commands. Not one of them would agree to travel with me to aid in your efforts."

He shook his head. "Impossible," he growled. "There has to be a female who isn't frightened of the bitches."

Her lips flattened. "I'm telling you the truth. I used every contact I have, trying to find a willing companion."

Muttering a curse, he crossed the room to grab his phone off the desk. Then, punching in a number, he paced to stare out the glass wall that overlooked

272

the Strip.

Twenty minutes later, he tossed the phone back on the desk.

"Dammit," he snarled, frustration thundering through him.

He'd called over a dozen of his most trusted contacts only to have them refuse to answer, or give him some lame excuse of why they couldn't travel to Vegas to be his companion.

"Not as irresistible as you believed?" Sloane drawled in sweet tones.

Tiege whirled, intending to snap back a reply. This was serious. More than serious.

If he didn't get a Nephilim to feed on...

His thoughts shattered as his gaze landed on her slender body and defensive expression as she prepared for his usual mockery. Abruptly he was struck by a thought.

A hideous, gloriously irresistible thought.

"You find this amusing?" he murmured, strolling back across the room.

"Why would I?" she demanded, making a half-assed effort to disguise her pleasure at the thought of him being turned down by the females.

"Because you love the thought of my arrogance being smashed?"

She snorted. "I sincerely doubt that anything could smash your arrogance. It's titanium plated."

His brooding gaze swept over her upturned face, lingering on her delicate features. He'd already had a sip of her energy. What would those lush lips taste like?

He was betting on honeysuckle.

Warm, sweet honeysuckle.

His cock stiffened, his balls tight as he envisioned those lips wrapping around the head of his erection to give him a slow, thorough suck.

"Perhaps," he said, his voice low and rough. "But just in case you're tempted to gloat, you should consider what this means."

She shivered, unconsciously reacting to the power of his sex pheromones. Sloane might have demon blood flowing through her veins, but she wasn't entirely impervious to his powers. A fact he fully intended to use to his advantage.

"I assume you'll have to feed on humans." She waved a hand toward the closed door, trying to disguise the delectable heat that was staining her cheeks. "Luckily you have a few dozen Thralls who are ready and eager to provide your dinner."

He stepped closer. It was his turn to shiver.

Now that he'd at last lowered his defenses, he could feel that raw, natural power pulse against him.

Goddamn. She would have been a favorite in the Harem.

"A human can't provide the energy I need for the ceremony," he said, his voice threaded with a golden power.

Not that he needed it.

The rich scent of her deepening arousal had far more to do with a female intrigued by a male than a Nephilim in the thrall of an Incubus.

"As I said, there's dozens of them out there," she stubbornly muttered.

A step closer. Close enough that the supple leather of her jacket brushed against his bare skin.

"It's not quantity, it's quality." His gaze lowered to where her pulse pounded at the base of her throat. "I need the power of a Nephilim."

She instinctively tried to back away only to jerk to a halt when her legs hit the edge of the bed. Tiege ground his teeth. Dammit. After tonight she wouldn't be so eager to try and avoid his touch.

He'd make damned sure of that.

"They refused to travel here. Maybe if you performed the ceremony near the temple you could feed—"

"It has to be here," he interrupted.

The hazel eyes smoldered with flecks of gold. "Surely your orgy isn't as important as the need to discover the truth about the pendant?"

"An orgy is always more important," he assured her, pressing a finger against her lips as she prepared to slay him with her tongue. "But I wasn't referring to being in Vegas. I need to perform the ceremony in the Mojave Desert."

She jerked her head, knocking away his finger. "Why?"

Again Tiege felt that intense annoyance at her rejection of his touch. He forced himself not to wrap his arms around her and jerk her against his body.

Patience.

"It's the spot where the barrier between life and death is the thinnest," he instead revealed.

A portion of her righteous anger faltered. "Oh."

"Yes, *oh*," he drawled.

"Perfect." She wrinkled her nose. "It seems we're screwed. I don't see how we're going to get a Nephilim unless you want me to try and capture one."

A slow, wicked smile curved his lips. "Actually, we already have one."

"You do?" Her brows snapped together. "Why didn't you tell me?"

"Because she just arrived." He allowed his gaze to lower, taking a slow, deliberate survey of her rigid body.

"Who—" She sucked in a sharp breath as she belatedly realized who the Nephilim in question was. "No. No way."

His hand reached to cup her cheek in his hand, the scent of honeysuckle wrapping around him as her body reacted to the promise of becoming his willing sacrifice.

Anticipation licked through him, igniting the sexual hunger he'd tried so hard to keep suppressed around this female. He gloried in the sensations. Christ, he hadn't felt this level of need for...six months.

Not since this female had appeared in his home with her defiant expression and ability to stir strange sensations that he sensed were too dangerous to indulge.

His thumb brushed over her lush lips, the sparks of energy shooting up his arm.

"Beggars can't be choosers."

Her lips parted, but before she could speak, his hands spanned her waist. With one fluid motion he had her lifted off her feet, then before she could yank out her obsidian blade and stab him in the heart, he tossed her onto the bed.

~ ~ ~

Sloane felt the air knocked from her lungs as she hit the mattress. Or maybe it was shock that stole her breath.

Or fury.

Whatever it was, it wasn't excitement.

Hell no.

How dare this male assume that she would allow him to feed off her? She wasn't a concubine. Or a willing Thrall.

She was a warrior.

"Have you lost your mind?" she rasped, pushing herself up to her elbows so she could glare into his beautiful face.

He placed a knee on the edge of the bed, hovering above her like an avenging angel.

Or more likely, a devil.

The lean, starkly gorgeous features had softened with a smoldering sensuality that glided over her like a warm caress.

A delicate hint of his Incubus powers.

"You were the one insisting that I concentrate on my duty," he reminded her, his eyes glowing like melted copper. The scent of exotic spices filled the air, clouding her thoughts. "Feeding is part of that duty."

She licked her lips, trying to clear her thoughts. Her body was softening as he leaned forward. Lust pulsed between them, battering through the barriers she struggled so hard to build between them.

"Not on me," she insisted.

His gaze lingered on her mouth that suddenly felt

swollen. As if preparing for his kisses.

"Why not?" he demanded, reaching out to grasp the sleeve of her leather jacket.

She was frozen as he tugged her arm out of the jacket. She should be knocking his hand away. And leaping off the bed. Or stabbing him with her dagger.

Instead she lay there like a stupid doll, allowing him to peel her out of her coat to reveal the miniscule muscle shirt beneath.

"I'm a Blade," she muttered. *Lame, truly lame.*

His lips twitched. "No longer."

"I've been trained as a warrior, not to…"

Her words trailed away as another blast of Incubus magic pulsed against her.

Christ. She was almost choking on her lust.

"Have sex?" he finished for her.

"Yes." Her teeth ground together.

"Don't worry," he assured her in low tones. "I'm an expert."

With a flick of his hand he tossed aside her jacket, grimacing as it hit the floor with a heavy thud. Well what the hell did he expect? She'd just pointed out she was a warrior. That meant she didn't wear little flimsy things. Her coat was loaded with her weapons.

Dismissing her lack of feminine appeal, Tiege planted his hand on the pillow beside her head, his molten gaze running a path of destruction down her rigid body.

"Wait," she breathed, trembling with an odd combination of fear and an intense, obnoxious yearning. "This is going way too fast."

"Have you ever fed an Incubus?"

"Of course not."

His fingers lightly stroked over her hair. "Are you a virgin?"

She flinched. There was no way in hell she was going to share her one, awkward attempt at sex with a drunken sailor. "No, but—"

"Was he human?"

She glared as he absently tugged the band from her ponytail so his fingers could thread through her hair. "It doesn't matter."

"You're right." His gaze scorched over her small breasts barely concealed by her tiny top, before he bent forward and allowed his lips to skim over her brow. "Any male who has come before me will soon be forgotten."

Her hands lifted, intending to push him away. Instead, they landed against the bare skin of his chest and promptly refused to obey the commands of her brain.

They didn't want to push the sinfully delicious creature away. They wanted to mold the chiseled muscles that were covered by bronzed skin that felt like polished silk. To explore down the hard planes of his stomach and discover exactly what was hidden beneath those black boxers.

"Arrogant bastard," she managed to breathe, her nails digging into his flesh as his lips nuzzled the tender skin of her temple.

"Arrogant, yes. A bastard, no," he murmured, his voice distracted as he absorbed the golden sparks that danced along her skin. An Incubus feeding. The knowledge sent a shiver through her. Not with horror. But with a raw, earthy pleasure. "My parents were mated."

Her mouth was so dry she could barely speak. "Master, this isn't funny."

His tongue traced a languid path over the shell of her ear. "I agree."

"I can't—"

"Why?" He nipped the lobe of her ear, his fingers tightening in her hair to tug back her head, leaving her throat exposed to his searching lips. "It's a natural exchange between our species."

It didn't feel natural.

It felt extraordinary. A rare, wondrous rush of sensations that she wanted to close her eyes and simply savor.

But she wasn't supposed to be melting into a puddle of goo beneath his expert touch, was she?

There was a reason...but what the hell was it?

"We don't even like each other," she at last managed to dredge out of the fog that clouded her mind.

"You don't have to like me to feel pleasure in my arms," he murmured, his lips closing over the pulse hammering at the base of her throat to give it a gentle suck.

Her back arched off the bed as a depraved need twisted her stomach and created a damp yearning between her legs. In the past few minutes the fading dusk had painted the room with vivid orange and violet shadows, increasing her odd sense of being whisked from the mundane world to a place of warm spices and golden magic.

"I—"

He released a low, sinful chuckle. "Hmm?"

Her hands slid to his shoulders, unwittingly squeezing the hard muscles. "This isn't going to happen."

His lips traveled downward, tracing the deep plunge of her neckline. "Did you swear fealty to my House?"

A sigh tangled in her throat. Lust continued to thunder through her, but it'd altered. Slowed and intensified until her blood barely trickled through her veins, like warm molasses.

She was melting from the inside out.

"Yes," she managed to mumble.

"Did you agree to do whatever necessary to protect me and the interests of my family?" he pressed, his tongue tracing the curve of her upper breast.

Somewhere in her muddled brain she knew he was leading her into a trap. Unfortunately, she'd lost the ability to think clearly from the second she'd landed on the mattress.

Oh, and the ability to breathe.

And move...

"Yes, but—"

His head lowered another strategic inch, allowing his lips to brush the tip of her breast that was poking through the thin material of her shirt.

"This is your duty, Sloane."

A groan was wrenched from her throat. Suddenly it made perfect sense.

This *was* her duty.

Oh. Her contract didn't say "You must have sex with Tiege." She would never have signed the stupid thing. But it was damned clear that she would do whatever necessary to protect and service the House of Furia.

And if she were being honest she would admit that if he'd been another Incubus she wouldn't have hesitated to offer her energy. She might be a warrior, but she was a Nephilim. She understood that the exchange of sexual energy had nothing to do with human morals.

But he wasn't just another Incubus. He was Tiege, Master of the House of Furia.

And the mere thought of having sex with him was...

Terrifying and glorious and so dangerously tempting that her instincts for self-preservation had kicked in and urged her to keep this male at a very respectable distance.

Now, she was being commanded to give him the power needed to perform the sacred ceremony. The perfect excuse to give herself permission to indulge in her deepest fantasies.

How the hell was she supposed to say no?

Truly the only sensible option was to accept that this was her duty.

Her hands traveled over his shoulders and up his neck to tangle in the silk of his dark hair.

Anticipation shimmered through her, completely drowning out the tiny voice in the back of her mind that whispered something about Hell and the pathways of good intentions...

CHAPTER THREE

Stripped of her coat and weapons, Sloane no longer looked like a lethal Blade.

Instead she looked indecently fragile as the fading dusk bathed her slender body in shades of soft violet and peach. A delicate creature that might disappear in a puff of smoke.

Tiege growled low in his throat, his hungry gaze sliding over her reclined body, lingering on the soft swell of her breasts that were visible beneath the muscle shirt. He'd always known she was tiny, but until this moment he'd never realized just how small she was. His gaze skimmed downward to the faded jeans that fit her with rapturous perfection. Absently, he reached to tug off her heavy boots, tossing them aside as his gaze lifted to study the pale face that was framed by the lush tumble of honey curls.

Her lips were parted in anticipation, and a golden, sexual heat was crawling over her skin, making his mouth water in anticipation of his feeding. But even in the growing shadows he couldn't miss the hint of bewildered innocence darkening her hazel eyes.

With a muttered curse, Tiege shrugged off his boxers and joined Sloane on the bed. His need was becoming a near-painful ache.

Stroking his fingers over her cheek, he allowed the taste of honeysuckle to seep through his veins. At the same time, he used his magic to block out the sounds from the outer room.

Nothing was going to be allowed to disrupt this moment.

Not after he'd waited for what seemed to be an eternity to get this female in his arms.

"Are you ready?" he asked in a low voice.

Her lashes fluttered down, hiding her expressive eyes. "As you've pointed out, it doesn't seem as if I have much of a choice."

Tiege snapped his brows together. "You're saying this is just duty?" he whispered, his fingers stroking down the length of her throat.

She shivered, a flush of arousal staining her cheeks. "I signed the contract. My job is to put the welfare of this House before my own wishes. If you need to feed then it's my obligation to provide you sustenance."

It was the precise argument he'd just given her. So why the hell did the sound of his words on her lush lips make him want to growl in frustration?

Because he didn't like the thought that she was feeling compelled to give in to her desire, he abruptly realized. Grim duty wasn't the same as active enjoyment.

He wanted her to accept the need that'd been smoldering between them for months.

Why it mattered was a question he had no intention of asking.

His fingers slipped beneath the narrow strap of

her shirt, absorbing the sparks of energy that leaped from her satin skin.

"And that's the only reason?" he prodded.

"What do you mean?"

His head lowered, his lips brushing over her forehead. "This heat," he murmured. "The passion." He kissed a restless path over her temple and down the curve of her cheek. "You feel it."

Her breath released from her body in a shaken rush as he sucked the tender flesh at the base of her throat, marking her as if she were an adolescent human. At the same time he weaved a more potent warning to other males by lacing his scent deep into her skin.

Tiege sucked in a deep breath. Oh...hell. She smelled of soap and honeysuckle and sweet innocence.

An intoxicating combination.

"Of course I feel it," she muttered, her hands lifting to grasp his shoulders. "You're an Incubus. You could create lust in a rock."

Annoyed by her refusal to admit the truth, he jerked up his head to glare down at her.

"It's not just my magic," he growled. "You've desired me since you arrived at my home."

She made a sound of annoyance. "Master..."

"Tiege," he sharply interrupted.

She blinked in confusion. "What?"

"You'll call me Tiege, not Master," he commanded, uncertain why he was determined to hear his name on her lips. "Say it."

"Tiege." Her eyes narrowed. "Satisfied?"

"Not even close." With a groan he lowered his

head to nip at the lush temptation of her lips. "Now admit the truth."

"What truth?"

He nuzzled the corner of her lips. "That this is more than just duty."

"What does it matter?" she stubbornly demanded, only to give a strangled gasp as his hands grasped the front of her shirt and casually ripped it in two. They both froze. Tiege in silent appreciation of her naked breasts tipped with berry-rose nipples. And Sloane in astonishment. "Tiege...what the hell?" she at last breathed.

His lips twisted into a fierce smile. Was she deliberately making herself a challenge? Did she know he would find it irresistible?

Or was she truly that innocent?

"You're going to admit that you want me," he warned, slowly lowering his head, holding her gaze as he licked one of the tightly furled nipples. "One way or another."

"Shit." Her nails dug into the bare skin of his chest, but not in protest. Tiege could feel the race of her heart and catch the scent of her arousal.

She might try to hide behind talk about contracts and obligations, but her body was already softening against him in silent need.

The flavor of her exploded on his tongue. Damn. She was as sweet as he'd anticipated.

He moaned deep in his throat.

Hell, he was on the point of explosion from the mere taste of her sweetness. "Honeysuckle."

"Tiege..." Her words trailed away as he suckled her, her heady power surging through him.

Her hands lifted to tangle in his hair, her back arching in blatant invitation.

"Yes?" he prompted, kissing a path up her throat.

"I..." She shivered as he traced her lower lip with the tip of his tongue. "Crap. I don't remember what I was going to say."

He chuckled against her silken skin, his hand skimming down her flat stomach to unzip the jeans. Then, with an expertise that came from centuries of experience, he had the soft material pulled down the length of her legs and tossed aside.

"That's okay," he husked, his gaze locked on the tiny bit of lace that was all that covered her slender body. He grasped the tiny thong and gave it a sharp tug, ripping the delicate fabric to expose the tender feminine flesh beneath. His heart thundered. "I'd rather communicate without words."

Dismissing the taunting voice in the back of his mind that warned he wasn't nearly as in control of this encounter as he was pretending, Tiege claimed her mouth in a kiss that demanded utter surrender.

She abruptly stiffened, floundering beneath his raw hunger. No big surprise, he silently chastised himself. He'd already sensed her innocence.

She might not be a virgin, but he'd swear she knew nothing of pleasure.

With fierce concentration he gentled his touch, his hand brushing down her naked thigh while his mouth teased at her lips until they slowly parted. Murmuring soft encouragement, he dipped his tongue into the moist heat of her mouth.

She stiffened again and he swallowed a hiss of

frustration. Dammit. Why was she fighting her own response?

Did she really intend to punish them both by denying the temptation of his touch?

Then, just when he was about to pull away, she gave a tiny sigh of pleasure and wrapped her arms around his neck.

Pure male satisfaction jolted through him at her unspoken capitulation.

I wasn't deceiving myself. She wants me.

Continuing to caress the soft skin of her inner thigh, Tiege nipped at her full lower lip before trailing a path of kisses down her throat. Heat blazed between them, the carnal energy transforming into power as it sizzled through his body.

She was so fucking potent.

Like drinking the finest champagne after a lifetime of cheap booze.

Her fingers clutched at his hair, her body shuddering with an unspoken plea.

His cock twitched in anticipation. Hell and damnation. He was ready and willing to give her what she needed. But there was no way he was rushing through this.

He wanted to savor every touch. Every kiss. Every soft sigh.

This female might have chosen to become a Blade, but she was a natural concubine.

And for tonight she was his.

Skating his mouth downward, Tiege captured the tip of her hardened nipple between his teeth, relishing the sound of her soft pants that filled the air. Had he ever heard sweeter music?

"Master," she rasped. "Tiege."

"Shh," he whispered, subtly feathering his fingers up her inner thigh, heading for his prize. "We can return to our battle later. For now, just enjoy."

She shivered, her hands running an impatient path down his back.

"As long as you remember this is just..." Her breath caught as his finger dipped through the moist cleft between her legs. "Oh."

He laughed softly, circling the hard tip of her nipple with his tongue.

"Your first lesson as a Thrall is to accept that your male always knows best."

She muttered something beneath her breath about arrogant Incubi and the pleasure of chopping off his manly parts, but she didn't try to suppress her cry of pleasure as his finger slid into the welcome heat of her body.

Tiege lifted his head to watch her pretty face flush with a sensual anticipation, lashes lowering and her lips parting as he stroked his finger in a slow, tantalizing tempo.

Had he ever seen anything more beautiful?

It didn't matter that he'd enjoyed females trained to bring him maximum pleasure. Or that she had no knowledge of how to feed his hunger. In this moment, he was utterly and completely ensnared by her tentative caresses.

Refusing to contemplate the dangerous realization, Tiege instead reclaimed her lips in a kiss of fierce demand. A burst of triumph raced through him as she willingly met the thrust of his tongue with her own, her nails sinking into his lower back as she squirmed beneath the spiraling tension.

She might want to pretend that this was nothing more than duty, but her body was anxious to give him exactly what he needed.

Absorbing the electric energy that crackled over her skin, he skimmed his lips over her cheek and down the tender curve of her neck. He paused long enough to lavish attention on her straining nipples before he scooted downward, teasing her belly button with the tip of his tongue. She made a choked sound, her hands jerking from his hair so she could grip the sheet beneath her.

He chuckled, settling between her spread legs as he explored the rigid muscles of her lower stomach. The air was drenched with the scent of warm honeysuckle and his own male spice, combining to make a new, highly erotic perfume.

Delectable.

Using the tip of his tongue, he traced the delicate line of her hip. Then, as she made a choked sound of need, he tugged her legs farther apart so he could discover the satiny skin of her inner thigh.

She wasn't as soft or curvaceous as his usual bedmates. Her body was honed with muscles and sinew that reminded him of a purebred mare. Perfect.

Sliding his hands beneath her tight ass, he angled her up, giving him perfect access to the sweet pussy that already gleamed with her arousal.

Ambrosia, he decided, licking through the thick honey. She gave a jerk at his intimate caress, her groan breaking the silence that filled the room. Tiege smiled in anticipation. He intended to wrench more of those enticing sounds from her throat.

Glancing up at her face that had lost the wary expression that constantly pissed him off, he dipped his tongue deep into her body, using her moans and sighs to guide him as he intensified her pleasure. Once, then twice, he urged her toward the cusp of orgasm, only to pull back before she could tumble over the edge.

He wanted her hot and needy and so lost in sensations she could no longer deny the passion that thundered between them.

Intoxicated by the taste of her sweetness, Tiege twirled his tongue around her sensitive clit. He intended to torment her for hours, but even as he settled in for the long haul, Sloane was taking matters into her own hands.

Reaching down, she grabbed his shoulders and with the strength that came from years of training, she was hauling him back up her body.

"No more teasing," she growled.

"Haven't you heard that good things come to those who—" He bit off his words with a low curse as she reached to wrap her fingers around his straining cock.

Her touch was firm, just short of painful as she gave him one hard pump. Her hand hit his swollen balls, squeezing them tight before she pulled her fingers back to the blunt head that was beaded with pre-come.

Okay. She was right.

Enough teasing.

Settling in position, Tiege tugged away her fingers before he was pressing his cock into the opening of her body and entering her with one slow thrust.

A rasping moan was torn from his throat. Holy shit. She was molten heat and exquisite tightness.

Perfection.

He forgot this was a feeding, even as he drank deeply of her power. Instead he concentrated on the exquisite sensations that shuddered through him as he pulled back his hips and plunged into her slick warmth.

Nuzzling a path down her cheek, Tiege nipped at the lobe of her ear, relishing the clean scent of her skin. Odd. He didn't realize until this moment how much he detested the perfumes the concubines drenched over their bodies. Having his senses filled with the delectable woman in his arms, and not a choking cloud of incense and oils, only intensified his pleasure.

Nearly overwhelmed by the intense rapture jolting through his body with every thrust of his cock, he struggled to concentrate on the sounds of her soft moans and the rasp of her breath. There was no way in hell he was coming before this female found her own release.

Burying his face in the curve of her neck, he kept his pace slow and steady, his hands spreading her legs so he could find a deeper angle. Her nails scored up his back, her body arching as she neared her climax.

"Tiege," she groaned. "Don't stop."

"Don't worry," he muttered in thick tones. "A fucking nuclear bomb couldn't stop me now."

Scattering kisses down her collarbone, he

lowered his head to suck the tip of her nipple between his lips, increasing his pace and urging her legs to wrap around his hips.

Tiege heard Sloane cry out in startled joy, the pulse of her release seizing around his cock. He clenched his teeth, his hips surging until he was buried deep inside her as a shattering climax slammed through him.

The world disappeared as he rode out the storm of sensations that assaulted him. Then, with a low groan, he wrapped his arms around her quivering body and rolled to the side, pressing her against his chest.

A silence filled the room, broken only by their heavy breathing as they both struggled to recover from the explosive coupling.

It's time to get on with the ceremony, a voice whispered in the back of his mind.

He was brimming with energy and night had fully descended on the Mojave Desert. Why would he wait?

But even as the thought of leaving passed through his mind he dismissed it.

The uncomfortable truth was that he was not fully *sated*.

Despite the thunderous orgasm, his dick was already growing hard and when she wiggled against him, as if she were attempting to untangle herself from his arms, he tightened his grasp and growled directly in her ear.

"This isn't done."

"Master...Tiege..." She tilted her head back, revealing the wariness had returned to her hazel eyes.

"You've already fed."

"It's not enough," he blatantly lied. Hell, his body felt like it could levitate off the mattress from the energy exploding through him. "I need more." He shoved his fingers into her satin hair, crushing her lips in a greedy kiss. "I need this…" He slid his mouth down the line of her jaw and then along the curve of her neck. She whimpered, her eyes fluttering shut as he continued his downward exploration, using his teeth and tongue to rouse her passion. "And this…" His lips closed around the tip of her nipple and all coherent thought ended.

CHAPTER FOUR

Sloane ignored Tiege's grim expression as he waited for her to climb into the Jeep the valet had pulled to the front of the hotel.

"I don't know why you're being so stubborn," he muttered, sliding behind the wheel of the car and pulling into the thick traffic.

Sloane didn't know why either.

A part of her wanted to remain at the hotel and recover from the past few hours.

Unlike Tiege, she wasn't used to losing herself in a mindless orgy of sensual desire. God almighty, she didn't even remember how many times they'd...what? Made love? No, that wasn't right.

Had sex.

Yes. That's what they'd done.

A fulfillment of hunger for an Incubus.

But it'd felt like more than that to her. A lot more.

Which meant she should be doing everything in her power to avoid the dangerous male.

She wasn't stupid. She knew that her shattering reaction to his touch wasn't just a female reacting to the magic of a sex demon. At least not entirely. She also knew she would be a fool to think for even second that she'd been anything more than a convenient meal for Tiege.

A clean break was obviously the wise choice.

Truth be told, she should have run six months ago. The second she caught sight of the Master of the House of Furia and sensed that he dangerously fascinated her.

Instead, she'd finished her shower that she'd refused to share with Tiege, and pulled out her phone to research the local desert, including the humans' secret military bunkers. Okay. She was an idiot, but there was no way she was going to let him go into danger without her.

The mere thought was enough to make her blood run cold. As if instinct was warning that something bad was going to happen if she wasn't close beside him.

With her decision made, Sloane had stolen one of his shirts to replace her ripped clothing, and tugged on her jeans and shoes. She'd just finished strapping on her weapons and was waiting beside the door when Tiege had strolled from the shower wearing a pair of black silk pants and a crisp white shirt. Naturally, he had to immediately decide that he didn't want her to come with him.

Contrary ass.

He wanted her, then he didn't want her…

Sloane didn't bother to argue. Instead she grabbed her leather jacket and headed out of the hotel room that had thankfully been cleared of the drunken guests, and down to the lobby. She was going. End of story.

Perhaps sensing that it wasn't worth the effort to

argue with her, Tiege had marched behind her, muttering his opinion of pigheaded, unreasonable Blades.

His muttering continued as he steered them away from the Strip that still buzzed with activity despite the late hour, finally picking up speed as they hit the edge of the city.

It was a half hour later before they'd at last left behind any hint of civilization. A thick darkness surrounded them, the silence of the desert broken by the distant call of a coyote.

Settling back in her seat, Sloane resisted the urge to grab the dash as they bounced over the dirt road. Instead she glanced out the window, blithely ignoring Tiege's frustrated glare.

"Tell me why you insisted on coming with me."

She hunched a shoulder, not about to admit the truth. "If you die then I have to find a new position."

He snorted in disbelief. "Petros hired you. He would keep you on no matter what happens."

"Not if you end up dead. No one wants a guard who can't protect their Master," she pointed out in a deliberately light tone.

His annoyance continued to sizzle through the vehicle. "I have a guard."

Her lips tightened. Why was he so bothered by her presence? Surely to him one warrior was like another? As interchangeable as the females who passed through his bed?

"I'm sure Jacob is a fine Watchman, but he wasn't trained at the temple." It was a fact he couldn't deny. No one offered better instruction than the priestesses' warriors. "And he doesn't possess my obsidian dagger."

A strange expression rippled over his beautiful face. "I'm beginning to think you care, Sloane."

She didn't bother to deny the charge. Instead her brows snapped together as he turned off the narrow path and parked behind a large rock.

"Why are we stopping?"

He nodded toward the elevated plateau just ahead of them. "That's where I need to perform the ceremony."

Her gaze scanned the endless desert around them. Drenched in silver moonlight it looked flat from a distance, but she knew it was an optical illusion. There were hundreds of small hills and valleys that could easily hide a dozen enemies.

"Fine." She reached to shove open the door, her hand slipping beneath her leather coat to pull out a handgun.

"Wait." His fingers wrapped around her upper arm.

Turning her head, she sent him an impatient frown. The vast space around them was making her itchy. The sooner the ceremony was done, the sooner he could be back to the safety of his private suite.

"What?" she demanded.

His jaw hardened, his lean face impossibly beautiful in the moonlight.

"You do as I say, when I say."

Anger jolted through her at his arrogant tone, but she bit back her hasty words. She was a guard. Which meant she was technically this male's servant. He had every right to give her orders.

Even if it did make her want to poke him with her obsidian blade.

"Certainly." She pasted a patently false smile on her lips. "Master."

His own expression remained grim as he studied her with a smoldering frustration.

"This could be dangerous, Sloane," he growled. "There's a very good chance our enemies followed me from Hong Kong. There's no telling how far they'll go to try and stop us from getting information that might pose a threat to the Sovereign."

She stiffened. Was he questioning her skills?

"I know what we're facing and I can assure you that I'm capable of protecting you," she snapped.

"I don't doubt your abilities," he snarled. "I just don't want—"

She scowled. "What?"

"I don't want you taking unnecessary risks."

Sloane blinked. Then blinked again. Was he...worried about her?

The thought was so ludicrous she instantly dismissed it.

"Master," she started, only to be interrupted by his rough sound of impatience.

"I told you to call me Tiege."

Okay, that was enough. She might be his employee, but she'd be damned if she'd be the whipping boy for his crappy mood.

"Are you always so irritable after a feeding?" she snapped.

He met her glare for glare. "Never."

So what did that mean? That she hadn't fulfilled his needs?

The thought was obscenely painful.

"I suppose you blame me for not doing it right?" she muttered.

His sharp, humorless laugh echoed through the Jeep. "I think we both know that if you'd done it any more right I wouldn't have been able to crawl out of bed."

She desperately struggled against the vivid flashbacks of being spread across the bed with this gorgeous male stretched above her, his eyes glowing with copper flames as he surged deep into her body.

However there was no avoiding the blast of Incubus heat that slammed into her, searing over her nerves with sparks of sensual anticipation.

She didn't think it was intentional. Just the side effect of being in such close proximity to a sex demon.

"Then why are you so pissy?"

He studied her in unnerving silence. "You disturb me," he at last admitted in grudging tones.

She jerked at the accusation. "What have I done?"

"You smell like honeysuckle."

He was disturbed because she smelled like honeysuckle? What the hell?

"Is that a bad thing?"

"It's a distracting thing." Frustration replaced the sexual vibes rolling off his rigid body. "I'm not supposed to want you. Not after I've already had you."

"Oh." She cleared her throat. He still wanted her? Good lord. That was…actually she didn't know what it was. She squirmed in her seat, feeling uncomfortably flustered. Was she blushing? So much for being a big, tough Blade. "I could use a different soap."

His nose flared, as if he was offended by her lame suggestion. "Change your scent and I won't be responsible for my actions."

Before she could recover from his sharp retort, Tiege was jumping out of the Jeep and heading toward the nearby plateau. Wondering if the male was playing some game to see if he could make her crazy, she swiftly followed up the narrow path toward the top of the hill.

Tiege had always been arrogant, mocking and downright annoying. But he'd never been psychotic. She could only assume he was under more stress than she first suspected.

Holding her gun in one hand, she came to an abrupt halt as they reached the pinnacle. The flat surface had clearly been used for centuries as a ceremonial spot for the House of Furia. The stone was deeply etched with a large circle that was filled with hieroglyphs that glowed silver beneath the vast sky splattered with stars.

Even from a distance she could feel the magic pulsing beneath her feet.

"Do you know how long the ceremony will last?" she demanded as Tiege headed directly toward the center of the circle.

He shrugged. "It depends on the spirit I'm trying to contact. Some come at my first call and others fight against my summons." He sent her a taunting smile. "Since I'm trying to contact a female I'm assuming she'll make it as difficult as possible."

She narrowed her gaze. As impossible as it seemed, he looked even more stunningly sexy in the moonlight. The wildness of the desert surrounding them emphasized the stark beauty of his face and the smoldering copper of his eyes.

A creature made of mist and magic.

A dangerous longing sliced through her heart.

"You're lucky you're an Incubus," she forced herself to mutter. "Otherwise a woman would have killed you a long time ago."

"That's why I have guards." Reaching into his pocket, he pulled out a silken handkerchief. Sloane assumed that the pendant discovered by the Master of House Ebarron was hidden inside it. With a last glance to ensure they were alone, Tiege sent her a questioning glance. "Ready?"

She gave a sharp nod. "Yes."

He nodded toward the etchings on the rock. "Don't step inside the circle no matter what happens."

Sloane frowned. It hadn't occurred to her that the ceremony could be a threat to Tiege.

"Will you be in danger?"

"Doubtful, but bringing a spirit into our world is always risky," he admitted. "If the spirit tries to escape my control then things could get dodgy." He waved a slender hand toward the darkness surrounding them. "While I'm interacting with the spirit I won't be able to concentrate on anything else. Which means you have to make sure nothing manages to creep up on me."

She frowned. She didn't need his warning.

"I know how to do my job," she muttered.

His lips twisted, his gaze making a slow, thorough survey of her stiff body. "And don't be sticking your dagger in my back."

She turned to head back down the pathway. "Don't tempt me."

~ ~ ~

Tiege waited for Sloane to disappear in the darkness before sucking in a deep, cleansing breath.

Not that it helped.

The air was still saturated with the tantalizing scent of honeysuckle and warm, delectable woman. Worse, his lips still tingled with the pleasure of stroking over her satin-soft skin.

Dammit, he was an Incubus. He used sex as a weapon, a tool and a source of power.

Never before had he been at the mercy of his own sensual need. But a few hours in bed with Sloane and suddenly he craved her like a drug. Even when he'd known that they'd had sex more than was safe, he'd continued to make love to her. Christ, how many times had he climaxed deep in her body?

Too many, a voice whispered in the back of his mind.

He'd come perilously close to making her his mate.

It was almost as if his body had taken control and was determined to bind this female to him in the most primitive way possible.

The knowledge made him frustrated, and short-tempered, and, as Sloane said, downright pissy.

At the same time there was a potent euphoria

303

that bubbled through him like the finest champagne. The strange sensation urged him to concede his inevitable fate.

Sloane was going to be his.

One way or another.

Giving a sharp shake of his head, Tiege forced away the distracting tangle of emotions.

Later he would deal with the female who was destined to change his life forever. For now he had to concentrate on the ceremony he was about to perform.

Lowering himself to his knees in the center of the circle, Tiege pulled the silk handkerchief away from the sky blue semiprecious stone that hung on a silver chain. The jewel was cut into a smooth teardrop that glowed in the moonlight.

Careful to avoid the silver chain that would sear his skin, he placed the gem on top of the elaborate hieroglyphs that'd been carved into the stone. Then, leaning back on his heels, he concentrated on the necklace.

He could sense the magic that pulsed deep inside the gem. It tasted of spice and power and sweet feminine energy.

The sort of magic that hadn't been in this world for a very, very long time.

Absorbing the energy, he released his own magic. It wasn't the dark, creepy sensation that most assumed when they discovered he could talk with the dead. Instead it was warm and soothing and so ancient it made his bones ache.

Sinking into his powers, he tightened his bond with the gem, giving it a mental "tug." Whoever had created the necklace was still connected to the magic, allowing him a direct link.

Seconds passed and then minutes. Distantly he was aware of the howl of a coyote, and the sound of Sloane's steady footsteps as she patrolled the area, and yet within the circle there was nothing but thick silence as he wrestled the reluctant spirit through the dimension that separated the worlds.

His teeth clenched, his muscles rigid as he watched a dark mist form directly in front of him. He could make out the vague female shape, but the features were impossible to determine.

He had a sense of age. And power. A lot of power.

Which was why he was struggling to maintain his control.

"Give me your name," he commanded. A name would offer him an added layer of control.

"Leila," the mist answered, the female voice filled with an innate arrogance. "Succubus from the House of Akana."

Succubus? Holy shit.

That would explain why the magic felt familiar and yet unfamiliar at the same time. The female sex demons had disappeared from the world centuries ago.

"An ancient and noble House," he murmured.

The mist swirled, the potent energy filling the circle. "You are...Furia," the Succubus at last said.

Tiege gave a nod of his head. "I am."

There was the sound of something that might have been a chuckle. "They always were handsome devils with the charm of an angel."

He flashed a wicked grin. Thankfully Sloane wasn't close enough to give her opinion of his supposed charm.

"True."

"And so modest." There was a pause as the spirit studied him with an intensity that Tiege could physically feel. "Why have you disturbed my rest?"

"I need information," he readily admitted.

"What information?"

Tiege pointed toward the gem. "Why you created this."

The mist quivered, as if the spirit was deeply affected by the sight of the necklace.

"Inanna's Tear," Leila at last breathed. "So the time has arrived."

Tiege felt a surge of hope. Clearly the gem was more than just a pretty bauble with a spell wrapped around it.

Now he had to pray it could offer him some way to destroy Marakel.

"Tell me what the magic will do."

"It was intended to counter angel magic."

"Angel magic?" he muttered. That wasn't what he'd expected. "Why place it in the pendant?"

There was a hesitation, as if the Succubus was considering her words. "To answer the question, I must reveal something that has been a closely guarded secret," she at last said.

"I will do my best to share only what is necessary," Tiege promised. He wasn't Jian from the House of Xanthe, who used secrets as weapons.

"I suppose it doesn't matter anymore. At least not to me," the female muttered before the mist seemed to solidify with an internal resolution. "There are a rare few within the House of Akana who possess the gift of foresight."

Tiege arched a brow. "I've heard whispers, although the House refused to confirm or deny the rumors."

"Can you imagine how tedious it would be to have endless petitioners lined outside our palaces, desiring a glimpse of the future?" Leila demanded. "As if we were their personal fortune tellers."

Tiege grimaced. She had a point. What could be more priceless than a glimpse into the future? Every demon in the world would be clamoring to know what their fate was going to be.

His lips twisted. And that didn't even begin to cover how valuable it would be to their various business ventures. Who didn't want to know which stocks were about to triple in value?

"You had the foresight?" he demanded.

"Yes."

"What was your vision?"

"I saw the Master of the House of Akana trapped in an angel's web."

Tiege rose to his feet, a sudden knot of fear lodged in the pit of his belly. Jian had warned that the angels were trying to influence Marakel and undermine the protection of the Obsidian Throne, but none of them had suspected the bastards had been directly responsible for attacking Akana and his men.

"What is an angel's web?"

"A spell that traps a demon in his own mind. He's alive, but unaware of the world around him,"

Leila explained before continuing with her story. "It seemed impossible, but there was no mistaking the image of the Master and two Watchmen lying in the darkness, surrounded by the magic."

"Damn." Tiege clenched his hands. He'd never heard of the spell before. Now it sent a shiver down his spine.

"I assume it came true?" the female asked.

"Yes."

The mist shuddered. Even in death the Succubus feared the mere thought of an angel invasion.

"Have they returned?" she breathed.

Tiege shook his head. "Not yet, but we fear they may be using the Oubliette as a meeting place to plot with Marakel." He paused, considering the impact of what he'd discovered. Unfortunately, he still had more questions than answers. "Do you know why the angels would target the House of Akana?"

"No."

Of course she didn't. That would have been far too easy.

"What else did you see?"

"Nothing, but I could sense that it would be imperative for the Master to be awakened, so I created the pendant."

Tiege bit back his disappointment. It wasn't that he wasn't happy as hell that they had a way to waken the Master of Akana. But he'd been so confident that the magic would be connected to Marakel.

He glanced down at the gem that shimmered at his feet. "Why didn't you tell someone what it was for?"

"If I had shared my vision then some fool would

have tried to alter the future, even though it's impossible," Leila said, disgust thick in her voice. Clearly she'd endured more than one person trying to alter their destiny. Or maybe she'd done it herself. "And another would have twisted my words to suit their own needs so they could waste the spell on some ridiculous plot to gain power." Without warning the teardrop necklace floated an inch off the ground, the air prickling with magic. "It was far better to wrap the pendant in a compulsion spell to reveal itself when angel magic touched this world."

Ah. So he'd been right in one thing.

It hadn't been a coincidence that the jewel had been found at this particular time. It'd clearly been triggered when Jian had brought the bodies of the Master of Akana and his Watchmen out of the Oubliette.

Careful to avoid the dangling silver chain, Tiege leaned down to grab the gem, wrapping his fingers around it. It felt warm against his skin, but not painful.

"This pendant will waken the Master?" he asked.

"Unless he's been physically harmed."

That was a question Tiege couldn't answer. Only Jian had actually seen the missing Incubi.

"Do you know why the angels would waste their magic to incapacitate a Master rather than just killing him?" he asked the question that'd been nagging at him since Jian first revealed he discovered the bodies.

"I would guess because a deathblow would have been felt throughout the demon world," Leila answered, her tone indicating that she was surprised he would have to ask.

"Damn," he muttered. It made perfect sense. The angels had clearly tried to keep their intrusion into this world a secret. At least until the bastards were prepared for a full-blown attack.

But why Akana?

The question was whirling through his brain when the sound of Sloane's voice sliced through the magic that filled the circle.

"Tiege," she shouted, the sound of her footsteps running up the hill echoing through the air. "Tiege, we have company on the way."

Shit. Tiege forced himself to concentrate on the mist that was already beginning to dissipate.

"How do I use the pendant?" he demanded.

"The magic is female," Leila said. "Only a woman can cast the spell."

His brows snapped together. He'd already sensed the magic was feminine in nature, but he didn't know that it could be created so only another woman could cast it.

"But there are no more Succubi..." His words were cut off as the mist slipped from his control and faded back into the hieroglyphs. "Hell."

Leila had created a spell designed to wake her distant descendant, but she hadn't seen enough of the future to realize there wouldn't be any females left who could cast the damned thing.

"Tiege." Sloane had reached the top of plateau, her urgency vibrating in the air. "We need to get out of here."

CHAPTER FIVE

Sloane watched as Tiege at last gave a shake of his head and turned to move out of the circle. She instinctively angled her body so she was between him and the approaching cars as she urged him to hurry down the narrow pathway.

The last thing she'd wanted to do was interrupt his ceremony. Even from a distance she could hear the low sound of his voice, which she assumed meant that he'd been able to contact the dead. But the second she'd caught sight of the flash of headlights, she'd known the vehicles were headed in their direction. The area was too isolated for a stray motorist to pass by at this time of night.

Now she led him toward the waiting Jeep, easily sensing his weariness.

Her concern increased when he crawled into the passenger seat without one protest. Rounding the front of the vehicle, she slid behind the steering wheel and started the engine. Then, shoving the Jeep into gear, she stomped on the gas and had them hurtling across the sand at jaw-breaking speed.

When Tiege remained silent, she glanced in his direction, grimacing at the sight of his tightly clenched features and the beads of sweat on his forehead.

"Are you okay?" she demanded.

"I will be," he promised in frustrated tones. Either his meeting with the dead didn't go as he wanted, or he was annoyed by the toll the ceremony had taken on him. Maybe both. "Can you tell who's chasing us?"

She glanced in the rearview mirror, her jaw tightening as she realized their pursuers were steadily gaining ground.

"I would guess Watchmen," she muttered, catching sight of the dark form perched on top of the nearest truck.

Only an immortal would take that kind of crazy risk.

"Damn." Tiege scrubbed a hand over his face, his body leaning heavily against the door of the Jeep. "I'm too weak to battle them."

"I got this," she assured him, stomping on the brake to make a sharp turn to the right. Then she had the gas pedal shoved to the floor as they bounced over a dune and headed down the bank of a dry riverbed. "Hold on."

"Shit." Tiege slammed his hands on the dashboard as she took a curve on two wheels. "You're enjoying this."

Was she? Sloane kept her gaze locked on the narrow path hidden at the end of the riverbed. Her adrenaline was thumping through her body and her heart was lodged in her throat. It felt good. Almost as good as being pressed into the mattress with Tiege between her legs...

She abruptly squashed the erotic images. Now

wasn't the time to be distracted with X-rated memories of sex with a gorgeous Incubus.

"It's my job."

"You are—" He cut off his words as she headed over another dune and entered the mining town that'd been abandoned years ago.

"What?" she demanded, glancing in the rearview mirror to make sure she wasn't being followed before she pulled behind one of the decrepit wooden buildings.

He released a long, hissing breath. "Going to be the death of me."

Her lips twisted into a smug smile as she caught a glimpse of the headlights moving north of the ghost town. She'd managed to shake them. At least for now.

"Not tonight," she assured him.

Tiege glanced out the window, taking in the half-dozen buildings that were a good breeze away from catastrophic collapse.

"How did you know this was here?"

"I did some research when you were in the shower," she admitted. She didn't say anything about being able to tap into the military satellite system. A woman needed her secrets. "I like to be prepared."

Tiege turned to flash her a wry smile, pulling out his phone to send a quick message. "I think we lost them."

Sloane nodded, but she waited until she was sure the vehicles weren't going to double back before slowly heading out of the town. Then, reaching a road that would lead them back to Vegas, she picked up speed.

"Did you learn anything of value?" she asked as he slipped the phone back into his pocket.

"Yes. We need to get the pendant to Jian."

She scanned the area ahead of them, refusing to lower her guard. Just because they'd shaken one enemy didn't mean another wasn't lurking in the dark.

"Why Jian?" she demanded.

Tiege held up his hand to reveal the tear-shaped gem that glowed with a pale blue light.

"The magic is supposed to waken the Master of the House of Akana. Jian is the only one who knows where he's hidden."

Sloane briefly inspected Tiege's pale face before returning her attention to the road. She didn't have to ask if he was disappointed. He hadn't made any secret of the fact he hoped the pendant could help him avenge Portia's death.

"So you're returning to Hong Kong?"

"*We're* returning to Hong Kong," he corrected. "I've already texted Jacob to have the jet waiting."

She frowned. She'd expected to return to the Greece villa now that the ceremony was complete. Tiege didn't need an extra guard to meet with his fellow Masters, did he? Once he was on the jet he should be safe.

Of course, he was still weak, she sternly reminded herself. Maybe when he was back at full strength he would realize there was no need for her to travel with him.

"You should feed," she abruptly announced.

She sensed his surprise at her words. Why? He was clearly drained from the ceremony and in dire need of regaining his strength.

"I know you're talented," he at last muttered, "but I doubt you can drive like James Bond and feed me at the same time."

She white-knuckled the steering wheel as shock jolted through her. Had meeting the spirit clouded his mind? He had to know it was impossible for her to risk feeding him. Not after they'd had sex more than once just hours ago.

"We could stop at the hotel—"

"No."

She blinked at his fierce rejection. "No?"

His exquisite face was impossible to read. "They'll be watching the hotel," he said. "We can't risk going back there."

She shrugged. He had a point. His enemies would no doubt be keeping a watch on the hotel, but that didn't mean they couldn't easily find a female willing to give him what he needed.

"You could have Jacob bring a female with him."

She could feel his anger blast through the air, prickling over her skin and twisting her stomach with raw lust.

"Why are you so eager to shove me into the arms of another female?" he rasped.

Sloane flinched. The thought of him with another woman was...hell.

Sheer hell.

Which was why she needed to get him on that plane and get herself back to Greece where she could thank Petros for giving her an opportunity, and then hand in her resignation.

The sooner she could put this male in her past,

the sooner she could try to build a new future. One that didn't include lethally gorgeous Incubi.

"You need to regain your strength," she pressed.

He gave a sharp, humorless laugh. "And you're not offering?"

Sloane was unable to prevent the shudder of longing that raced through her body. Why was he tormenting her? Did he have any idea of what it cost her to deny his request?

No. He couldn't.

To him, the feeding was nothing more than sating a need. While she was aching for something that could never be hers.

"I…"

"Well?"

She licked her dry lips, acutely aware of Tiege's heated gaze as it monitored the sudden heat staining her cheeks.

"I thought Incubi avoided feeding from the same source. You know…" She coughed, feeling oddly reluctant to say the word. "Because of the…"

"Mating?"

Something painful sliced through her heart. Sloane grimaced, forcing herself to concentrate on angling the Jeep off the road and toward the empty tarmac at the back of the airfield.

"Yes," she muttered, her voice thick with an emotion she didn't want to name.

Perhaps realizing she was fragile enough to shatter beneath his mocking, Tiege sucked in a deep breath.

"I'll worry about feeding later," he muttered. "All that matters right now is getting to Jian."

"Fine."

"Park here," he abruptly commanded. "We'll walk the rest of the way."

Sloane obediently stopped the Jeep and turned off the engine. They were still shrouded in darkness, but less than a few feet away the bright lights that surrounded the airport turned the night to day.

With a swift efficiency, she double-checked her weapons, holding her gun in one hand as she shoved open the door of the vehicle. She wasn't worried about the human guards. She had enough demon blood in her veins to avoid their unwelcome attention when she wanted. But she wasn't stupid enough to think that whoever was hunting Tiege wouldn't have eyes watching the airport.

She could only hope that she and Tiege could slip past before their enemies realized that they were here.

"Let me go first," she commanded in low tones.

"No way in hell," Tiege snapped.

She turned her head to meet his dark scowl. "I'm your guard," she reminded him. "It's my duty to make sure there aren't any traps waiting for us."

The copper eyes flared with a fierce emotion. "You're fired."

"I'm…fired?" She studied him in confusion. She'd done everything in her power to protect him, including feeding him when that wasn't in her job description, and now he wanted to fire her? Anger, and something that felt perilously close to betrayal flooded through her. "Why?"

He grimaced, no doubt sensing her pain. "Shit." He glared at her in frustration. "Okay, you're not fired. But you are about to get a new job title."

His bizarre words only intensified her bewilderment. Why would she want a new job title? It wasn't like she could become one of his Watchmen. Unless he meant he intended to make her a household servant?

No. Way.

She was a warrior, not a domestic drudge.

"What does that mean?"

He made a sound of impatience at her blatant suspicion. "We'll discuss it later."

She gave a shake of her head. "Did that ghost rattle your brains?"

"I spoke with a spirit, not a ghost," he snapped, continuing to glare at her. "And she's not the female responsible for rattling my brains."

~ ~ ~

Tiege knew he was acting like a crazy man.

Unfortunately, he couldn't think straight. Not when his emotions were tangled into a painful knot.

Right now he was running on primitive instincts. And those instincts demanded he keep this woman safe.

Perhaps sensing that she would be wasting her breath to convince him she should go first, she rolled her eyes. "Are you ready?"

"Wait," he muttered.

Her brows snapped together, her expression concerned. "Did you see something?"

"No, but I don't doubt they're out there." Flinching as the silver seared his skin, he looped the pendant over her head and settled the chain around her neck. The silver wouldn't bother her. Then, pulling back, he studied the gem that settled between the gentle swell of her breasts. "I want you to head straight to the jet."

Of course she couldn't just accept his order. This female was created to be a pain in his ass.

"What about you?" she asked.

He shrugged. He couldn't see the Watchmen lurking in the dark, but he could feel them. So far they were content to wait, but as soon as Tiege headed toward the waiting jet they were going to attack.

"I'll transport myself," he lied. Unfortunately, he was too drained to call on the power necessary to magically transfer himself from one location to another.

Her eyes narrowed. "No. I won't go until I know you're safe."

He leaned forward, his nose touching the tip of hers. "That was a direct order."

She grimly held her ground. Hell, she didn't even flinch. He was a ruthless Master who could make grown Watchmen crap their pants with one glare, but not Sloane.

Which was no doubt why he found her so fascinating.

Well, one of the thousands of reasons he found her so fascinating.

"I'm here to protect you," she said between clenched teeth. "I can't do that if you're trying to do something stupid."

Tiege knew better than to try and convince her

that he didn't want her in the line of fire. She considered it her duty to act as his guard. Besides, she clearly thrived on danger.

Something that was no doubt going to put him in an early grave.

For now, he had to offer a rational excuse.

"You're a Blade," he growled, his hand lifting so he could wrap his fingers around the teardrop gem. He sucked in a sharp breath. Lust blasted through him at the enticing warmth of her satin skin and the feel of her heart beating against his knuckles. *Later*, he silently promised himself. Once they were back at his private villa he intended to take her to his bed and never let her out. "And right now the most important thing in the world is that pendant. Your duty is to protect it."

She drew in a quivering breath. "Tiege."

Angling his head to the side, Tiege brought a sharp end to her protest by the simple process of capturing her lips in a kiss of sheer possession. She stiffened, her hands lifting to grasp his shoulders. But even as he prepared for her to shove him away, she gave a soft sigh and melted against his chest.

Briefly allowing himself to savor the sensation of drowning in sweet honeysuckle, Tiege at last pulled back to give her a gentle push toward her open door.

Dammit.

"Go."

Sloane wavered, clearly torn between the realization that the pendant needed to be kept safe, and her instinctive need to remain at his side. Then, with a muttered curse, she leaned forward to press a fierce, far too fleeting kiss to his lips before she was jumping out of the Jeep and running straight for the airfield.

At a much slower pace, Tiege stepped out of the vehicle. He was weary from the ceremony, and far from his full strength. Thankfully, however, he was a Master. Which meant that a mere Watchman couldn't hope to match his power.

At least that was the hope.

Moving forward, he released a breath of relief when the shadows stirred and two forms abruptly appeared before him. He'd depended on the fact the warriors were waiting for him instead of following Sloane, but there was no way he could be certain until now.

Pretending he was unaware of his companions, Tiege walked forward, not halting until a large form was suddenly standing directly in his path.

"Stop," a deep voice sliced through the darkness.

Tiege halted, taking a quick survey of the males. Both were wearing matching camo pants and black T-shirts. Both had oversized, muscular bodies and arms tattooed with the sigil of the House of Marakel. But that's where the similarities ended.

The one closest to him had long, dirty-blond hair and a bluntly carved face that gave him the appearance of a caveman. His pale blue eyes glittered with a lust for violence, and a blatant lack of intelligence. One of those "all brawn and no brain" sort of Watchmen.

The one who hovered in the shadows, however, had buzzed-cut hair and a lean face that held a cunning that warned he was the more dangerous of the two. He was at least smart enough to remain at a distance and use his idiot friend to keep their prey distracted.

Tiege folded his arms over his chest, conjuring his most obnoxiously arrogant expression.

It wouldn't take much to piss off the nearest male. Which would make it that much easier to kick his ass.

"Who are you?" he demanded.

The male flexed his muscles. "Gunnar, a Watchman for the Obsidian Throne," he said in proud tones. "I have been sent to find you."

Tiege arched his brows. "Why?"

The male deliberately rested his hand on the hilt of the dagger that was strapped on his hip.

"The Sovereign believes that you have a talisman that should rightfully belong to him."

Tiege swallowed a curse. It was exactly what he'd been expecting, but that didn't prevent the stab of annoyance.

There was no way to keep recent events entirely secret. Already the demon world was whispering about the turmoil surrounding the Obsidian Throne and the growing suspicion that the temple was involved. But the fact that Marakel knew about the pendant and had managed to follow him to Vegas meant that someone with inside information had been sharing their secrets.

A traitor?

The mere thought was enough to make him tremble with the need to hunt down the bastard and destroy him.

"The Sovereign is mistaken," he smoothly lied, waving a dismissive hand. "Now step aside."

Gunnar puffed out his chest. Tiege snorted. Was the idiot trying to intimidate him?

"I have no desire to hurt you," the Watchman said, holding out a beefy hand. "Give me the object and you can be on your way."

"I told you." Tiege regarded the male with open disdain. "I don't have it."

Gunner stepped forward, his expression hard with determination. "Then you won't mind if I search you."

With lightning speed, Tiege had his fingers wrapped around the male's wrist and was squeezing with enough force to crush the bones.

"Touch me and I can assure you it will be the last thing you do," he snarled, his free hand reaching to grasp the handle of Gunnar's dagger so he could yank it out of the sheath.

The Watchman made a choked sound of pain, stumbling back as Tiege abruptly released his mangled arm.

"If you don't have it then where is it?" the male demanded, cradling his arm against his chest.

Tiege shrugged, covertly glancing toward the airfield. Had Sloane managed to locate Jacob?

"I heard that Sorin of House Ebarron had acquired a new bauble," he mocked, pretending to examine the blade on the dagger he'd just stolen. "You might ask him."

Gunnar hesitated. The encounter clearly wasn't going as he'd expected. "Then why were you in Vegas?" he finally blustered.

"Why any male is in Sin City." Tiege flashed a taunting smile. "Sex. Booze. Sex."

"Lie." Gunnar scowled, clearly itching for a fight despite the fact that Tiege had just broken his wrist. "You came to use your powers."

"Careful, Watchman," Tiege drawled, relief racing through him as he caught sight of his jet pulling onto the nearest runway. No matter what happened to him, Sloane and the pendant would be safe. "You're about to piss me off."

Tightening his grip on the dagger as he prepared for the fool to attack, Tiege was caught off guard when the dark-haired male abruptly stepped forward.

"The female has it," he said in harsh tones.

Gunnar frowned. "What?"

"He's been distracting you so the female can escape, you fool."

The male ignored Gunnar's baffled expression as he turned to sprint toward the plane.

Shit.

Tiege didn't hesitate as he leaped forward and used the dagger to slice through Gunner's throat. The blow might not kill him, but it would keep him incapacitated long enough for Tiege to take care of the Watchman's partner.

Ignoring the blood dripping from the blade, Tiege managed to catch up with his prey just as he reached the chain-link fence that blocked the path to the runways.

He reached out, intending to grab the male's shoulder, only to be forced to leap to the side as the bastard abruptly turned and slashed a silver dagger toward Tiege's face. He felt the tip of the blade scrape his jaw, but he'd already struck out with his own dagger, slicing through the Watchman's lower stomach.

The male sucked in a pained breath, but he didn't hesitate as he swept his leg toward Tiege, trying to knock him off balance. Tiege easily hopped out of the path, but he couldn't avoid the blade that slashed toward his shoulder.

Pain exploded through him as the male sliced through his flesh and muscle.

Dammit. His lingering weakness had made him sloppy. Now he was paying the price.

Jerking back, he felt his arm go numb.

He had to end this. Now.

Clutching the dagger, he slashed toward the male's face. Predictably, the Watchman jerked his head backward, leaving his upper torso vulnerable. Tiege instantly struck, driving the blade deep into the center of his chest.

He hit bone, and then the lung, but he missed the heart. Which meant the bastard was still capable of fighting.

Moving back, Tiege called on the dredges of his swiftly fading strength. He would have one last chance to—

Tiege's dark thoughts were interrupted as the male made a strange gurgling sound, his eyes going wide as he stared at Tiege in disbelief. Then, seeming to move in slow motion, the bastard tumbled forward, landing flat on his face at Tiege's feet.

Tiege muttered a curse, his gaze locked on the obsidian blade sticking out of the Watchman's back.

"Sloane," he muttered, stepping over the dead male's body and awkwardly climbing the fence.

He managed to make it over the top, but he lost his grip on the way down, tumbling onto the hard ground.

Instantly Sloane was at his side, wrapping an arm around his shoulder as she urged him to his feet.

"You're injured," she chided, as if angered that he was bleeding like a stuck pig.

"I told you to get out of here," he snapped, hating the fact that she was seeing him at his most vulnerable. For the first time in his very long life he actually cared whether or not a female found him worthy of her respect. "Even you should be able to obey a simple—"

"Not now," she rudely interrupted, half dragging him toward the waiting jet.

Tiege groaned, trying to remain conscious as he sensed someone joining them.

"I've got him," Jacob muttered, grabbing Tiege around the waist and tossing him over his shoulder.

White-hot agony shuddered through him as he was carried up a narrow ramp. But even as his lips parted to protest the rough treatment, the world began to recede and a ruthless darkness sucked him under.

CHAPTER SIX

They were eight hours into the flight when Sloane heard the faint sound of a groan from the back of the jet.

Instantly she was on her feet and heading into the small bedroom. It didn't occur to her to allow Jacob or any other member of the staff to check on their Master. She wasn't really thinking at all.

Who could blame her?

She'd gone through hell after she'd left Tiege and located Jacob, who had the jet fueled and ready to go. The aggravating brute had promised to transport himself, but she'd known he was lying even before the jet had moved into place for takeoff. A part of her had known she should do as Tiege commanded and leave with the pendant, even if he wasn't on the jet. It clearly was important that it be taken to Jian. But even as the jet revved its engines, she'd been forcing open the door and racing back to join in the fight.

Tiege might be furious, but there was no way she could leave him behind.

Period.

Halting next to the bed, she gazed down at the male lying flat on his back.

Earlier Jacob had stripped him of his filthy clothes and washed away the blood before gently placing him on the mattress. Now Sloane studied the wound on his shoulder that had healed to an angry red scar, and the lingering pallor of his skin.

If he hadn't been so drained he would be fully recovered. Instead...

Her heart abruptly lodged in her throat as Tiege's thick lashes lifted to reveal his stunning copper eyes. Heat filled the cabin and her clinical inspection of his injuries altered to something far more dangerous.

Suddenly she was vibrantly aware of the silky black hair that looked as if it'd been rumpled by a lover's fingers. And the shadow of a beard that darkened his jaw with a scruffy sexiness.

And the hard body that was completely naked.

She shivered, a raw, earthy need pulsing through her.

"Are we in the air?" he asked in a husky voice.

She nodded, lowering herself to perch on the edge of the mattress. "Yes."

"Good." His hand lifted, as if he intended to touch her, but he gave a startled grunt when she curled her fingers into a fist and punched him on his uninjured arm. He blinked in shock. "What the hell was that for?"

Sloane grimaced. She hadn't actually meant to strike him. But dammit...she'd been so freaking worried about him.

"Because you're supposed to be selfish and arrogant and absorbed with your own pleasure," she snapped.

He arched a brow, an unexpected amusement

smoldering in his eyes. Almost as if he suspected the reason for her ridiculous burst of anger.

"Have you been told your bedside manner sucks?"

She scowled at his impossibly handsome face, her heart thundering in her chest as his fingers brushed her hair behind her ear.

"You aren't supposed to be a hero," she informed him.

In the dim light his eyes looked like melted copper as his fingers trailed down the arch of her throat.

"Good." His fingers cupped her nape, gently tugging her head down so he could trace her furrowed brow. "I'd far rather be the villain."

She trembled, allowing him to wrap his arms around her. She'd been so terrified that she'd lost him in some idiotic attempt to save the demon world.

Now she didn't have the strength to pull away.

Or at least that was the excuse she was using as she melted against his chest, her fingers running through the raven satin of his hair.

"You need to heal," she murmured.

"That's exactly what I intend to do," he assured her, his hands skimming beneath her leather jacket.

Sparks blazed between them as his mouth lightly teased over her face before settling on her lips. Perhaps she would never be his destined mate or prevent the disaster that was looming, but for the moment she could give Tiege the strength he needed to survive until they reached Hong Kong.

Shutting her mind to the bittersweet emotions

tugging at her heart, Sloane pulled back so she could shrug off her jacket, allowing it to slide to the ground. Then, with more haste than elegance, she was tugging off the rest of her clothing so she could stretch onto the mattress next to him.

Even knowing that every second she spent with Tiege was destined to entangle her renegade heart more tightly, she couldn't deny his hunger that she could feel with every burning kiss and every stroke of his hand.

In return she offered a fervent response that made him groan with approval, gathering her close as he rolled onto his side.

"Sloane..." he whispered, gazing down at her with a vulnerability that seared away any lingering barriers she tried to place between them. "My beautiful warrior."

She shivered. She'd never felt so vulnerable. Or so perilously exposed.

Holding his copper gaze, she reached up to stroke her fingers over his exquisite face.

"Am I giving you what you need?" she whispered, aching for his reassurance.

"All I need is you," he promised her softly, bending down to claim her lips in a kiss of raw hunger.

The simple words made something expand deep inside her, and desperate to divert her mind from the treacherous emotions, she focused on the sensation of his hands gliding down her back. Pressing closer to the heat of his body, she explored the chiseled muscles of his chest, smiling as she felt the vibrations of his groan beneath her palms.

She might never have Tiege's heart, but his body was ready and eager to belong to her.

Refusing to consider how many other women had known him just as intimately in the past and how many were yet to know him in the future, Sloane tilted back her head as he trailed a path of kisses down the sensitive line of her throat.

Until they landed in Hong Kong he was hers. Completely and utterly.

His mouth traced the curve of her breast before he captured the tip of her nipple between his lips, making her gasp in sharp pleasure.

"Yes," she muttered in approval.

Continuing to tease the sensitive peak, Tiege reached to grasp her hand, guiding it down to his straining cock.

Sloane smiled, curling her fingers around his hard length. She felt smugly powerful as he gave a shaken groan.

Tiege muttered a low curse as she stroked from the tip to the wider base, taking time to discover the soft pouch beneath his erection before stroking upward.

"Shit," he breathed, his hands moving to grasp her thighs so he could tug apart her legs. "You only have to touch me and I am drowning in desire."

He was not the only one drowning, she acknowledged as his hand sought the heart of her femininity, already damp and aching with need. A moan was wrenched from her lips as a slender finger dipped into the heat of her body, her hips instinctively lifting in silent invitation.

Oh, yes. Her eyes fluttered shut. Already she

331

could feel the delectable pressure beginning to build in the center of her womb, and her fingers tightened on his arousal, making him moan in pleasure.

"Wait, Sloane," he pleaded, covering her hand.

She frowned. "Wait?"

"This is too important to rush," he murmured, his lips teasing along the line of her shoulder as he gently turned her so she was lying on her side.

"Important?" she breathed in confusion.

"I intend to remember this night for the rest of my life," he said, his lips brushing her ear as he molded himself against her back.

Sloane frowned at his words. The rest of his life? Was he implying—?

Her thoughts shattered as he gently tugged her leg up and over his hip.

Later she would worry about what he meant. For now all that mattered was the feel of his lips nuzzling at the curve of her neck, and his hands expertly exploring her full breasts, tugging her nipples into full arousal, before they were sliding down her body with wicked intent.

She swallowed a gasp as his fingers slid between her legs, parting her most intimate flesh. Then with exquisite slowness he pressed his erection deep into her moist channel.

"Oh…lord."

She struggled to form her words only to have them snatched from her lips when his fingers discovered her clit and he stroked her in tempo with his shallow thrusts.

"Do you want more, Sloane?"

More? She whimpered, not certain she could

bear more without shattering into a thousand pieces. Then he shifted the angle of his thrusts, plunging deeper, and she reached backward to dig her nails into the muscles of his hip.

"Yes."

The rasp of their heavy breaths filled the air along with the scent of exotic male spices and passion. Sloane squeezed her eyes shut, her body moving to meet his thrusts with increasing urgency.

"Sloane," he groaned, his hips slamming upward as his seed poured into her, triggering her own release.

She cried out in ecstasy, indifferent to their cramped surroundings or the staff that waited just outside the door.

For now nothing mattered beyond the feel of Tiege's arms wrapped around her and the wild beat of his heart against her back.

Keeping her eyes closed, Sloane sensed Tiege slowly pull out of her body and lay her flat on the mattress. She felt as if she was floating, still lost in the heat of their pleasure.

Nestled beside her, Tiege allowed his fingers to stroke over her shoulder, tracing the curve of her breast before brushing against the necklace she'd forgotten she was wearing.

"This is glowing," he murmured softly.

Forcing open her heavy lids, she glanced down at the pendant that was shining a bright blue.

Odd.

"What does that mean?" she demanded, belatedly realizing there was a warm light that surrounded the gem.

"I don't know," he murmured, his fingers absently toying with the pendant. "Maybe nothing."

She hid a grimace as she quivered beneath the feel of his light touch. She'd just had the orgasm of her life, and already her body was eager for more. Clearly she needed a distraction.

"Jacob heard from Jian while you were sleeping," she forced herself to say.

"What did he want?"

"He said he would meet us at the airport."

"Good. The sooner we can hand over the pendant, the sooner we can return to Greece," he muttered. "For now...I want to discuss us."

She felt her heart miss a beat. Maybe more than one.

"Us?"

His fingers slid to cup her chin, tilting her head back so he could inspect her pale face.

"More specially, about our future."

Her muscles tensed. Was this the big kiss-off? Was he about to tell her that she'd overstayed her time in his household?

"What future?" She pasted a teasing smile to her lips, determined not to allow him to see her pain. "You said I was fired."

"I also said I had a new job in mind," he corrected in husky tones, his gaze sweeping down her naked body.

Her mouth went dry, a strange sense of breathless anticipation tightening her chest.

"What job?"

A slow, utterly intoxicating smile curved his lips. "Mate."

Sloane trembled, caught between shocked disbelief and a desperate hope.

"But you don't even like me," she breathed.

His hand tenderly cupped her cheek, his features softened with an emotion she never dreamed possible.

"I've craved you from the second I caught sight of you. Which was why I worked so hard to keep you at a distance." His lips twisted with regret. "I was just too arrogant to accept that I might have met my match."

Sloane knew exactly what he meant. Hadn't she done her own share of denial?

And in the end, all she'd accomplished was making herself miserable.

Still, it seemed crazy to think that he'd been enduring the same torment.

"Mate." She licked her dry lips. "You're sure?"

"Never more sure," he swore, lowering his head to press a slow, lingering kiss on her lips. "You are the only woman I want in my arms. Tonight and forever. Say yes, my sweet Blade."

There was only one answer. Lifting her arms, she wrapped them around his neck.

"Yes."

~ ~ ~

Tiege wasn't happy.

After arriving in Hong Kong, he'd expected to remain just long enough for his jet to be fueled and the pendant to be handed over to Jian. He wanted to be in Greece where he could lock the doors to his villa and spend the next few centuries alone with his mate.

Instead he'd discovered a limo waiting for him that whisked him across the crowded city to a home hidden behind high brick walls and several layers of security. His mood wasn't improved as he was led by a uniformed servant to the elegant office at the back of the house and left to wait for nearly twenty minutes.

Usually he would have appreciated the floor-to-ceiling bookcases that lined the walls, along with the stunning view of the nearby beach.

Not today.

Dammit. He'd done his part, hadn't he?

Time to enjoy his reward.

The memory of Sloane sleeping on his bed, her naked body covered only by a thin sheet, seared through his mind. He'd hoped to be done with this exchange before she woke. She was still getting used to the idea of being his mate.

Now he had to worry she would wake up and freak out because he wasn't lying beside her.

At last there was the sound of approaching footsteps, and Jian entered the room looking fresh as a fucking daisy in his designer suit while Tiege was rumpled, jetlagged, and casually dressed in jeans and a cashmere sweater.

"What the hell is going on?" Tiege groused, tossing the necklace on a lacquer table. "I told you I would meet you at the airport to give you the pendant."

Jian smiled as he slowly strolled toward a door behind the large desk. "I needed to show you something in private."

Tiege clenched his hands as he followed his friend. "Dammit. Hurry up. I have a beautiful mate waiting for me."

"Mate?" In the process of unlocking the door, Jian glanced over his shoulder in surprise. "Congratulations."

Tiege felt a tingle of pleasure race through him. Mate. It still stunned him.

He'd seen how close his brother had been to Portia. And a part of him had always envied their relationship. But he hadn't truly understood just how deeply he would be connected to Sloane.

It was as if she'd filled a hole he hadn't realized existed.

"I don't want your congrats," he muttered, plagued by a restless ache at being separated from Sloane. "I want to be in bed with my woman."

"You'll want to see this." With a dramatic motion, Jian shoved open the door and waved Tiege into the shadowed sitting room.

With a roll of his eyes, Tiege stepped over the threshold and glanced around the room that he abruptly realized was filled with the various Masters. Obviously there was a powerful spell that had muted their presence. Otherwise he would have sensed them from the minute he'd entered the house.

His lips parted to demand an explanation, only to snap shut when he realized the Masters had turned their chairs to face the front of the room, where a male with dark eyes and dark hair was dressed in casual slacks and a white shirt, leaning against a marble fireplace.

The Master of Akana.

Tiege shook his head. The last time he'd seen the male he'd been lying unconscious, his hair faded to a deep red and his skin a sickly ash color.

"Holy shit," he breathed, glancing toward Jian who'd moved to stand at his side. "How did you wake him?"

"He just woke about eight hours ago and Taka brought him back here," Jian said, folding his arms over his chest. "I'm assuming you did something with the pendant that broke the magic surrounding him."

"I..." Tiege bit off his denial, suddenly remembering the soft glow that'd surrounded the gem after he'd had sex with Sloane. When Leila had claimed the magic would only work for a woman, he'd assumed it had to be cast by another Succubus. Now he realized the power could easily have been triggered by their lovemaking. A Succubus, after all, was a sex demon. Aware of Jian's searching gaze, he gave a shake of his head. "Don't ask."

Jian's lips twitched. "I don't need to."

Tiege nodded toward the male who'd disappeared centuries ago. "Does he remember what happened?"

"He doesn't know who attacked him, or how he ended up in the Oubliette."

Tiege muttered a curse. Once again his hope that they would have some evidence against Marakel was doomed to disappointment.

"What does he remember?" he demanded.

Jian leaned to speak directly in Tiege's ear. "He remembers having a vision."

Tiege felt a chill of premonition inch down his spine. "Did the vision have anything to do with the Obsidian Throne?"

Jian nodded. "He says he witnessed the Throne smashed beyond repair, and Marakel kneeling at the feet of an angel."

Tiege grimaced, any hope of returning to his private villa with his mate completely destroyed.

"Oh…shit."

~ * ~

ABOUT THE AUTHOR

ALEXANDRA IVY is the *New York Times* and USA Today bestselling author of the Guardians of Eternity series, as well as the Sentinels and Bayou Heat that she writes with Laura Wright.

After majoring in theatre she decided she prefers to bring her characters to life on paper rather than stage. She lives in Missouri with her family.

Visit her website at **www.AlexandraIvy.com**.